D1373597

GLITTER
BURN

HEYWOOD
GOULD

POCKET BOOKS

New York   London   Toronto   Sydney   Tokyo

POCKET BOOKS, a division of Simon & Schuster Inc.
1230 Avenue of the Americas, New York, NY 10020

Copyright © 1981 by Heywood Gould
Cover photo copyright © 1989 Mort Engel Studio

Published by arrangement with the author
Library of Congress Catalog Card Number: 81-8752

ISBN: 0-671-66592-8

First Pocket Books printing August 1989

10 9 8 7 6 5 4 3 2 1

POCKET and colophon are trademarks of
Simon & Schuster Inc.

Printed in the U.S.A.

GLITTER
BURN

It was early June and New York was already
a ghost town. The rich had departed at the first sign of a
Puerto Rican with a transistor. Politicians hung in to turn
on a few fire hydrants and pose with some wet Third
Worlders before taking off on junkets that kept them away
until after Labor Day. Commerce slowly ground to a halt as
vacations, long weekends and holiday vaginitis depleted the
typing pools. The illuminati fled at the first unseemly
prickle of sweat to play out their romances in various
Saratogas and East Eggs. The rest of the population scram-
bled for exits like people in a burning theater. The five
million or so who remained were like the aged and infirm
abandoned to a conquering army. Summer provided a
devastating social litmus for them all. They were either too
poor, too maladroit or too gauche to get away. A city full of
pariahs. And they knew it.

The journalists, of course, remained, peddling their sor-
did jeremiads to the perspiring masses. They needn't have
bothered. There are no great crimes or crises during the
summer, the perpetrators of such all being away recreating.

It's a lean time. The public, grown gouty on a winter's diet
of drug busts, sex crimes and errant legislators, comes
limping to the newsstands demanding more. So the expert
gleaners like myself go to work prowling the streets, ransack-
ing the bureaucracies in search of a pervert or malingerer. It
isn't long before a disgruntled civil servant appears to
inform on his coworkers. A headless torso in a tube top, rolls
out of a disco doorway. A welfare mother is discovered with
three Picassos in her living room. After nine years in the

service of the *New York Event*, a tabloid founded by Aaron Burr and recently acquired by a Midwestern conglomerate which also owns supermarkets and funeral parlors, I knew that the dog days would not pant too long before we had our shot of the macabre.

In the meantime, the corpseless, cataclysmless days grew longer. One morning the only news was a Volkswagen that blew up in the middle of the Brooklyn Battery Tunnel. I made it sound like the wreck of the *Hindenburg*. For human interest I added a few asphyxiated firemen and a neurosurgeon who dropped dead leaning on the horn of his 450 SL. A lot of sound and fury, even if it was strictly for the back pages. TRAFFIC JAM CLAIMS DOCTOR'S LIFE, they called it.

I usually lunch at the Stacked Exchange, an in time bistro on Wall Street. The barmaid is a basso in a bikini, who throws down straight shots of testosterone. I sit at the bar with my elbow in a puddle and feed her lines.

"It's so dark in here you have to drink by the braille system."

"The only thing fresh on this hamburger is the rat's footprints."

"They oughta call this place Mount Palomar. You need a telescope to see your drinks."

There's a Puerto Rican girl, about sixteen, with a slack, sallow body, who parades nude on the bar. Put a dollar in her garter belt, and she squats in front of you offering her scraggly, pubescent patch for inspection. I prefer her relief, an angry redhead who could be twenty-five or ninety. This is the kind of woman who hates her dimples. She's been around the block so often she's got stretch marks on her spiked heels. I go for a fin whenever I see her. She stands splaylegged over my bloody bullshot as I place the money with trembling hands. Then she squats, sneering all the while, grabs my head and gives me a gander. I'm not a stranger to female genitalia, but I've never been permitted to survey the area without making an insertion or an explanation. Here nothing is expected of me. My five bucks buys thirty seconds of uninterrupted perusal. This woman is positively Delphic in proportion. I get the feeling if I holler a stupid question in there, I'll get a stupid answer.

For a postprandial treat this afternoon I repaired to the executive office of the *Event*, thirty floors above the noisome apocalypse of the street. From there I could watch the rotting barges ply the dishwater Hudson while Stanley P. Grissom, executive editor of the *Event*, stuck pins in my byline.

Grissom is a red-faced ectomorph, just the type to have a hemorrhage in the middle of a good laugh. The object of his mirth was my application for a leave of absence. I had managed to connive a job as journalist-in-residence at the University of Hawaii, and needed his approval.

"I love this line 'going back to the earth for renewal,'" he said. "The only earth you know is the Coney Island sand you've got up the crack of your ass."

"I need a change," I said. "I've spent thirty-three summers in this town. One more and I'll go nuts."

"Nobody'll notice," he said.

"I'll commit ritual suicide. I'll fall on my pencil in the middle of the city room."

"We'll work around you."

"You've granted leaves to three men with considerably less experience than me. . . ."

"Of course," Grissom said. "They were expendable. I can always get some jerk to interview a movie director in an air-conditioned hotel room. Or go to a gourmet food show. Or cover a new fall opening of one of those fag designers. That's not for you."

"Why not? I like air-conditioned gourmet fags. . . ."

"No, you're my bread and butter. My man in the ghetto. The master of messy homicides. And I know we've got one coming, too. I can smell it."

"The only messy body you smell is mine," I said. "I'm stagnating. Nine years on this job, and the only things I've learned to do are throw up with a cigarette in my mouth and write the same sentence in a story three times. . . ."

"Don't be modest," Grissom said. "You're also an expert

expense-account padder. You have no equal in your ability
to make up phony names and addresses, to put words in the
mouths of fictional people that they never said anyway. I've
seen you stand perfectly motionless for hours without a
thought in your head. You're definitely a man of parts, an
indispensable member of my team, and I'm not letting you
go anywhere you might conceivably have a good time."

"It's one thing to hate me," I said, "but to be unfair . . ."

"The two usually go hand in hand, don't they?" he said.
"Oh, but now you've gone and given me a twinge." Grissom
broke a cheekbone trying to look contrite. "They're feeding
pellagra to a bunch of volunteers at the Mississippi State
Pen. You can always go down there and take potluck."
Grissom laughed so hard his temporal artery began to
flicker. "Listen, I'm doing you a favor. You're the kind of
New Yorker who gets bitten by the tsetse fly when he crosses
the George Washington Bridge. You just stay nice and safe
and warm here in the Rotten Apple. There's nothing wrong
with you that a good old-fashioned blackout won't cure.
Meanwhile," he grinned fiendishly, "you can keep busy
covering the weather."

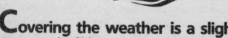

Covering the weather is a slight improvement over the Chinese water torture. Flaubert, who tore his
hair out over a comma, would have been bald as a cue ball
after a week of trying to dream up six fresh paragraphs a day
about the weather.

"Temperatures rose for the fourth straight day
yesterday. . . ." How many times have I written that sentence, or an inelegant variation of same? The trouble starts
when you get epigrammatic and put words together that
have no relation to wit, accuracy or the weather, for that
matter, but might get you a better job on a news magazine.
"It was a day for thick shakes and girl watching. . . ." or
"The mercury had wings, but New Yorkers needed flippers

today as a sudden thunderstorm . . ." What you really want to do is explode in a Faulknerian torrent: "Groaning under the quotidian burden of tragedy and triviality, a pestilential admixture that blurred the senses in fruitless ratiocination, contemplation of a commuter's destiny whether or not it bore any resemblance to the overheated pavement, the clouds of dusty afterbreath that floated around them in the Stygian din of the subway, New Yorkers cared little for the weather today as . . ." One fateful day the temperature finally breached the hundred mark. I spent the morning sweltering in a crowd of thousands on Wall Street watching an exotic dancer named Sugar Cohen take a bath in a vat of Brazilian Banana, some ice-cream chain's Flavor of the Month. At three o'clock I headed for the *Event* office at Manhattan police headquarters. The whole city seemed suspended in a globule of sweat.

Air-conditioned bars glittered like igloos in an inferno, but I pressed on and was soon rewarded by the sight of the Medusa heads—a more accurate metaphor for Justice than a blindfolded cheerleader—on the Gothic facade of the soon-to-be-demolished headquarters building.

Reporters used to work in a tattered two-story taxpayer on a narrow back street behind police headquarters. On hot days we would take our beers outside and heckle the handcuffed prisoners being herded out of the paddy wagons. Once, a large, humorless mass murderer took exception and charged across the street at us. After that, we switched to counting the steaming turds dropped by police horses and could be quickly detoured from that by an irate whinny, police reporters not being celebrated for their pluck.

All this was a mere four years in the past, but it seems to have happened in the Dark Ages when I contemplate our present surroundings. We've got green carpeting, desks with typewriter bays, water coolers in every office, air conditioners and push-button phones. We've got hot and cold running press officers, who try to keep us from talking to the cops at the precincts. It's like working at the White House.

This day had been too hot even for crime, at least the kind you had to break a sweat to commit. The ticker tape which

11

records mayhem from every precinct in the city was silent. I heard nothing but the harmonious gurgle of water coolers, the snap of beer cans.

In the *Times* office a blond policewoman had her skirt hoisted to demonstrate a new thigh holster. Flashbulbs were popping. The entire press corps was in attendance. The policewoman had nice legs helped along by high heels and brown mesh stockings, all regulation police issue, believe it or not. Her blouse was one button off the mark. An American flag was pinned to her breast pocket, a silver crucifix gleamed in her cleavage. Doris Day with a .38, and you'd better not get fresh.

"Cute little Cossack, isn't she?"

I had my own private blonde, lounging with her feet up on my desk in the *Event* office. It was Jill Potosky, formerly of the *Event,* now a celebrity journalist with the *Times.* I hadn't seen her for over a year, but she wasn't the type for a big hello.

"What are you doing down here with the proles?" I asked.

She scratched lazily at a sunburned calf. "Covering that pussy holster for the woman's page. I couldn't take the heavy breathing."

"Tough talk," I said. "The fuzz is having fun."

"She's showing herself off to a roomful of men. What woman in the world could resist that?"

"Is this the man-hater I used to know?" I asked.

Potosky scratched a little higher. "Oh, I still hate men. I've just added most women to my list."

I tried to find a vantage point from which I could look upon that golden limb without being obvious. For the year of her employment at the *Event,* Potosky had been the star of all my drunken fantasies. By day she was fresh-faced and professional, an up-and-comer who quite properly had no use for a has-been like me. But at night in fitful inebriate slumber, or even struggling in the embrace of someone more accessible, she would appear to do my bidding. My adventures with this woman could have formed the syllabus for a graduate course in great cultural moments of the twentieth century. I had bound her with Isadora's scarf, fondled her with Freud's cigar, chastised her with Krafft-Ebing's walking stick, spanked her with Harlow's fur slipper, even kissed the hem of her garment in the anteroom of the Winter Palace.

At times Frederick's of Hollywood did her wardrobe, but there were moments when only nurse's shoes and see-through whites would do. And, of course, in moments of extreme emergency there was the old standby, the knee socks, plaid skirts and middy blouses of the Catholic school succubi of my adolescence—the girls from Our Lady of the Spilled Seed. Yet no fantasy she abetted was more intriguing than her own persona: the sinister virgin on the make, the woman whose head, heart and hymen are ineffably linked and will remain intact until all three are simultaneously vanquished.

Potosky had swept into the *Event* city room a strident, arrogant, twenty-one-year-old blonde with a Phi Beta Kappa key and an ass like a petunia. During her first year she straddled the profession like a colossus trying to force enlightenment through an unlikely orifice. There wasn't an editor, Neiman fellow or anchorman who didn't get a seminar. This might have been sound epistemological strategy in academe. Professors will happily abandon sherry and spouse, even jeopardize promotion for one publishable peccadillo. The ardor increases proportionate to the consequences. Newspapermen, unhappily, have nothing to lose and are prone to long, boring confessions followed immediately by malodorous dozes. Repeated encounters with these celibate rakes gave Potosky a rather cynical view of the profession, so that when my number bobbed up, I, the one man who could have made her happy, was tarred with the same limp-bristled brush as my colleagues.

After a year Potosky had quit the business, professing herself "tired of the grind," although she didn't say which one. There followed a short, appropriately disastrous marriage, and then an assignment from the *Times* to cover the plight of the woman of the underdeveloped world, or vice versa, I could never get it straight. First, we had "Ms. Nanook" from Greenland. Then "Prisoners of Purdah" from North Africa. And finally pay dirt. While hunting discarded clitorises after a Watusi fertility rite, Potosky was captured by a band of pygmy guerrillas, who were just a shade taller than their Russian machine guns. She spent forty days in a mud hut with forty Hutus and a Belgian nun. When the little revolutionaries had been overrun, the mercenaries and the network mobile units arrived to see Potosky, safari suit barely sullied, helping her limping Belgian sister over the redoubts of diminutive corpses.

This adventure made Potosky a national celebrity. She became the only Western expert on the left-wing pygmy movement. Her campus lectures were SRO. She hit all the major talk shows. Everyone wanted to hear how the Hutus had kept nightly vigil around Potosky and her pet nun, fanning them with the broad leaves of the pupu tree, sharing their scant rations of yam and pickled monkey's foot.

"I've been following your career," I said. "You're a regular Sheeny, Queen of the Jungle, aren't you?"

"That's a new one, at least," she said.

"Is it true that pygmies have horizontal penises?"

Her reply was obscured by the clinking of the fire signal. In the old headquarters it was a bell that could awaken the dead. Here it was an apologetic clunk, which went on endlessly and without apparent rhythm unless you knew the code, and then you could get the magnitude, location and number of alarms of the fire.

"What is it?" Potosky asked.

"It's either a drunken timbal player, or Times Square seems to be burning down."

It was definitely the end of the world.

Smoke poured out of subway grilles as far down as Twenty-third Street. Herald Square was like a gigantic parking lot, rows of cars standing in glistening immobility as far across town as the eye could see. Macy's was partially obscured in exhaust fumes. Shoplifters, clutching handkerchiefs to their noses, ran back and forth into the store.

Fire trucks were parked at crazy angles in front of the subway entrances on Times Square. Ambulances turned onto the sidewalks, scattering pedestrians like frightened pigeons.

I had run all the way up from the twenties with Potosky huffing along behind me. And I'm the guy who gets winded when he walks to the bathroom. A battalion chief was retching into a red hankerchief. I flashed my press card. "What's going on?"

The chief looked at me as if I were a false alarm. "I left my frankfurters in too long," he said.

"May I quote you?" I said and hurried away before he could answer.

Culhane, the fire commissioner, was standing in the middle of the street with a fireman's poncho over his pin-striped suit, waiting for someone to take his picture. As soon as he saw me, he began barking commands.

"You spell your name with a C or a K?" I asked. That question always gets cooperation.

He spelled his name twice for me. "A switching line short-circuited," he said. "Now we've got passengers coming out of there saying the train exploded. We've got so much electrical smoke we can't figure out what went on."

Firemen streamed out of the subway kiosk, carrying coughing, shrieking passengers on their backs and dumping them in the arms of policemen and ambulance attendants.

"A human bucket brigade," I scribbled on a piece of copy paper and was so pleased with the felicity of the phrase that I looked around for more devastation to describe.

Potosky had cornered a weary fireman. "How bad is it down there?" she asked.

The fireman gagged. Tears ran in sooty trails down his red-leather cheeks. "Not that bad," he said. "At least there ain't no spics or niggers around to throw garbage at us."

I slipped around a police barricade and headed for the subway entrance. Acrid, black smoke blew out at me. Hot motes of soot settled like gnats out of hell on my forehead. The celestial trombones tuned up in my brain.

"Subway's closed, buddy."

A fireman on the end of a stretcher butted me back into the clean air. A Puerto Rican girl with bottomless black eyes was lying on the stretcher staring at me. She gasped for breath and clutched at her throat, but she never took her eyes off me.

"Laser," she wheezed as the firemen trundled her by. The blue veins stood out on her neck as she reached for me. "Laser."

"You know her?" the fireman asked me.

I shook my head and followed them to the ambulance. The girl twitched on the stretcher. A tiny drop of blood rolled out of her mouth. She looked imploringly at me.

"This woman is dying," I screamed.

A pimply intern sauntered over and put his stethoscope to her chest. A pulse flickered on her neck like a beacon. She moved her lips, shaping the word "laser," then passed out.

The intern called to a muscular Puerto Rican. "Nurse!"

The nurse had a scar on the bridge of his nose and a Marine Corps tattoo on his forearm. He was not my idea of an angel of mercy. "Paramedic, man, you know what to call me," he said. "I'm a paramedic."

"Take this girl to the hospital," the intern said, not at all intimidated.

The paramedic squinted down at the girl. *"Hermana,"* he said. *"Puedes hablar, hermana?"*

The intern looked upward for divine guidance. "I didn't say take her phone number. I said take her to the hospital."

The paramedic looked at the intern, trying to decide which way to split his head. "We're just sending a bus up to Hoover. We can bump one of those old ladies. . . ."

"I didn't say that," the intern said. "Just get her on the next one. . . ."

The paramedic began to vibrate. "Sure, one less spic pussy in the world, huh, doc? One less mouth for welfare to feed. . . ."

The intern looked to me for sympathy. "Would you say there was a crisis in health care in this city?" he asked.

"One empty apartment so the Jew landlord can raise the rent," the paramedic ranted.

"No point in provoking people," I advised the intern. But he obviously hadn't gotten to that point in his training where he had learned how to act like a human being.

"Schmuck," he shouted at the paramedic and then turned away to two policemen. "Could you please get this woman on an ambulance right away?"

"I'll handle this," the paramedic said. He grasped both ends of the stretcher, jerking it off the ground. The girl's head lolled over to the side.

"What's wrong with that girl anyway?" I asked.

The intern looked at my press card, his pimples glowing like warning lights. "She's got polyglottis of the blowhole," he said, trying to push by me.

"She kept saying laser," I said.

"She's a nuclear physicist, couldn't you tell?"

"Why would she repeat this one word?"

"The woman was delirious," he sputtered, dousing me in a cloudburst of Listerine. "She could have been saying razor because she didn't shave her legs this morning, or eraser because she spelled her name wrong. . . ."

"Got a gusher over here," a fireman called. They were bringing an old man out on a stretcher. He had a round bloody hole the size of a basketball in the middle of his blue serge suit. Aside from that, he was a neat, austere old man, a

17

bit pale perhaps, a bit distracted as well, his watery gray eyes roving wildly, his thin blue lips pursed prissily as if he had just heard a vulgar story. There was a thick, livid scar around his neck; his hands flopped over the sides of the stretcher, crisscrossed with scrapes at the wrists and knuckles. He groaned and tried to speak. A noise like that of a squeakily closing door came from somewhere within him. He frowned, as if concentrating on an intense problem, and coughed up a few chunks of aorta.

I stepped back and went two rounds with my breakfast. "I think he's dead," I said.

"Albert Schweitzer's got nothin' on you," the intern said.

"Is that a rope burn around his neck?"

The intern turned the old man's head. Blood flowed in a crimson freshet out of his mouth. Grimacing, the intern pushed the head back.

"He has them on his wrists, too," I said.

The intern lifted one limp arm. The scars were so deep it hurt to look at them.

The intern's name tag said Fliegenspan. "Let's find out who this guy is, Fliegenspan," I said.

It took him a few seconds to figure out how I knew his name. "Why?" he asked.

"You want a second opinion?" This guy looks more like he came off a battlefield than a burning subway."

"So?"

"So aren't you curious to find out who he is?"

"For God's sake, I can't search him. . . ."

"You're a doctor, you can do anything."

That put the serum in his hypodermic. He slipped his hand under the blood-soaked jacket and felt around in the man's jacket pockets. Then he went into the pants and came up shaking his head.

"Nothing," he said.

"Okay," I said, "tell me it's not weird that a clean, well-dressed old man gets on a subway without an ID, and just enough money to pay his fare."

"These people live on fixed incomes. . . ."

"And then gets his chest blown off."

"Now, we don't know that for sure. . . ."

"C'mon, Fliegenspan, there's something fishy here, and you know it. The cops will trace him, and you'll sign the death certificate. All you have to do is tell me his name."

Fliegenspan suddenly went shrewd on me. "Why should I?"

I put my arm around him. "Isn't there a story you'd love to put in the paper? A burning issue that's been ignored by the media. Orgies in the maternity ward. Rusty bedpans. White slavery in geriatrics. . . ."

"As a matter of fact . . ." Fliegenspan said but then looked doubtful. "I've been through this with the *Times* and the *News,* but they both put me on hold."

"Trust me, Fliegenspan," I said. "I'll get you banner headlines."

Now he got earnest; I liked it better when he was shrewd. "You see, the quality of outpatient care has been steadily eroded by a conspiracy of . . ."

Jill Potosky was striding purposefully through the barricades toward us. I grabbed Fliegenspan by the stethoscope. "I can see the headlines now," I said. "Outpatients Eroded, story page three. But we've got to keep this a secret, or we'll destroy the impact. Now there's a girl from the *Times* coming. I won't tell her about the outpatients if you keep mum about the old guy. Deal?"

Fliegenspan grabbed my hand in a clean, surgical grip. "Deal," he said.

And Potosky was upon us. "I'm trying to get an estimate of the number of injured," she said.

"Good idea," I said. "I was just asking Dr. Henderson here about that."

Potosky copied Fliegenspan's name off his lapel tag. "Henderson? That must be the Old English spelling. Can you give me any idea how many people have been evacuated from the subway so far, Dr. uh . . . Henderson?"

"How does he know?" I asked with all the lofty scorn I could muster and backed her up with a pedantic forefinger. "This isn't the jungle, you know, where stories drop out of the air like coconuts."

I turned to Fliegenspan. "Where are all these people going?"

"Hoover Memorial Hospital," he said.

"Well, there's your answer," I said to Potosky. "There's where you should be. And you too, Doc."

It took him a while. And when he got my drift I wished he hadn't. "Oh, yes . . . yes . . . of course, I have to leave right now." He winked twice and gave me a knowing glance as he backpedaled toward an ambulance.

"Friend of yours?" Potosky asked.

"He is rather a nice fellow, isn't he?" I said. "Actually, we've just met."

"The way he winked and shook your hand. Your mother wouldn't like that."

"Why? He's a nice Jewish boy. A doctor, too."

"What were you two talking about?" she asked.

"High colonics. We both love water sports."

She shook her head hopelessly.

"I don't know why you insist on being competitive on a simple story like this."

"Maybe it's not so simple," I said. "See you at Hoover."

I could feel Potosky's curious stare as I flounced off. Me and my cute little exit lines. I'd never be able to work this story in peace, thanks to my own big mouth. I needed medical help, too. Only they hadn't discovered a cure for terminal bravado.

Hoover was damned from its inception. A hospital named after Herbert Hoover can never hope to recover. It had been built in 1928 when that laissez-faire engineer was still a hero to the free enterprisers of the booming twenties, most of whom defenestrated within a year, cursing him all the way down. It rose on Tenth Avenue and Forty-fifth Street, a neighborhood that's been an unregenerate slum since Peter Stuyvesant threw out the first ball against the English. It was designed by a functional architect of the Art Deco School (imagine a tipsy ballerina trying to get through *Swan Lake,* and you've got the functional architects of the Art Deco School). From the outside it looks like a mansion in search of a moor. Its interior was laid out with that conspiracy against silence and sunlight that characterizes most public architecture of any period. Tiny, wire-reinforced windows line the dark green corridors. Hollow walls and crawl spaces magnify every sound. On a clear day you can hear the janitor farting in the boiler room, typewriters clattering, filing cabinets slamming shut, a veritable cacophony of the civil services. Buildings like this are no place for the sensitive, the frail, the unstable. Which is why they're used for schools, hospitals and welfare centers.

The emergency room, already bulging at the seams with battered babies, stabbed spouses and nodding junkies, now had to accommodate the hundred-odd casualties of the subway fire. People lay underfoot gasping into oxygen masks, vomiting from heat prostration or just staring bleakly in shock. Reporters canvassed the carnage for an articulate eyewitness. Definitely the amateur approach. Victims can never describe their ordeal; they were usually unconscious through the best parts. Only someone who wasn't there, someone with a fertile imagination and total disregard for the facts, can give you the big picture. And it helps if that person doesn't exist at all.

I brought Mrs. Bessie Schildkraut, a sixty-seven-year-old grandmother from Canarsie, into the fray. Mrs. Schildkraut is my most inspired invention. She's articulate, has total recall and really gets around for an old lady, having been present at every natural and man-made disaster in the metropolitan area over the last nine years. She's a grandma (everybody knows that grandmas don't lie—what could they lie about?) and comes from a section of Brooklyn so amorphous that not even its residents know where it is.

"The train stopped short," Bessie said, "and in came all this black smoke. People were screaming. The heat was so bad I thought I was going to faint. One man started singing 'The Lord's Prayer.' I saw a woman fall; she didn't get up.

21

GLITTERBURN

Then there was an explosion and all the windows blew out. An old man fell into my lap bleeding like he'd been stabbed or something. Then these firemen battled through the smoke. Such brave men. As scared as I was, I felt proud to be a New Yorker."

A brilliant description. Who needed hysterical passengers to confuse me with the facts? I wasn't a stenographer taking down the idiot rantings of the commonality, but an artist whose impressions meant more than a thousand eyewitnesses.

I sneaked around trying to find a free phone. There were three in the community service office, guarded by a huge black nurse, munching Tootsie Rolls and reading the *National Star*.

I flashed the old press card. It made me as popular as a runaway urine specimen. "Can I use the phone?" I asked.

She looked me up and down with profound West Indian contempt. "No way. We have to keep these lines open for crisis intervention."

"Give him a line, Brenda."

It was the militant paramedic, Angel Vasquez, according to his name tag. He was standing, arms folded, blocking the doorway. He had a woman's purse over his shoulder, a rather disconcerting addition to his wardrobe, which set my innards atremble. "Make your call, man," he said, "then we'll have a little talk."

I try to avoid tête-à-têtes with muscular ex-marines carrying purses. "Well, I wouldn't want to interfere with a crisis," I said, inching toward the window.

Brenda gave me a farewell look. Her starched uniform crackled as she eased off her chair and waddled out of the office with elephantine dignity. Vasquez stepped back to let her pass, then resumed his position blocking the door. "Make your call, man," he said.

"Certainly will," I said. "And thank you for interceding in my behalf."

I called the *Event* and dictated the story for the last edition. Then I got myself switched over to Seymour Levinson, the night assistant editor.

"Go home," Levinson said. It's the only thing he can say without becoming automatically responsible for my expenses during the next eight-hour period.

"I'm not ready for that," I said.

"There's nothing more for you there, so go home," he said.

"But there have been some interesting developments," I said, smiling and nodding at Vasquez, who just stared at me like a cigar-store Indian.

"What development?" Levinson asked.

"I'm not at liberty to say," I said.

"Stop pullin' my prick and get to the point, willya? You're on your own time anyway."

"Mr. Vasquez of the hospital staff is standing right here with me."

"That's code, right?"

"Right."

"All right, asshole, I got nothin' better to do than play twenty questions with you. You can't talk 'cause this guy's standin' there, so gimme a hint."

"An incongruous fatality," I said. "A senior citizen got hit by a pitched ball, and what a shot! He had to be taken out of the game and put on the inactive list."

"Sorry, I lost that one in the sun."

"He took a basketball in his chest, a jump shot," I shouted. "And he dribbled off the court. A personal foul is indicated."

"Okay," Levinson said, "some old guy got shot on the train during the fire and bled to death."

"Two points," I said. "Now it so happens that I am the only spectator who saw this little play, so I'd like to stick around. . . ."

"And look up nurses' skirts for a couple of hours on company time," Levinson said.

"If that's what it takes to straighten this thing out," I said with sober dedication.

"Our own fearless correspondent. Our own Ernie Piles. . . ." I heard the excited murmur of voices. A bad sign. "Hold on a second, Scoop," Levinson said and put his hand over the phone. Then he was back on. "You wanna work so bad, I got something for you. They just found a severed hand in a collection box at an Iglesia Pentecostal in Spanish Harlem."

"So send the religion editor," I said. "Sounds like a miracle to me."

"The only miracle is I get you to sweat all night on a hundred-and-thirteenth street," Levinson said.

"Look, you've only got a fraction of a stiff," I said. "I got the whole thing. Where you gonna be working tomorrow when every paper and station in town is carrying the story, but the *Event?*"

"All right, putzo, dig your grave," Levinson sneered. "You're on overtime as of now. And you'd better make the murder story pay off, even if you have to go out and kill some *alteh cocker* yourself. . . ."

"Vasquez advanced on me, brandishing the pocketbook. "See this?"

"Yes, and it's quite lovely. Is it a Gucci?"

"That's all that's left of that little girl they brought out of the subway."

"What do you mean?"

"That girl," he said louder, as if I hadn't heard. "The one who kept talking about your blazer. She's dead." He threw the purse on the desk.

There was a length of coiled clothesline in the purse and nothing else. Vasquez stared at me with furious concentration. "She died in the emergency room while the doctors were foolin' around with all those old Jews. I found the purse on the floor."

"Did you see the girl die?" I asked.

"No, no, no." Vasquez shook his head as if talking to a slow-witted child. "Listen, they stashed the body somewhere, 'cause they know they had a negligence or malpractice suit on their hands. That's the first thing these creeps learn in medical school is how to cover their asses. And don't think they don't stick together. . . ."

"Did you check admissions?" I asked.

"I never got her name in the first place."

"She disappeared almost as soon as she got here."

"Well, how about the morgue?"

"Can't get near it," Vasquez said triumphantly. "Cops all over the place. Detectives inside. It's a cover-up." He leaned forward threateningly. "Now what are you going to do about it?"

Now was my chance. I slammed my hand on the desk so hard I startled Vasquez. "Expose the bastards," I shouted. "C'mon, we'll get to the bottom of this."

I pushed by him and dashed down the hall for the exit. When I turned back, he was standing in the doorway. I flashed him the clenched fist and hit the stairs. Another prime example of underclass paranoia, I thought. Lucky for me I'd gotten away. But in the same rush of alpha waves I wondered why there were cops guarding the morgue. And also realized that clothesline could make rope burns.

Ah, what the hell, I could take a little side trip to the morgue. The walk would do me good.

Morgues are afterthoughts to the people who build hospitals. They always have the facilities nicely laid out until some wet blanket says: "All well and good, but where are we going to put the stiffs?" So they wedge a room in between the employees' lockers and the vending machines.

The Hoover morgue was not on the hospital directory so I had to sniff it out. I ran down to the basement. The off-white walls got grayer. Patients lay in ghastly calm, four to a room. The fluorescence dimmed and the paint peeled. An emaciated old man in a stained hospital shroud asked me for a cigarette. I gave him the pack. An elderly nurse with rouged cheeks and a blond wig was having a coughing fit behind her desk. I knew I was heading in the right direction.

A tiny electric sign whispered out of the gloom at me. "Mo-gue;" either the "r" was missing or it was a Southern

25

hospital. Outside, on the ramp leading up to the driveway, there were a few drab detective Plymouths among the flashing emergency vehicles. An overweight patrolman stood guard in front of the morgue. There were patches of sweat on his shirt, and he was breathing hard from the effort of standing on his feet.

"What's goin' on?" I asked. Behind the frosted windows wavery forms moved in a blur and voices were barely audible.

"They're havin' a barbecue," the cop said.

I showed him my press card.

"Got any pictures of your kids?" he asked.

I made a mental note to stop flashing that goddamn card. "I guess they're doing an autopsy in there," I said.

"I think they're doing their laundry," he said.

I tried another tack. "Could you get somebody to come out and give me a statement . . ."

"About what?"

"The Puerto Rican girl."

"Oh, I can make that statement," the cop said, clearing his throat for a recitation. "The Puerto Rican girl is a strange, beguiling creature. . . ."

Fliegenspan rushed out of the morgue.

"I've got to talk to you," he said, jabbing his finger in my chest.

I threw a gloat at the policeman. "He's going to tell me everything he knows."

"See ya in a second," he said.

Fliegenspan drew me into a musty alcove near the Coke machine. "Boy, is this your lucky day," he said.

"Is it about the girl?" I asked.

"What girl?"

"The Puerto Rican girl, dummy."

Fliegenspan gulped in outraged incredulity. One just can't call a Jewish Prince a dummy. "You're the dummy around here, buster," he whispered vehemently. "I'm talking about the old man, the one with the hole in his chest."

"What about him?"

"He's . . ." Fliegenspan stopped and jabbed me again. "Does that deal we made still go?"

"Sure, sure, the eroded outpatients . . . Now, what about the old man?"

"He's Cyrus Wilkins."

It took me a moment to riffle through the cerebral index cards. Cyrus Wilkins, seventy-eight, chairman of the board of Global Paper, a multibillion-dollar multinational. Wilkins, himself a self-made billionaire. Started out as a card cheat in the Yukon, fleecing miners out of their claims, buying and selling until he owned millions of acres of forestland in Canada and the Northwest. A lunatic right winger, owns his own radio network which sends out the Gospel according to John Birch to fifty affiliates throughout the country. Cyrus Wilkins brings his lunch to the office in a paper bag, doesn't drink fluoridated water, disinherited his son for marrying a Catholic. Runs a nonunion shop. Doesn't go for a nickel in raises or benefits to his employees, but if you goosestep into his office with a sheet over your head you get the keys to the vault with browsing privileges. What the hell was Cyrus Wilkins doing on a New York subway?

"Can't be," I said.

"It is," Fliegenspan said. "His executive assistant just made positive identification."

"How'd they pin him so fast? His face isn't that well known."

"The cops knew who he was, that's all I know," Fliegenspan said. "And the cause of death . . ."

"And the cause of death . . ."

"Embarrassment," Fliegenspan hooted, "because his shirt was all bloody from the howitzer that hit him in the chest."

"Murdered," I said.

"It could be suicide if you can imagine a guy putting a shotgun to his chest and getting off both barrels, because that's how big that hole is."

Cyrus Wilkins murdered with a double-barreled shotgun aboard a burning subway. Not even Bessie Schildkraut could have thought of this. "Fliegenspan, this is a big one. Now I've just got to get an official confirmation. . . ."

"Whoa, wait a minute, what about my story?"

"We're gonna spread it all over the paper," I said, backing away toward the morgue.

"Well, that's fine," Fliegenspan said, "because if I'm not speaking to a reporter from your paper within an hour about the deplorable conditions in the outpatient program— which, incidentally, I consider a good deal more crucial to this city than some meaningless piece of sensationalism . . ."

"And I agree. Wholeheartedly. In an ideal society outpatients would make the front page while murdered billionaires on burning subways would be lucky if they got in at all. Now you just wait here; we'll send our medical reporter up with an ambulance escort."

I ran back to the morgue. A new cop was on duty. He had an angry shaving rash under his third chin, and one look told me he lacked the wit of his predecessor. Before I could stop it, my hand zoomed to my wallet in that old vestigial reflex and flashed the press card. The cop looked at it like it was a malignant tumor and shook his head.

"No," he said.

"Why are you saying no?" I said. "You don't know what I want."

"I don't care what you want," he said. "The answer is no."

"I want a policeman. Somebody's mugging my grandmother."

The cop dug in and squared his shoulders.

"Lieutenant Duffy in there?" I asked.

"Only if he's dead," he said.

"Duffy, you asshole!" I screamed.

The cop flushed under his whisker burn. He balled a fist the size of a volleyball and moved on me, but he went sprawling as the morgue door swung open, and Detective Silas Grey strode out to see what was happening.

Grey is probably the toughest man on the Eastern seaboard. He's as black as a comma, stands six eight and carries

a good three-hundred pounds, none of which seems to have
settled around his midsection. He has more strength in his
lower lip than I have in my whole body. When he stands still
it looks like somebody left the pipe rack in the suit. When he
walks you hear the sounds of a distant avalanche. He
functions as chief head buster and food taster for the chap
whose malicious visage peered out from behind his back.

Lieutenant John Duffy looks like a monsignor with a
hangover. He's the kind of public servant who finds the
public a hindrance. He wishes half the population would be
murdered so he could arrest the other half.

"Who invited you?" Duffy said.

"You get the only air-conditioned room in the city, and
you throw a cordon around it," I said. "Is that fair?"

"Take a walk," he said.

"Isn't this the press preview of *Gone with the Wind?*" I
asked.

"Take a walk," Grey said.

Him I listened to. "Sure I will, but first tell me what Cyrus
Wilkins was doing on the subway."

Duffy's head jerked in angry surprise. "Names of the
victims have not yet been released. . . ."

"Never mind the catechism," I said. "I've got it all. I was
there when he came out. . . ."

"You can't print any of this without official corrobora-
tion," he said.

"Smarten up," I said. "This is the yellow press. Print first
and settle out of court later is our motto. I just want to put
your name in the paper next to some particularly acute
quote about this whole business."

"You'd better stay away from this one," Duffy said.

"Keep talking," I said, scribbling away. "You want to
elaborate on that threat a little?"

Duffy turned back to the morgue. "If this turkey stays
around five minutes longer, wring his neck," he said to Grey.

"You'll never get to the top of your profession if you
antagonize the fourth estate," I shouted after him.

"My, my," Grey said, shaking his head. "You holler loud
enough to wake the dead."

"Tell your boss he's an asshole," I said, backing out of punching range.

"He's only trying to do you a favor," Grey said. "This could definitely burn you, baby. Burn you bad."

Grey nodded soberly. He never lied and he never exaggerated; the toughest guy on the Eastern seaboard doesn't have to do that.

"Maybe you could forget about how mean you're supposed to be and drop this story," he said.

"Can't do that," I said.

He shrugged and turned away as if I were already in the obituaries.

New Lead Fire, I called it. I dictated to Ishkowitz, a summer intern from the Missouri School of Journalism, a pear-shaped Jewish kid who had decided to hero-worship me until Labor Day.

"Investigators probing into the cause of the fire on the IRT yesterday have produced a mystery of their own," I dictated.

"Far-out lead," Ishkowitz said.

"Just take it down," I said. "Late yesterday afternoon detectives under the command of Lieutenant John Duffy, Manhattan South Homicide, sealed off the morgue at Hoover Memorial Hospital, denying access to reporters and hospital employees as well. . . ."

"Hey, this sounds great," Ishkowitz gushed. "Wait until Mr. Levinson sees this. He said it was just a crock of shit."

I managed to get through the story with a minimum of exclamations until the last paragraph.

"The mystery deepened with the disappearance of a young woman who was taken off the train with Wilkins. Eyewitnesses reported the woman kept screaming 'laser, laser' as she was taken on a stretcher to an ambulance. One of Global Paper's subsidiaries has been engaged in classified laser weapons research under a secret contract with the Pentagon for years."

Suddenly Levinson was on the line. "How do you know they're doing secret defense work?"

"If they're not, this story will give them the idea," I said. "I might even get a finder's fee."

"The only thing you're gonna find is the subway to the South Bronx," Levinson said. "They just found a hand in the meat department of the A&P on Intervale Avenue."

"Was it on special?" I asked.

"Find a subway, Krales."

"I've got time. Until they find a face, they won't know who it is."

"Krales . . ."

"I'll go up there," Ishkowitz said.

Levinson snorted, "You? They've never seen anybody who looks like you up there. They'll think you're something to eat."

"I'm sure Ishkowitz is quite capable of covering this," I said.

"Thank you, Mr. Krales. . . ."

"You're welcome, Ishkowitz," I said.

"Listen, Krales, this sounds like another one of your novelizations. How can we prove the dead guy is Wilkins if the cops won't admit it?"

"I have my sources," I said.

"The only source you have is on your tie. Now get up to the Bronx where we got a story you can get your teeth into."

"A frozen hand? Seymour, we're talking about Pulitzer Prizes here. Woodward and Bernstein, move over. Levinson and Krales break the biggest story of the year."

"I want proof, Krales," Levinson said. "And not from Bessie Schildkraut, either."

I was looking for a subway token before he hung up. A night in the South Bronx, the garden spot of New York, awaited me.

"Hey, Krales!"

Fliegenspan was bearing down on me, waving a piece of paper. "I thought you were sending a reporter up to speak to me."

"I am," I said. "Our ace medical man. Would have been a doctor, but he can't stand the sight of money. . . ."

"Because I've got something big here. I've got something that's going to blow the roof off the medical establishment of this city. . . ."

I snatched the paper out of his hand. It was Wilkins's death certificate. The cause of death was listed as "asphyxiation leading to cardiac arrest." Not a word about a couple of large bullets that caused a very large hole.

"What do you think of that?" Fliegenspan fumed. "I guess a few heads will roll when you print this."

"No," I said. "We can't print this."

"What do you mean? We have to. It's our duty . . ."

"It's our duty to improve outpatient care in this neighborhood, isn't it?" I asked.

"Yes. . . ."

"Stick with me, and there'll be an oxygen tent on every corner. People will send out for a colostomy like they do for a pizza." I ran for a phone, Fliegenspan in hot pursuit.

I dialed the hospital and asked for the morgue. Grey answered, and I asked for Duffy.

"I think he's in conference," Grey said.

"Tell him I've got a copy of Wilkins's death certificate," I said.

There was a muffled rumble, then a maddened cry.

"Where are you?" Duffy screamed.

"In a phone booth staring at a felony," I said. "It is a felony to falsify a death certificate, isn't it? It certainly isn't grounds for promotion."

"That greasy little intern," Duffy raged.

"That man is the closest thing to Hippocrates this corrupt age will ever produce," I said.

Duffy's voice was thick with menace. "This is the end of you, Krales."

"Stuff and nonsense," I said. "Just give me official confirmation that the deceased is Wilkins, plus enough about the death to make a few plausible paragraphs."

"And what'll you give me?"

"A thousand and one pieces of death certificate."

"You bastard," Fliegenspan screamed and tried to get into the phone booth. I closed the door on his hand.

"What's that?" Duffy asked.

"Hippocrates is having hysterics," I said. "C'mon, give."

"Why not? It'll never be printed anyway," Duffy said. "Wilkins was murdered on the train during the commotion of the accident. He was blown up by a small plastic explosive that might have been strapped to his chest with a detonator electronically controlled."

"That's a nice little toy," I said, scribbling furiously.

"There were rope burns around the wrist, ankles and throat like he'd been hog-tied," Duffy said. "Bruises and lacerations in the upper cranial area. Traces of dried sperm along the inner right thigh."

"Whose?" I asked.

"Obviously, he's not in a position to give us a free sample," Duffy said. "We assume it's his."

"A man in his late seventies?" I said. "You're a wet dreamer."

"There are indications that the deceased had a seminal discharge," Duffy snarled. "You want details?"

"Not if it's going to upset you, darling," I said. "Besides, I've got enough to keep me out of the South Bronx."

"But not off the unemployment line," Duffy said. "I gave you the rope, Krales. Now go hang yourself."

Fliegenspan managed to extricate his hand while I was dialing the *Event*. Just as I got Levinson on the phone, I turned to see him bearing down on the booth, brandishing a standing metal ashtray.

"I'll have to call you back, Seymour," I said and just managed to slip out before Fliegenspan's momentum carried him into the booth.

"Help, mad doctor," I screamed, running down the corridor. A security guard, his Afro sticking out from underneath his cap, quashed a reefer and tried to act authoritative.

"What's going on here?"

I pointed to Fliegenspan, who was running full tilt, the ashtray raised high over his head. "That man is impersonating a physician," I said and dashed out of the building. The last thing I saw was Fliegenspan with a face full of mace, shouting, "I am a doctor. Look at my name tag."

I hid in the Iron Lung, a bistro around the corner from the hospital. Doctors and nurses stood around, talking about afterbirths and ski weekends. I sat in a phone booth screaming at Seymour Levinson.

"Cop, you hear? Bobby, *gendarme, polizei*, Cossack. I got one on my side. Lieutenant John Duffy says yes, indeed, that stiff is none other than Cyrus Wilkins. Now put me on with a rewrite man, and send some other poor slob to the Bronx. . . ."

"Josh?" These were Grissom's honeyed tones. "I'm on the line here with Sy."

"Gollee, my first conference call," I said.

"We think you've done a fantastic job on this story, Josh, but unfortunately there are some legal problems with it."

"Not anymore," I said. "I've got a quote from a cop, and also the death certificate right here in my hot Hebrew hand."

There was a moment of silence as Grissom reached for his Rolaids. "Is there no end to your initiative?" he said sourly.

"Not in your lifetime," I said.

"I hope those people at the University of Hawaii appreciate you as much as we do."

That sounded like a bribe. "I thought I wasn't going to Hawaii."

"Why not?" Grissom asked. "I can think of no better man to carry the banner of the *Event* to foreign climes."

"I can't either," I said.

"A man of talent and discretion," Grissom said. "A man who knows the value of silence."

"I just burned the death certificate," I said.

"May I be excused?" Levinson asked disgustedly.

"Certainly, Seymour, and thank you," Grissom said. "Now, Josh, why don't you come in tomorrow, and we'll arrange for a first-class ticket . . ."

"I just forgot Duffy's quote," I said.

"And a substantial expense allowance. . . ."

"Hold it," I said. "One more perk, and I'll forget my name."

"After all, we want you to do us proud in the tropics, uh . . . Professor Krales," Grissom said.

"That has a nice ring to it," I said.

"And no one can better live up to the title," he said, cloyingly expansive about the whole thing.

"Thank you," I said.

"Thank you," he insisted.

It was all crudely but effectively done. I was being bought off, but not with a twenty-dollar bill or a couple of tickets to a fight. For the first time in my life the price was right, and so for the first time in my life I would succumb.

The story had to be big. Grissom was foregoing one of his greatest pleasures in life—tormenting me—just to keep it out of the paper. If I ran it down, maybe I'd win a Pulitzer, topple the government, get those fellowships and starlets that had always eluded me. But that would mean sweating and hustling and haranguing my way through another summer in New York. And for what—the truth? How much better to be lolling on the sands of Waikiki beach, expatiating on the First Amendment to a class of love-starved *leilanis*.

"Krales, you're nothing but a whore," I thought. That had a nice ring to it, too.

I stepped out into the Iron Lung and joined the party.

Clams Chinese style had been my undoing.

Not the six martinis I chugalugged with Loretta, a two-hundred-pound dental technician from Brooklyn. Not the evil-smelling reefer I shared with an ear-nose-and-throat man from Trinidad. Not the kilo or two of olives, peanuts and tiny bricks of moldy cheddar I consumed. No, everything had been going swimmingly until someone suggested Chinatown.

It's an old custom—get drunk and go to Chinatown. And like many old customs of obscure origin, it's the worst possible thing you can do under the circumstances. If you've managed to keep your head and your cookies during hours of dissipation, a few minutes in a Chinese eatery on the Bowery will make you lose both.

There was a group of us. Or was it only me and the two-hundred-pound dental technician? All I know is it was a tight fit in the back seat of a Checker. Darkness was peeling off a fresh day. Garbage sautéed in fragant piles on the sidewalks. Bums retched along the byways. Orientals slouched by, eyes downcast. The relentless cityscape cut through the booze euphoria like a phone call at three in the morning. Bad news.

We went to a place that was so brightly lit the cockroaches did a song and dance as soon as they hit the Formica. If it had been Akron I would know it was a dream, but it was New York—Chinatown—and I know I saw a man with skin so transparent every capillary stuck out in his head like dead ends on a road map. The Chinese are a comely race, but not under fluorescence. Caucasians could use a little backlighting as well.

A busboy with arms like Loretta's fingers brought a steaming cauldron of arcana. It tasted like Mao Tse-tung's bathing suit. A group of emaciated chaps in the corner

36

pointed at me and giggled, obviously under the impression that I wouldn't know they were making fun of me because they were doing it in Chinese. Old Capillaries looked up from the *Racing Form* and bared a mouthful of brown teeth. Then he said something to the emaciated chaps, causing a faint wave of mirth to pass over them like a breeze over the gingko blossoms. After watching Loretta shovel mollusks into her maw for about three years, I decided I needed a spot of cold water on my wrists. The bathroom was at the bottom of a long, steep stairway. It was much too long a walk, so I plunged down like a kamikaze and spent a very pleasant weekend with my forehead pressed against the cool porcelain of the urinal.

The rancid taste of my spittle brought back a jumble of sense memories. A purple nipple hove into view. I made a speech about fat women. A massive bosom thrust me down a dark hall like a cowcatcher shoving a dogie. There was the vicious hum of an electric toothbrush. Snores and whispers. Then escape. How often have I slipped out of darkened bedrooms away from women whose names I could hardly remember? All very well to bemoan it, but it's the thing I do best in the world.

I had escaped from a sublet on Seventy-fourth and Second, the Girl Ghetto, they called it, wherein nurses, stewardesses and secretaries jammed four to an apartment. Circumnavigating a sullen roommate clutching a Tampax. Slipping through the living room where a pair of nacreous legs arched over the sofa while a dark form writhed in silent fury between them.

Outside, denimed janitors hosed the sidewalks. A doorman with more gold braid than a Montenegrin field marshal whistled for a cab. Ahead of me loomed the eerie greenery of Central Park. I crossed Fifth Avenue and flopped on a bench. Already, the city was like a preheating oven.

The streets were thronged with joggers, cyclists and dog-walkers, the new acolytes of health. I saw America striving, the varied regimens I saw. The housewives battling cellulite. The executives aerating their lagging livers. The homosexuals pursuing eternal youth. The oldsters forcing blood through sclerotic arteries. Couples being conspicuously "together." Singles being defiantly alone, and liking it. I heard America grunting. The thwack of the Pumas, the swoosh of the wheels.

And only a few steps within the sinister foliage I sensed America coiling to spring. The criminals checking for the glint of a chronometer. The perverts with *Walpurgisnacht* ringing in their ears. Malnourished, diseased, chain-smoking drug addicts panting clouds of polluted breath as they lurked in ambush. No vitamins for them; the only pills they took got them high. Eschewing bicycles and barbells, they stayed in shape by pursuing those superbly conditioned middle-class athletes who strayed into their midst.

It was a melancholy sight, this ingenuous defile marching into the flora to be debauched by the fauna. It was certainly nothing to laugh at. But someone disagreed.

The laugh shattered the orderly morning calm. It was an absolute shriek of desperate merriment. A few heads in the herd of joggers turned. A cab driver leaned out to take a look.

A blonde in a white evening dress was running barefoot up Sixty-fifth Street, holding a white high-heeled shoe in each hand. She spread her arms out and vaulted a fire hydrant, her dress trailing over it in regal caress. Some contemporary flapper, no doubt, with a noseful of cocaine, fleeing a night of bliss with her Racquet Club Romeo. She was tall and moved with the grace of an athlete.

In the middle of Sixty-fifth Street a gray-thatched, black chauffeur labored sedately out of a brownstone mansion over to a forest-green Silver Cloud parked at the curb. He looked up at the blonde. . . . It was her chauffeur. My God, I thought. A blonde in white with a green Rolls and a black chauffeur—the colors of priapism if I ever saw them.

I got up and ran toward her. Now a hunched, double-chinned gentleman in a homburg marched out of the brownstone toward the Rolls. He, too, turned to watch her before entering. He had a swarthy, sneering face with a hooked nose that was Goebbels's dream. The Semitic financier. The hairy-handed, herring-breathing beast with the heavy charm. So that was what she was fleeing.

She was running at full tilt now across the street, while Mr. Swarthy Homburg got into the Rolls and the chauffeur closed the door gently behind him. They had forgotten each other.

"Hey, miss," I shouted. I didn't know what I was going to say. All that mattered was to get her attention.

She turned in midstride. "You." She laughed and ran toward me.

The Rolls ignited with a discreet purr. A puff of genteel white smoke belched out of the exhaust pipe.

The girl was upon me. Her skirt billowed around her legs.

"You!" she cried with a manic shriek of hilarity and raised her hand over her head.

The Rolls-Royce eased away from the curb. Her blue eyes glittered like uncharted tropical seas. Feral teeth flashed in her suntanned face. The tap on the edge of her high heel glinted. The Rolls gleamed. Everything was light and movement and excitement.

And then everything exploded.

>

Dying is almost worthwhile if it's hot, you're broke and they let you write your own obituary. Lolling on the sidewalk, looking at a suspiciously celestial path through the trees to the cloudless heavens, a thousand rolling tympani heralding my arrival in the netherworld, I realized that I was being given these few precious moments to leave my last words to the world. I've worked under deadlines before, but this was ridiculous. I had to hurry before they took away my ectoplasm, and I'd only be able to slam doors and knock people's hats off.

EVENT REPORTER MARTYRED, read the black-bordered

headline I composed. "Crushed by love's juggernaut in the person of a spiked heel at point-blank range, reporter Josh Krales expired on a sidewalk near Central Park today," read the lead.

But wait . . . I climbed a few rungs of thick morning air. Purgatory bore an astonishing resemblance to Fifth Avenue. I had a very unseraphic bump on my noggin. I was alive, I decided, but somebody else wasn't. The joggers had reversed their field, sirens were wailing, there was a festive feeling in the air. Everyone converged on the spot in the middle of Sixty-fifth Street. It wasn't a hit show, and they weren't giving anything away. The only thing that draws such a devoted crowd is a nice fresh corpse.

Staggering across the street, I was swept up in a blue surge of policemen and deposited in front of the smoking wreckage of what had once been a forest-green Silver Cloud. The man in the homburg was spread over the back seat like shad roe over a Triscuit. A limbless jacket with a few flakes of dandruff on the shoulders sat stolidly behind the wheel. A black face—I assumed it belonged to the jacket—was on the floor, staring balefully up at the steering column as if trying to locate a squeak. Bystanders threatened to vomit or swoon if they tarried another moment, but nobody moved.

I had to be the first reporter on the scene. Better hurry before the mobile units arrived and everybody went into their media act.

I walked resolutely up the sandblasted steps of the brownstone as if I'd made the journey a thousand times before. A vigilant policeman made censurious noises.

"I'm the family physician, officer," I said. "I was called. . . ."

The cop led me into a quiet paneled vestibule where a wrinkled lady in a black dress was trying to fit her large, warty nose into a handkerchief. She tore a clump of white hair out of the back of her head and added it to a growing pile on the floor. Her voice creaked like the hinge on a coffin. The cracking sound sounded Greek to me. I pointed a limp medical finger.

"And this, I assume, is . . ."

"Mrs. Agamisou," the cop said. "I thought you said you were the family doctor. . . ."

"This lady would never let me near her," I said quickly. "Depends on old-country remedies, turtle turds, chicken lips, things like that. . . ." All the while I was trying to place the name. Agamisou, Agamisou.

"Alcibiades Agamisou," I said aloud.

The cop was in a philosophical mood. "Guess his money ain't doin' him too much good now."

Perhaps. But it had been quite useful to him while he was alive. This was Agamisou, the original Greek Tycoon.

Alive, he'd always been Page One. Dead, he'd really stop the presses. And who said nothing happened during the summer.

Agamisou's bio read like a handout from a demented press agent. He was a kid from Athens born in a slum in the shadow of the Parthenon to a family famous in the neighborhood for rickets, incest and psoriasis. His father, looking upon the havoc he had created, deserted the family when little Alcibiades was four. Mom just sat in the vestibule and cried all day, and the rest of the family was too dumb to steal and too ugly to whore, so Alcibiades had to provide.

He got his start as a bootblack in the Athens shipping district. Thirty years later, by his own proud admission, he had ruined every man whose boots he had blackened. He was the single largest shipper in the world, gulping down companies at two or three a month. He didn't care where it was or what it did; he wanted it. Plus the ground it was on, and the bank it borrowed from as well. Of course, there was the usual double dealing: a little bribery, an occasional murder (they're called assassinations when more than a million dollars is involved) and some kind of unpleasantness with the German occupation, which necessitated his absence from Mother Hellas for several years.

Actually, only a fraction of Agamisou's wealth had come from duplicity and intrigue. No, the lion's share had been inherited from his wife. While barely out of his teens, Agamisou had married the daughter of Democritus Dolmas, a shipping magnate of an earlier era. In this, Agamisou

41

shown himself a true romantic. For although his new wife was twenty years older than he, with a bow and a stern that would rival any of those on her daddy's ships, his undying love conquered all.

Their marriage was idyllic but short-lived. A scant three months after they took the vows, the little woman was washed up on the rocky shores of Smegmos, a little Aegean island that had been included in her copious dowry. She had been carried off in the undertow, her grieving husband explained. No one asked about the bruises on her head and face—they were obviously caused by the rocks. Or about the tiny puncture wounds in her abdomen. There was a variety of man-eating sardine indigenous to these Aegean waters—a distant relative of the piranha fish, Agamisou's physician explained. He immediately became the proud possessor of a nursing home in Salonika. These minuscule manslaughterers had been portrayed on certain urns of antiquity, a local archaeologist reported. He immediately moved to Athens where he became curator of everything over the age of sixty-seven. Although no one had ever seen these voracious creatures, their existence was confirmed by several fishermen who hydroplaned from the inquest in their new speedboats.

Agamisou turned Smegmos into the red-light island of the Aegean. He had the wealth of a renaissance prince, so why not the morals and the enthusiasms as well? The simple, pious fisherfolk became accustomed to the champagne bottles and bikini tops that floated by their shabby barques. They ignored the occasional mangled fetus that fouled their nets. On summer nights when the wind was right the cries of imported chorines could be heard as far down as Corfu. An investigative reporter was burned beyond recognition while a guest there, the result, said a local constable, of the eruption of a long-dormant volcano under his bed. There were no complaints brought against the *seigneur* of this little island. He was a wealthy man, and this was how the wealthy lived.

Agamisou was no philanthropist. No research centers or

children's hospitals bore his name. He didn't support artists or preserve landmarks. He didn't collect treasure; he squandered it on boats, cars, houses and women—an admirable program in my eyes. He had bedded and booted every leading lady in Europe; had been seen sour and saturnine on the arm of every titled beldame under the age and breadth of forty; had bought his way out of scandals with fourteen-year-old schoolgirls in Sardinia; and supported chanteuses, masseuses, soubrettes and minettes in every civilized country in the world.

Now Agamisou, the voluptuary, the shameless profiteer, had been dispatched with the same frank, brutal finality with which he had lived.

Through the window I saw platoons of cops turning out to guard the building. They would keep the press away. I alone would be privileged to traduce the bereaved family. Josh Krales, a nosy, vindictive son of a bitch who hated the rich, disdained the poor and had a modish horror of the middle class; who wrapped himself in the First Amendment to justify every sort of villainy he could safely perpetrate. I was unscrupulous, mendacious, selfish . . . and quite pleased with myself.

It was an old Fifth Avenue townhouse, built during the gilded age when life was simpler and the Protestants had all the money. The banisters were of polished mahogany. A few Monets lined the walls, just so nobody would get bored walking up the stairs.

The second floor looked like the late Mr. Agamisou's office. In one dark, heavily shaded room a solid oaken desk stood on an Oriental carpet. There was a huge Mercator on the wall with little clock insets showing what time it was in all the capitals of the world, put there, no doubt, so Agamisou could awaken his oppressed subordinates in the middle of their nights. Adjoining was a boudoir in which Louis XIV would have happily laid his *pot de chambre*. A soft, golden carpet swallowed your feet. Curtains of golden velour halted the sun's rays. A huge gold-plated fourposter dominated the room, veiled by a diaphanous golden curtain that drooped to the floor. It was here that Agamisou had accomplished his seductions, here that he had tumbled that lethal, blond heel wielder.

But something clashed. A tiny puddle of darkness, a black hole that let in the universe. It was on the golden armchair by the bed. A throwaway sheet, the kind street hawkers thrust into your hand. On it was a grainy photograph of a gutted tenement, and under it, in the crazily mixed lettering of a ransom note, the caption: GET ON THE GUILTWAGON.

I slipped the sheet into my pocket.

"Doctor, doctor . . ." A slim brown lad stood in the doorway, bleating and faltering like a newborn fawn. "Come quickly, it is Hippolytus. . . ."

He led me up the stairs to the third floor and into a flagrant salon darkened by a torrent of silk curtains, redolent of hashish and sexual excrescences. In the shadows sat a tiny medicine ball of a man, keening and wailing with the skill of a Cretan grandmother. His torso gleamed white and hairless through a filmy black kimono. Fat-boy breasts sagged over his belly; flesh hung in dowager's folds from his arms. This was Hippolytus, the first born of Alcibiades Agamisou, heir apparent to his father's conglomerated empire. Hippolytus, known as Polly to his closest friends, or the Queen of Athens to the horde of journalists who chronicled his dissipations. Polly, who had proclaimed his deviance to the world, risking disinheritance and banishment. Who had boasted to a reporter: "I haven't seen my father in seven years. The longer I stay away, the bigger the checks get." Who had been excommunicated when he arrived for Easter Mass on the arm of a fifteen-year-old Maltese boy. "The Metropolitan was jealous because my date was younger than his," he later said. At the moment he wasn't saying anything more quotable than, "Papa, I've been bad . . . Papa, forgive me. . . ." He held out his hand to me as if to a dancing partner. "Are you the doctor?"

"Yes," I said.

"Will you give me a shot?" he asked.

"You mean a sedative?" I asked with a medical frown.

"Anything you've got," he said with shrill impatience.

"Darvon, demerol, pentathol, thorazine, if you have any. Oh, my God, you don't have thorazine. No, that would be too much to ask. Oh . . ." He clutched his stomach and resumed his keening. "I'm in pain, doctor. My papa . . . my papa . . ."

"Your papa just got blown to bits, and all you can think about is getting high."

I turned to see who had authored that harsh remark and recognized the undisputed star of the family, little sister Clytemnestra.

She advanced on her brother, hands on hips, a cigarette drooping from her lips. She was short and broad like her father, with a small waist and large, expressive breasts that stirred with every change of emotion. Now they were swaying back and forth like twin pendulums against a tight T-shirt that reached a heartbreaking inch below her buttocks.

Hippolytus came out of his trance long enough to snarl at her in French. She snarled back in Greek, something that sounded like "multihieroglyph panglossitis achoo."

"I will not speak Greek," Hippolytus shrieked, leaping to his feet. "That language is only good for selling fish or insulting somebody's mother. I will not. . . ." He stamped his foot and closed the kimono around himself.

"How did you get in here?" Clytemnestra asked me.

"I was just passing the scene and volunteered," I said.

"Come with me," she said, turning on her heel and marching out of the room.

Hippolytus sobbed plaintively and held out his hand. "Doctor, please stay."

He didn't have a chance.

I followed the bouncing buttocks out of the
room and up the stairs. The fourth floor was curiously plain,
as if the decorator had run out of steam.

"These are the servants' quarters," she said, reading my
mind. "I prefer it up here."

Her room was self-consciously Spartan; it looked as if she
had deliberately set out to make herself uncomfortable. The
floor was bare, the walls covered with radical posters
proclaiming obsolete slogans, rallying cries of a few years
before, which now seemed centuries old.

There was a narrow cot in a dark corner of the room. It
was neatly made up, three-cornered in military style.
Strange, to make one's bed so neatly after one's father has
been blown up. But then the rich are different. . . .

"You sleep on that?" I asked.

"It's quite comfortable," she said.

"Are you punishing yourself?"

"I'm atoning," she corrected.

"For what?"

"I don't have time to raise your consciousness," she said,
ripping the blanket off the cot and lying down. "What kind
of doctor are you anyway?"

"I'm a gynecologist," I said. As busy as she was, there was
always the off chance that she hadn't had her yearly Pap test.

She spread her legs, looking for the imaginary stirrups.
"You don't look like a gynecologist."

"It's only a way station," I said. "I started as a chiropo-
dist. In a couple of years I'll be a brain surgeon. . . ."

"What's your name?" she asked.

"Fliegenspan," I said.

"You know who I am, don't you, Dr. Fliegenspan?"

"Everybody does. . . ." As indeed they did. "Clitty" was
her jet-set *nom de guerre*. Although only twenty-five, she'd
been making headlines for ten years, ever since she'd played

the thumbsucking, pink-pantied nymphet in a porno film which had a limited but lucrative audience—her father, who bought up every print. She'd been married three times. The first to a Moroccan deckhand on her father's yacht, who died from an overdose of couscous. Second to a Ugandan pole vaulter, who vaulted from his penthouse without his pole; and the third time to a Turkish tennis pro, who had such an explosive serve that the entire clubhouse blew up. With every liaison her despairing father had put more money in the trust fund, and more distance between himself and his rebellious daughter. "The incorrigible Clitty," she was dubbed by the English gossip sheets. She became the corespondent in so many divorce scandals, staff and distaff, that an English MP proposed a law exempting anyone who had intercourse with her from a charge of adultery. Of late she'd been rather quiet. No scandals, no marriages . . . There'd been rumors of a reconciliation with her father; others spoke of a mysterious involvement in radical politics.

"I'm in shock," she said.

"You seem perfectly lucid to me," I said.

"If you know who I am, you know that I don't want to be goggled at by a lot of sleazy policemen," she said.

"And the courtyard is full of them, Your Highness," I said.

"Well you can cut them off for the time being," she said. "I want to bribe you into telling the police that I can speak to no one. Now how can I do that?"

"You can't," I said. "I'm incorruptible. And you're in shock. We'll discuss my price later."

I slipped out, closing the door gently. Assuming the proper medical demeanor, I marched down the stairs. At the third-floor landing I had to slide past Hippolytus, who was threatening to jump. "I want to die," he squealed, his kimono falling open onto one of the most unappetizing fish-white paunches I had ever seen. "Don't hyperventilate," I advised.

The second floor was crawling with sleazy policemen, dusting, photographing, stealing. One of them, a very large, very black gentleman, was prowling through Agamisou's office, checking something out for his boss, whose irate buzz-saw voice whined from the bedroom.

"Hey, Grey, get in here. . . ."

I whizzed past the office door as Lieutenant John Duffy came out of the bedroom holding a cigarette butt between a pair of tongs. "He had a broad in here," Duffy said indignantly, as if this were reason enough for the man to have been booby-trapped to smithereens.

Outside, firemen were hosing down the smoking Rolls. Two ambulance attendants were packing decapitated torsos and loose limbs into body bags.

"I got a black thumb here," one of them said.

"Well, don't ever try to plant nothin'," the other one said. A cop standing nearby guffawed and ran down the street to relay the joke to his buddies. Alcibiades Agamisou's nearly severed head flopped back on its neck. His eyes glittered like a stuffed bird's. Even dead he didn't look like a good man to make fun of.

There are some toes in Spanish Harlem," Levinson crooned over the phone.

"Several million at last count," I said. I was standing in a phone booth up the block from the Agamisou house, watching the street slowly fill with police emergency vehicles. There still wasn't a reporter in sight.

Levinson's good humor was unbreachable. He really thought he had me. "These were found at a construction site on First Avenue this morning," he said.

"Maybe they're hammer toes."

"Go up there and find the feet that go with them."

"No can do, white man," I said. "I'm going to Hawaii. . . ."

"By way of East Harlem," he said. "You're still working for me until your leave of absence comes through."

"Well, then, what am I going to do about Agamisou?" I asked, savoring the moment.

"Who?"

"The Greek shipping billionaire," I said. "It's the damndest thing, but he just got blown out of his Rolls-Royce up here on Sixty-fifth Street not twenty minutes ago. The chauffeur went along for the ride as well. It's a mess, Seymour. Talk about toes . . ."

Levinson moaned. "And you just happened to be passing when this happened."

"Better than that. I saw the bomber. She was a blonde in an evening dress. I'm an eyewitness, Seymour."

"Do you pay people to get killed when you're in the neighborhood?" Levinson asked plaintively.

"And then I told the cops I was the family doctor, so they let me in the house, and I got quotes from the sissy son and the nympho daughter. All exclusive. . . ."

Levinson called out for somebody to check police headquarters to see if there'd been an explosion. "I'm giving you one more chance to get on my good side," he said.

"Seymour, he's got an all-gold bedroom. And the daughter lives like a Weatherwoman on the fourth floor. . . ."

"All right," Levinson said. "Give in your story, but don't disappear on me."

Ishkowitz came on the wire full of breathy gratitude. "I got some great stuff from that Dr. Fliegenspan," he said.

"That was yesterday," I said. "Journalism knows one tense, the present." That wasn't bad. I'd have to include that in my Hawaiian seminar. I could see a whole row of coeds going over, legs in the air, after hearing that line.

"Thanks to you, I've got my first byline, Mr. Krales," Ishkowitz said.

"Are you typing, Ishkowitz?" I asked.

"I just wanted to tell you how grateful I am. . . ."

"You aren't important enough to be grateful," I said.

"I know you act tough with everyone, but deep down . . ."

"Deep down I wish I could act tougher," I said. "Deep down I wish I could torture and rape and pillage, but I haven't got the guts. Now take this: 'Greek shipping magnate Alcibiades Agamisou was killed early today in front of his East Side townhouse when a bomb exploded in his limousine just as he was entering it. . . .'"

I gave him the story, including a graphic description of the townhouse and the mourning siblings.

And then I added the zinger. "Police believe that Agamisou entertained someone in his lavish all-gold bedroom on the second floor of the townhouse last night. A tall blond woman wearing a long white dress was seen running out of the house a few minutes before the explosion."

Gurgling with admiration, Ishkowitz took the last paragraph down. "Mr. Levinson is reading the story now," he said. "He says you shouldn't disappear."

"Goodbye, Ishkowitz," I said. I hung up and disappeared.

I wandered down Madison Avenue looking for Hawaiian shirts. A thousand boutiques between Sixty-fifth and Fifty-ninth, and not one shirt with a pineapple on it. A thousand limp-wristed clerks with their jacket collars pulled up as if it were raining, and they all told me to go to Alexander's.

I worked my way to the Upper West Side and ended up in my least favorite place—my apartment. I'm working on being an absentee renter. The place depresses me. It reeks of helpless mama's boy, who can't keep his room clean. Every time I walk in I think the FBI has been searching it. They haven't. It always looks that way. I used to have a maid, but I was ashamed for her. Now I'm waiting for the place to reach Dirt Zero, that point at which it can't get any messier. Then I'll turn it over to the Smithsonian and move to a hotel.

I pushed two hundred pounds of yellow newspaper off my bed and tried to find a clean place on the sheets to lay my head. My eyes had barely closed over Clytemnestra Agamisou cavorting in her T-shirt when the phone began ringing. It persisted like a nagging wife long after the caller should have surmised that I wasn't at home. I never pick up a phone that rings more than fifteen times—no well-wisher would stay on the line that long.

I took refuge in the bathroom. An advance party of cockroaches was reconnoitering the toilet; their antennae waved like frantic semaphores at my approach. I rinsed the pupae off my razor and shaved. A chunk of plaster had fallen into the shower in my absence. There was a sodden clump of blond hair in the drain. One of my amours must have had radiation poisoning. The phone was still ringing.

I cowered by the bed in my jockey shorts. Even my creditors would have given up by now. The paper sent telegrams. The cops would have shown up in person. I handled the receiver like a leprous limb.

"Putz, I need you." It was Reva St. James, the paper's gossip columnist. "I'm working on Agamisou. The paper says you got a Ph.D."

"It's all in the piece, Reva," I said.

"Don't be gallant, sweetface. I'm covering a garden party in New Jersey, a biggie, and your presence has been particularly requested."

"Who by?"

"You mean there's more than one? My God, who'd a thunk it? La Agamisou herself, the grieving daughter . . ."

"I'm going to Hawaii, Reva," I said.

"You're coming to New Jersey with a syndicated columnist, who also has her own TV show. Mr. Grissom is green-lighting the trip. Everybody on the *Event* humors Reva, peaches, even you. Now climb into your morning coat. I'm downstairs with the limo. Bring your diary; I want all the juicies."

So you're the new rage," Reva St. James said, peeking out of the back seat of her limousine like a quizzical Pekingese. "What's your secret?"

"Premature ejaculation," I said. "I climax with awe-inspiring swiftness."

Reva's chauffeur, a bull-necked, deadpanned Sicilian, held the door for me. He scowled at my ribaldry.

Reva grabbed my hands as I settled into the velour

cushions. "Let me check your thumbs out, Valentino. So what's your gimmick?"

"I sleep with my sweat socks on," I said. "I won't do anything the missionaries wouldn't do, and I fill the after-glow with stories about my ex-wife's infidelities. . . ."

"Hmm . . ." Reva sucked one of her three-inch vermilion nails. "You're smart, that's what it is. Looks like I'm going to have to dust off the rumpled, intellectual type again. Last time we used it was for Marilyn and Arthur. Hmmm . . . Boozy, not overly clean. Nowhere in sartorial department. Not sportif and a klutz at the discos. Have I got it so far?"

"Like you've known me all my life," I said.

"Hmm . . . It looks like the girls are going to try the meaningful route for a while. Trust little Clitty to come up with a rara avis."

"We try harder," I said.

"I already gave you smart, love. Now you're working on too smart."

I took out a cigarette.

"Oh, and he smokes Camels," she said. "He's a regular throwback, isn't he?"

"They're chocolate Camels," I said.

Reva hiccuped and made a naughty-little-girl face. "I think you actually made Reva laugh," she said.

"Do I get funny?" I asked. "Or too funny?"

"Don't be funny," Vito said, sideswiping a young mother with a baby carriage as he turned onto the West Side Highway.

Now Reva gave me the cute-cunning face she'd probably been using since the third grade. "Vito protects me. Isn't that sweet?"

She was one of those tight, tiny women who sit with their legs folded under them. Tan and falsely blond, she was the type who lived with her mother until one of them died and then married her male equivalent across the hall (if his mother had just died, that is). But somehow a chromosome had gone wild. Reva had gone into the newspaper business and was now the most powerful gossip columnist in the country. The star attraction of the *Event,* her column "Guess Who" was syndicated in hundreds of papers throughout the world. She had a syndicated TV show, "Reva's Reverie," that people fought to get on. She was a "maker and a breaker," to use one of the many phrases of her own invention. But she came from Brooklyn, from my neighborhood. As a teenager I had ignored girls like her, leaving them to their private crushes, their marathon phone calls; I still couldn't take her as seriously as she wanted me to.

"Like the wheels?" Reva asked.

"I was just wondering how you got the accountants to spring," I said.

"My dear little sex object, Reva won't set her size fives down on any piece of wilderness outside of Manhattan without the limo, the driver-cum-bodyguard and the week's supply of Maalox. On the continent I require an armed *garde de corps* from the elite regiment of the host country. In the Middle East a roundup of all suspected terrorists must precede my arrival by at least forty-eight hours." She sneaked a look to see how the routine was going. "It's very hard to lead *La Dolce* these days, what with inflation, terrorism and controlled substances. I'm telling you, my sources are dropping like flies. Either they go broke, or they're kidnapped, or OD or find Christ. . . ." She stopped for a breath. "Or they get themselves murdered in the most grisly fashion." She batted her dacron eyelashes at me.

I turned away like a sailor from Medusa's head. "I guess Agamisou was good copy," I said.

"And so was Cyrus Wilkins," Reva said. "If you like American Grotesques. And I do." Reva poked me with her dimpled fist. "Reva's not supposed to know about that one, is she? And neither is America."

"Well, if Reva doesn't know, it's not Joshie's fault," I said, mimicking her.

She drew back, hurt, and became very businesslike. "When you're a household word you'll have the right to refer to yourself in the third person."

"The Wilkins story was killed at the paper," I said. "Believe me, I worked very hard to let America know all about it."

"Oh, I know you did. I read a dupe of your story. As a matter of fact . . ." She pulled a few folded sheets out of her bag. "Here it is. I've already put in an order for the Agamisou piece as well."

"What do you mean?" I asked.

"That story won't run either. At least, not quite the way you dictated it. A shame, too; your prose is quite deathless."

"There's no reason to kill the Agamisou story. That's a straight hard-news piece. . . ."

"So was Wilkins," Reva said.

"They found sperm on his leg," I said. "He was probably out doing something he shouldn't. . . ."

"At his age, sweetie? The market would go up before he would."

"He probably owns a piece of the *Event,*" I said.

"Not a farthing's worth. . . ."

"Well, it's something political."

"Oh, now, don't be so newspaperly," Reva admonished. "Don't be such a bore. We've got ourselves a good old one hundred percent American conspiracy. When the Agamisou piece gets bowdlerized, you'll see . . ."

"How do you know it will?" I asked, angered by her smugness.

"Vito," she called to the chauffeur.

The glass partition came up, and Reva moved so close I could smell her Dentyne. "I wouldn't want to be a rich man these days, darling," she whispered. "They're dying like flies."

"Two does not an epidemic make," I said.

"How about four?" she said. She took a clip out of her pocket. It was an obituary: J. C. MCCLENDON, CHAIRMAN COMPUTECH, 73. The story described the death by heart attack of one of New England's leading philanthropists.

"You'd have a heart attack, too, if someone was caving your head in with a rock," Reva said.

"How do you know?"

"You get more than a tax attorney when you hit the eighth figure, brown eyes. You get Reva. These boys look in my column every day to find out if they're still alive."

She flipped me another obit: EDMUND PRUNEAU, 46.

"The crayfish king," I said. "From New Orleans . . ."

"A soft-spoken Southern gentleman from the old school," Reva said. "Liked his women black, his whiskey old and his competitors dead."

"Died in an automobile accident," I said.

"You'd find it hard to drive, too, if somebody had cut your brake linings," Reva said. "No, my dear, you'll have to face up to it. Somebody is murdering millionaires, and somebody else doesn't want America to know about it. Don't you find that interesting?"

"I'm going to Hawaii," I said.

"If some relevant details are left out of the Agamisou story . . ."

"Like what?"

"Like his name, snookums," Reva said. "Will you be interested then?"

"With all the cops and eyewitnesses, they wouldn't dare . . ."

"I didn't ask you to recite the Constitution. If there's no mention of Agamisou's name in the story of a mysterious explosion and an unidentified body, will you help me out on this story?"

"Yes," I said.

Reva smiled and pinched my cheeks with the savagery of one of my sadistic-solicitous maiden aunts. Any second now I expected a kiss that would engulf my entire cheekbone. I recoiled from those glistening auntly lips with the disquieting feeling that I had just been set up.

"All right, then, fasten your seat belt, cupcake, we're heading into the twilight zone."

The landscape changed with drastic suddenness as we turned off the highway onto a narrow country road.

"Welcome to Terra Rica," Reva St. James said with a flourish. "The land of the superrich."

There was no heraldic fanfare, only the crack of exploding gravel under the tires. Huge evergreens rose up on both sides of the road. I shivered. Vito turned off the air conditioner. We seemed to be heading into the mouth of a primeval rain forest.

"Where are we?" I asked.

"Short Hares, New Jersey," Reva said. "The county seat of the Blodgett family."

"Dismal place."

"Uncharted territory," Reva said. "The Blodgetts have been making the bucks since Great cubed Granddaddy burgled teepees in the Hudson Valley. They came over on the *Mayflower,* and were buying and selling and stealing before the anchor dropped."

"Never heard of them."

"Of course you haven't, silly," Reva said. She opened her purse and took out a sheaf of yellowing clips. "This is it for the past three hundred years. Why, the Kennedys make more news in a half hour. Look. Births, deaths and marriages, and not a whole lot of those either. The rest they keep hushed up."

"So who are they?" I asked.

"The superrich. The super-duper-illionaires, puss. They're not on the map, period. You don't find them in Newport, Palm Beach, Portugal or Barbados. They're so rich they're invisible. I mean, take this town. Out here in the famous horse country of New Jersey nobody knows where Short Hares is, not even the state police. I had to look it up in an old state atlas because it isn't even on the road map.

Now that, *mon petit chou,* is *La Classe.* We are not on the planet earth, so throw away your ideas about wealth. I'm the biggest society columnist in the free world, plus parts of Poland and Hungary. I know everybody. *Evvveryyyboddy* . . . But I've never been to a Blodgett party. Or handled a Blodgett item. I've never even met a Blodgett. They won't have anything to do with me." She paused triumphantly. "Now that's class."

The road ended abruptly in front of a solid wall of trees. Two soldiers stood guard by an iron gate. American soldiers in battle dress with M16s over their shoulders. A trim, grizzled black sergeant laden with hashmarks and field ribbons appeared, carrying a clipboard. "Name, please," he barked.

"Reva St. James and Josh Krales of the New York *Event,* captain," Reva chirped.

"Sergeant," I corrected in a clenched whisper.

"I'm doing Billie Burke," Reva whispered. "They love it."

"Take them in," the sergeant said to one of the sentries. "No stops."

A fresh-faced lad looking like a little kid wearing his daddy's gear popped into the front seat and doffed his pot. "Straight down the road," he said curtly to Vito.

A thick wall of foliage lined the corduroy access road. Through an occasional chink in the trees I saw low-slung farm buildings, garages, tool sheds, barns. A black man on a rusty tractor inched out of a hidden driveway as we passed.

"Looks like a broken-down old family farm," I said.

"Six thousand acres of it," Reva said. "Worth at least twelve thousand an acre in this neck of the woods. Bascomb Blodgett the Third, Boomer's grandfather, bought it during the Depression for a song."

"Who's Boomer?"

"Why, our host, Sunny Jim, our host. Boomer's the best-kept secret of the Blodgett family. Or was, until today. It seems he's the scion with the destructive tendencies— every superrich family has one. He went to Hurd Prep, that supersnob boarding school in the Berkshires. The headmaster at the time was dismissed for fondling the fourth formers. He can't get his memoirs published—the Blodgetts just won't permit it—so he just funnels all the juices to me. Well . . ." She took a deep breath and wet her lips. "Boomer was a problem. One semester he blew up all the toilets with cherry bombs. That's when the other kids gave him his *nom de querre*. Well, the Blodgetts donated a new set of pipes to the school, plus a tiny stipend for the endowment, and Boomer got another chance. Next semester the first three rows of the auditorium went up about a minute before the students arrived for morning prayers. Well, a slap on the wrist was definitely called for. Boomer was banished to the new dorms the Blodgetts so obligingly built. A psychiatrist was called in. A little sports therapy was recommended, you know, to give the outlet for his aggression—not that he hadn't already found a better one. Boomer went out for the basketball team, but alas, he wasn't good enough. So he set fire to the locker room. With the team in it, of course. A few of the lucky ones came out with third-degree burns and incomes for life. The poor chaps who got out unscathed had to settle for college tuition and extras."

"When was this?" I asked.

"About five years ago," Reva said. "Boomer's been in seclusion ever since. Shock treatment, a Zen monastery, nobody knows where. And now he's out just in time for his twenty-first birthday. And you know what that means."

"Enlighten me. . . ."

"Twenty-one, you little plebe," Reva said. "The magic number. The moment when the rich kid gets to play with his own income, or at least a part of it. Boomer gets control of his own piece of the Blodgett Life Trust today. I mean, I'm sure they've cut him off as much as they could. Which means he'll probably only be good for a million a year until some relatives start dying off. That's tax-free, of course. Now little Boomer's called a press conference, which is a super transgression against the Blodgett tradition right there. Something big's going to come out of this, I know it."

A platoon of soldiers were double-timing along the road with field packs and camouflage gear. "What are those guys doing here?" I asked our military escort.

"We're Army Rangers, sir," he said. "Alpha, Bravo and Charley companies. We're stationed here."

"But this isn't military property," I said.

"The Blodgett family has kindly permitted us the use of its grounds for training maneuvers," the soldier said. "The terrain makes a perfect simulation of the forests found in France and Germany, as well as the Soviet Union."

"Are the Rangers expecting to invade Europe?" I asked.

The soldier nodded soberly. "We have a counterinsurgency preparedness in that area, sir."

Reva was beaming at me. "Do you get it now?"

"I get it," I said. "The Army uses the farm as a training base and in return guards the whole place for them. They get the best security in the world, and it doesn't cost them a nickel."

"The rich never pay for anything, my dear," Reva said. "It's undignified." She patted me like a bright student who was beginning to pick things up. "Now, what planet are we on?"

"Terra Rica," I said obediently.

"That's a good boy."

We followed the yellow dirt road right up to disillusion. Expecting the serpentine prelude to culminate in a Wasp Mahal the likes of which I had never seen, my breath quickened as the road wound into a sudden clearing. Acres of pastureland stretched to the mountains at the horizon. Dark clumps of grazing cows pocked the pleasant landscape.

A long, low, frame building appeared to the right. It looked like a chicken house, but TV antennae sprouted from its shingled roof.

"Servants' quarters," I whispered to Reva. "Uh, where is the main house, my good man?" I asked the soldier.

He pointed with the barrel of his rifle. "Right here, sir. Mr. Blodgett lives here."

The house was covered with ugly gray sores where the paint had peeled and the lumber had been left to rot. Blinds were drawn around most of the windows except for one on the second floor, where a gaunt, white-faced old man in a dark suit steadied himself on the sill.

"The place was a boarding house for farm workers when Mr. Blodgett bought it," the soldier said. "He just left it the way it was."

"Where do the farm workers live now?" I asked.

"Oh, they have split-levels off the road," he said. "They have a little rec hall and a swimming pool. . . ."

"And the Blodgetts live like hired hands in the nineteen twenties," I said to Reva.

"That's real class," she said. "I've never seen such class before."

We turned into a parking area where dusty pickups and cannibalized jalopies clustered around one shiny, magnificent old Rolls.

"That's a twenty-seven," Vito said, showing his first sign of enthusiasm.

"It's got no insides," the soldier said. "Just the frame. The family uses those old station wagons to get around."

We followed the noise to the back of the house. The entire press corps—ink, wire and tube—was represented. A couple of bridge tables had been put together, and a fat, dour, old woman retainer in a gray uniform was dispensing doughnuts and lemonade in her own good time.

"Some exclusive," I said. "Every ink-stained freeloader on the Eastern seaboard showed up for this bash."

"I smell the sweat of an anxious press agent," Reva said, her lips pursed petulantly. "And accustomed as I am to working in luxurious solitude, I don't like it."

Morrisey of the *News* swayed in front of the old domestic like a mesmerized cobra. "Got anything harder than this?" he said, waving a doughnut. I slipped an afternoon edition of the *Event* out of his hand and looked through the paper three times before I realized that my story was the innocuous little box on page eight: TWO MEN KILLED IN EAST SIDE EXPLOSION, which explained in three halting paragraphs that two unidentified men had been killed when their unidentified car blew up earlier that morning on an unspecified East Side street.

The wire service people were getting the vital statistics on the place from a few old black men in work clothes. The TV guys were standing around touching their makeup and cutting up Dan Rather. Jill Potosky had cornered a pinched old man in overalls. We could have been at City Hall, or in the puddle of a quadruple homicide. It was business as usual. Only it wasn't. The *Event* was suppressing the story. Did that mean my expense account would be censored as well?

I wandered back to Reva. "You were right. Agamisou's name isn't mentioned."

She gave me a smug, secret smile. "Somebody's managing the news, snooks," she said. "In a big way."

"But why?" I asked.

"Oh, we'll find out," Reva said. "Maybe Boomer will be able to shed some light." She pointed to a ragged youth who was lurching purposefully through the crush like a drunk on a secret mission.

The scion to the Blodgett "superillions" looked like he was on a three-day pass from skid row. With his frayed work shirt and baggy green pants he could have been a handyman in training, except for his unworkmanlike hair, every strand of which looked as if it had been soaked in oil and hung out over his forehead to dry. Patches of blond beard roamed his face like tumbleweed looking for a chin. He was Dachau-thin, his clavicle jutting painfully; I could sense the serried ribs beneath the floppy work shirt. He was a mess. But his billions gave the act an air of mystery, as if something deeper than mere sloth lurked beneath it all.

"Reva St. James," he called. He had a querulous preppy voice that made you want to punch him in the mouth.

Journalists stepped aside as this patronizing scarecrow bore down on us. Up close he was even more grotesque. His pale blue eyes bulged, desperate to escape his head. His breath smelled as if he'd been brushing his teeth with sheep dip, and you could have started a truck farm under his fingernails. I, who have bathed in many varieties of effluvia, stepped back, but Reva let this filthy specter put his arm around her tidy little shoulders.

"You're the guest of honor here," he said, leading her away. "I watch your show all the time." Over his shoulder he talked down to the plebes. "There'll be a press conference in the garden. If you'll all step this way."

Boomer took us around in back of the house. An ancient black man with a wooden leg came out and watched us glumly.

"Be careful walkin', Mr. Blodgett," he called.

The bones of an elaborately landscaped garden were visible beneath the neglect. There had been fruit trees at its perimeters; their dry, bent trunks still waved forlornly. Crushed stalks and dead leaves lay in dusty furrows. We had to sidestep fallen trellises with nails protruding. Even the weeds were crowding themselves to extinction. The place had been abandoned to nature. And nature would restore it. Pioneer succession would soon set in. The old house would disintegrate, and the entire estate would turn into a primeval hemlock forest awaiting a new millennium of despoilers.

For now, Blodgett led us past a gazebo where ladies with parasols might have dallied before the Blodgetts put a stop to such *parvenu* frivolity. A pungent cloud of marijuana wafted by. "We're ready," Boomer called, and three women came out of the gazebo in a hail of giggles.

They were led by a tall, angular brunette, her hair cropped close. Behind her trooped a dainty, giggly blonde, vaguely familiar, wearing cut-off jeans and a midriff top.

"Helene Sanders, the actress," Reva whispered. "She plays the dumb blonde in that TV show, the 'Feminine Bureau of Investigation.'"

The third lady out was Clytemnestra Agamisou, conspicuously ungrieving. And why not? Nobody knew her father was dead. She was wearing a tight orange T-shirt that had GLITTERBURN printed on it in flaming capitals, tight black jeans and soft leather boots that folded over her knees.

The skinny brunette took off her shoes and ran across the pasture, while the other two trod more carefully among the thorns and rusty nails.

"Be careful, Athena," Boomer Blodgett called; but she ran on, laughing, her feet striped with blood and dirt.

"Who?" I asked Reva.

"Athena Stuart, sweetface. Don't tell me you don't know her!"

Of course I did. What downtrodden middle-class American male didn't know Athena Stuart, California feminist, track star and media personality? She had broken up more homes than the Bloomingdale's bill. Her two best-sellers were *The Myth of Sexuality,* which declared that women had been talked into the farce of romantic sexuality just to keep them enslaved; and *Getting It On Without John,* which prescribed alternate ways of achieving physical satisfaction, like running, hydrotherapy, "subjective masturbation," etc. Her every book, article and rant had been lovingly collected by my ex-wife. I had hurled scores of snarling ripostes at her from across the television set. And here she was, running to embrace my other nubile nemesis.

"Potosky," Athena Stuart cried.

"Stuart," shrieked Potosky.

Stuart put an arm around Potosky's shoulder and walked her off for a private explanation.

"Hiya, doc . . ."

Clytemnestra Agamisou was looking saucily up at me.

"I guess I ought to explain," I said.

She had other ideas. "Wanna be the first guy on your block to ball an heiress?" she asked.

"I live in a pretty hip neighborhood," I said.

She squeezed my arm—she was remarkably strong for a little girl—and pulled me off balance.

"Come with me to the gazebo," she said.

Dead vegetation snapped like old bones under our impetuous footsteps. The gazebo was decorated in early spider. An imperious garter snake refused to make room on the moldering bench.

"Give me a cigarette." She took the pack out of my

pocket, lit a cigarette and threw the match onto a pile of dead leaves in the corner. The leaves began to crackle, so I hastened over and did a quick fandango. HEIRESS BURNT TO DEATH IN GAZEBO. REPORTER DIES LEAPING FROM WINDOW: I didn't like the headline.

"You took advantage of me," she said, shaking her finger.

"A lot of good it did me," I said. "The paper hasn't printed my story."

"And it won't, either."

"Excuse my callousness, but you don't seem too broken up about your father's death," I said.

"He's broken up enough for both of us." Clytemnestra giggled and touched her left breast with a kittenish pout that went right to my prostate. "Looking at something?"

"Your T-shirt," I said. "What does that Glitterburn stand for?"

"This." She ditched the cigarette, and I did another dance on the dead leaves. Crossing her hands at her waist, she peeled the sweater off. Her globular bosoms were crowded onto her chest with very little room for cleavage.

"Somewhere a seven-foot Amazon is running around with your boobs," I said.

She giggled and dropped the T-shirt with a stripper's coyness. "I knew you were a phony, you know, but I didn't care. Phonies turn me on."

"I'll bet you need a can of turpentine to get out of those pants," I said.

"Just watch me," she said. She pulled the jeans over her hips, wriggling a bit to get them over her buttocks, never taking her eyes off me. Every move was another nail in my libido. Still, she was working a lot harder than she had to. There was a butterfly tattooed on the inside of her thigh.

"Is that a butterfly?" I asked.

"Yes, and if you wait any longer it will be a caterpillar."

Her lepidoptery was faulty, but I got the message. I was stalling, and she knew it. I'm just not used to freaky millionairesses with porno bodies doing primal presents in front of me.

"Don't tell me you're gay," she said.

"I wasn't when I came in here," I said. "And I haven't seen anything to make me come out of the closet."

She turned. The jeans dropped over boot tops. "So what's the problem?"

"I guess I have a headache," I said. I had a crazy thought. Clitty was putting on this act to keep me away from the press conference, which was about to begin. But why? Why keep me away from a story that would be on all the wires in fifteen minutes anyway?

Clitty followed my look, then shuffled across the gazebo to me, her jeans dragging through the leaves.

"Afraid you'll miss something?" She unzipped my fly and removed my tentative member.

"Doesn't look like I will," I said. "Don't you want to get back to your friends?"

She rested the increasingly decisive gland in the palm of her hand. "I have time," she said, dropping suddenly to her knees. "I just might be able to fit you in. . . ."

That tore it. Once oral retention began, I'd be a goner. I would accept fellatio from a polar bear in a blizzard. I pulled away quickly.

"Business before pleasure," I said, hastily zipping my fly. I had one brief, heartrending view of a seminude, wholly horny heiress on her knees in the middle of the gazebo before I dashed out to Boomer Blodgett IV and his revelation.

"And it better be good, Blodgett," I snarled. "It better be good."

Behind every great fortune there's a great crime," Boomer Blodgett IV solemnly informed the gentlemen of the press. "For the descendants of criminals this is a hard thing to bear. . . ."

He seemed stoned on a little bit of everything, lurching like a drunk, preaching like a speed freak and scratching like a junkie.

"It's hard to look back over your family history, over the bones of millions of exploited Indians, slaves, workers. It is hard when you hear their screams of agony coming across the pages of history"—I added a dash of LSD to Boomer's formula—"and you smell the stench of their hovels, breathe in the soot and dust of their company towns. . . ."

The cameras were grinding, the pencils flying. It wasn't anything you couldn't hear every day in Union Square—and better—but Boomer had a couple of billions to back it all up.

"As the fifth-generation descendant of a family of criminals, I was born with a silver spoon," Boomer continued.

Now the stuff was getting hackneyed. Time for a little hard news. "Just how much is the Blodgett family worth?" I called out.

"More than *you* could ever imagine," Boomer answered coldly and then went back to work on his breast without missing a beat. "I never knew greed. I didn't have to. I didn't have to lift a finger for the rest of my life, and my every need would be seen to. I didn't have to be rapacious or homicidal. The crimes of my ancestors had provided for me. Believe me, it isn't a comfortable situation."

There wasn't a dry eye in the house.

"Are we running a benefit for contrite millionaires?" I called out.

My colleagues turned to me with a collective "tsk." How could I persecute this poor little rich boy?

"I have learned never to seek sympathy," Boomer said.

"Why seek when you can buy?" I said. The "tsk" turned to a low roar.

"We're curious about where you've been over the last three years," a TV mannequin said in a pointed change of subject.

"I will have something to say about that," Boomer said. "But first, to reply to the gentleman . . . uh, what is your name, sir?"

"Barbara Walters," I said.

Boomer didn't like being kidded. His lower lip began to curl, and his eyes narrowed. I couldn't tell if he was going to burst into tears or blow up the estate. "I can sympathize with the gentleman's attitude," he said. "Wealth is not popular in this country. . . ."

"It is with me," I shouted.

"We'll never reach our goal of equality and full employment as long as there are people—well, let's face it, people like me—who have disproportionate incomes. In my own small way I hope to redistribute some of this wealth today. To start a trend that will end in a mass movement of love and revolution."

Everyone was quiet now as the realization dawned that the lad was a psycho.

"In the last three years I have undergone a radical change of consciousness," Boomer said. He reached into the weeds and came out with a battered old suitcase. "I have emerged with a new understanding of myself and the forces that shaped me. I know now that I must acknowledge the guilt of my class and make restitution." He opened the suitcase. It was crammed with packs of new bills. "There's a million dollars in this suitcase," he said. "My entire yearly allowance taken from the portfolio of tax-exempts that the trustees of my father's estate have purchased for me. I had no part in the earning of this money and no say in its use until I reached my twenty-first birthday." He slammed the suitcase shut. "Today, is my birthday, and as a present to myself I will return this money to the people from whom it was stolen." He raised his arms to the heavens. "Today," he shouted, "I'm jumping on the Guilt-wagon. . . ."

"Let's get this straight," I said. "You're going to give this money away, is that right?"

"That's right," Boomer said. "All of it."

That woke the rest of the media up.

"Who to?" Morrisey asked.

"To the people," Boomer said, his eyes rolling, his arms outstretched to exaltation.

"What people?" Morrisey asked.

"The news people," I said. "That's why we were invited."

Boomer favored me with an unreasonable facsimile of a smile. "I doubt if many news people live in Newark," he said. He raised his hand to stanch the flow of questions. "Let me explain further. I have traced the roots of my family fortune. In seventeen forty-one, my ancestor Ephraim Blodgett established a trading post in what is now Newark, New Jersey. Within twenty years he had acquired substantial land holdings. We know that he fled to Canada during the Revolutionary War but managed to return richer than ever. My forebears had a talent for making money, right up to my grandfather, Bascomb Blodgett II, who is sitting up there in that decrepit old farmhouse right now. I kinda feel sorry for him. He's spent his life covering up the shit his descendants made of their lives. My father's suicide, my mother's alcoholism . . ."

"C'mon, Boomer, lighten up. . . ."

The voice pulled young Blodgett up short. He flashed the sheepish grin of a suburban husband caught telling a boring story for the hundredth time.

Athena Stuart came striding into the garden.

"Let's get on with it, babe," she said.

"Right," he said, hefting the valise. "Now I'm going into downtown Newark, back to the exact location where my ancestor began his pillage. . . ."

"That's a heavy black ghetto," someone behind me whispered.

"You're all welcome to come along if you want," Boomer said. "I have ten thousand hundred-dollar bills in this suitcase, and I'm going to distribute them to the people in the community one by one. I'm not going through the power structure on this. I'm going to make direct penance to the people." He picked up the valise and moved quickly toward the garage, shouting: "Pull out the Guiltwagon." Her shoes still in her hand, Athena Stuart galloped over to join him. An old van painted stark white, with GUILTWAGON embla-zoned in red letters on both sides, backed out of the garage crunching gravel, an old poker-faced servitor at the wheel. Helen Sanders, still working on her girlish giggle, came out and hopped into the bus. Clytemnestra Agamisou, her ensemble restored, came out of the gazebo. She walked by me without speaking, her perfume lingering like the sting from a slap in the face.

Everyone dashed madly for their cars. I ran out into the parking lot. The limo door was open, and Vito was gunning the motor. I hardly had time to close the door before he peeled down the dusty access road.

Reva was sitting on her legs again, a sure sign that she was pleased with herself. "So what's new?" she asked.

"Boomer's going to give a million dollars away," I said.

"That's class," Reva said. "Definitely class."

Givin' a million to a buncha niggers," Vito fumed. "As if the government didn't give them enough. The guy's nuts."

"Don't be so sure, Vito bubby," Reva said. "The rich always have a good reason for what they do. That's what separates them from the poor people who just blow along in the wind."

"Boomer doesn't look very purposeful," I said.

Reva patted my hand. "It's in the genes, love. He knows what he's doing."

"And you do, too, don't you?" I asked. Reva looked too smug, even for Reva.

"He's so observant," Reva said. She pinched my cheek until my eyes watered. "He's such an observant little man. . . ." Then she settled back into the velour cushions. "I have a crazy idea, Joshie baby. We'll let it percolate for a couple of days, okay, sweetie? I just want to make sure I'm right before I tell America."

Newark grew on us like a fungus. Huge, dynastic oil tanks —EXXON, SHELL, MOBIL—lined both sides of the highway. Smoke spread in gray blotches from the refineries. The atmosphere bristled with pollutants, flirting with oxygen, leaving the air rancid with their frottage. Houses, too, grew among the tanks. Small and frame, TV antennae reaching through the smog, bicycles sprawling in the driveways, old men puttering on the porches.

The arteries to the diseased heart of the city were clogged with industrial debris. In the ghost suburbs, stunted houses hovered over the narrow gutters as pale and broken as the immigrants who had once sought respite within them from punishing eighty-hour weeks. Off to the right, the black waters of Newark Bay lapped the morbid shore. Nothing lived in that swamp except the carcass of a tugboat long since set adrift. Ahead in the city were desperate black youths doled into a state of manic energy. Their frenzied roar sounded faintly in the stillness, growing louder as we penetrated into the inner city, and the buildings grew taller and closer together, as if closer to an energy source; the noise came out of open tenement windows, record stores, out of the shouts of pedestrians.

"A million dollars isn't going to save this city," I said.

"The million dollars is to save Boomer," Reva said. "The city will have to look after itself."

The Guiltwagon led us to a street within shouting distance of City Hall. Bottles broke and garbage crackled as the limo slid into a parking space. Vito reached for a sawed-off pool cue. Reva squinted into a diamond compact. I was suddenly overwhelmed by melancholy. There were ten thousand one-hundred-dollar bills in that suitcase, and I wasn't going to get one of them.

Boomer jumped out of the Guiltwagon and set up a little table like a street hawker. No sooner was the valise opened than he had drawn a crowd. Lanky teenagers, their black, incurious faces contrasting with the shrill colors of their clothing, padded up on elaborate sneakers. Pugnacious children danced out of the tenements, mumbling oldsters shuffled over for a look, winos bestirred themselves from doorways, hostile faces appeared at the window of a bar across the street.

A burly lad wearing a purple T-shirt with "The Sensual Spades" on it sauntered over to Boomer, the promise of quick, lethal violence implicit in his every movement.

"What you sellin', man?" he asked in a surprisingly high voice.

"Not selling anything," Boomer said, looking away from the boy, afraid to engage his glance. "I'm giving something away. . . ."

"Sheet," the boy said. "Nobody gives nothin' away. . . ." A radio car rolled by and almost ran into a lamppost as the two black policemen got a look at the contents of the valise. The patrol car proceeded to a corner and stopped, the driver speaking frantically into the radio.

The sensual spade returned. "That ain't real money, man. . . ."

Boomer looked around, desperate for help. It was probably the first time in his life he had come in contact with a nonservile Negro. But the Fourth Estate wasn't going to ease him through this rite of passage. Pencils were scratching and cameras were rolling on this historic confrontation. If Boomer got cut from his ear to his kneecap, we would do nothing but record the time and place of the act, and the name of the malefactor—if apprehended, of course.

"It's real money, and you'll get some of it, too, if you back up a little."

It was Athena Stuart, assertive and utterly undaunted, waving her finger like an angry schoolmistress in the boy's face. "Who are you, bitch?" the boy asked, retreating a few steps.

Athena cracked a pack of bills and gave one to the boy. "Tell your friends," she said. "Bascomb Blodgett the Fourth is here to give a million dollars away. There's a million dollars in this valise. And you'll all get a piece of it if you step back and give us some room."

The boy just stood there, marveling at Athena's audacity. "I got your room swingin', bitch, you know what I mean?"

Athena looked him up and down with obvious disdain. She walked over and jammed her finger in his sternum, shoving him back a few steps. "I don't need what little you got, my man," she said.

My heart throbbed, desperate to escape my already doomed body. "We're dead," I whispered to Reva.

"Athena knows what she's doing," Reva said.

"She's setting Boomer up," I said. "She's setting us all up." The boy took this rebuff with frightening equanimity. He turned and walked down the street. Even in broad daylight he moved with stealth. Athena turned to the crowd.

"We have a million dollars to give away. This man"—she pointed to Boomer—"this man may look like a dirty hippie, but he's one of the richest men in America. . . ."

Boomer stretched out a hand overflowing with fluttering bills.

"He wants in some way to atone for the crimes his people perpetrated on your people," Athena said. "A hundred dollars apiece. Just form a line and it's yours. . . ."

A bent old man in work clothes stepped forward. "Hell, I'll take the fool's money," he said and snapped a bill out of Boomer's hand.

"Sure, you will," Athena said. "Take what you can get. That's the American way, isn't it?" There was a collective grumble of assent. "Get yourself some food, or use it to pay the rent, or buy clothes. Hell," she shouted, "just go out and get high with it. . . ."

The crowd roared now. Clenched fists sprouted here and there. There was laughter. A teenager as thin and black as a railroad tie bopped forward, pulling his cap over his ears. Pantomiming a sneak thief, he snatched the bill out of

Boomer's hand. The crowd now broke the ranks they had astonishingly maintained up to this moment. Boomer and his valise disappeared in a maze of shoving black bodies. Athena hopped gingerly away from the stampede.

"If you'll all keep in line," she said with a smile. She knew they wouldn't. Who would? Boomer's panicky croak came from somewhere within the black depths. "My friends, if you'll just wait your turn . . ." She was sacrificing him, throwing him to the mob. . . .

The sudden whine of a hundred sirens froze the crowd. A convoy of police cars, their lights flashing, came rolling down the street. At the rear of the convoy was an official-looking limo. The crowd parted. Excited voices proclaimed the arrival of the Mayor.

Red-faced cops adjusting riot helmets, brandishing shotguns, jumped from the cars and formed a double line. The mayor, a short, stocky black man in a rumpled gray suit, got out of the limo behind two massive white men in similarly abused clothing, whose heads swiveled in angry, birdlike movements, surveying and threatening the crowd.

Mayor Henry Ellender was the first black man to be elected mayor of a major city. If that distinction meant anything to him, he didn't show it but walked very quickly, his head down, ignoring the calls of his constituents. After a year and a half in office, the only emotion he had left was suppressed irritation, and this was what showed in his face as he confronted Boomer Blodgett.

"Good afternoon, sir," he proclaimed in the euphonious basso of a man constantly on the edge of an oration. "I am Mayor Henry Ellender."

"Get to the back of the line, Henry," some rebellious soul called out. "You're gettin' enough down at City Hall."

Mayor Ellender turned and regarded his brethren without censure or judgment. It looked as if he was counting the house.

"You are Mr. Blodgett?" he inquired courteously.

Boomer backed up, his eyes turning like pinwheels.

"We don't normally experience this type of"—the mayor

chose his words carefully—"direct philanthropy in Newark. If you had informed us ahead of time, we would have tried to dissuade you. . . ."

"Dissuade me?" Boomer shrieked indignantly. He moved forward to demonstrate, then backed up even further.

"Yes, sir, that is correct," the mayor said. "A sizable gift like this might do wonders for your conscience, but it won't help the people in this community. You see, we need jobs here, not occasional charity. We need a spirit of hope. We need to inspire our people to produce for themselves. . . ." The mayor looked around and decided not to waste a speech. "Perhaps we can find a more practical channel for your generosity. . . ."

"Are you telling us to leave, Mayor Ellender?" Athena Stuart asked. She had a few inches on the mayor and used them.

"Ah, yes, Athena Stuart," he said. "Welcome to Newark."

"Will you answer the question?" she said. "Are you telling us to pack up our money and go?"

The mayor looked at Athena's head, silhouetted against the skyline of downtown Newark. It seemed to have a calming effect on him. "I'm suggesting it for your own safety, Miss Stuart. I'd call you Mizz, but that brings unpleasant racial memories."

"I'd call you Uncle Tom," Athena said, "but that might do your namesake an injustice."

Mayor Ellender digested this with nary a gulp. "You are holding a parade without a permit, inciting to riot and disturbing the peace," he said quietly.

"We are exercising our right of free assembly," Athena Stuart said. "And if you try to stop us, we'll use this million and millions more to run you out of politics. We'll investigate you and your colleagues. We'll buy so much TV time you'll have to go on between sermonettes and the test pattern. We'll pick a pretty, young, untainted black man. We'll crucify you, Ellender."

The mayor nodded. "You make an effective point, Miss Stuart," he said. He turned and pursued Boomer around the valise, finally catching him and pumping his hand enthusiastically as the flashbulbs popped. "Come and have tea with me when you've finished down here, Mr. Blodgett," he said. Then he turned to his bodyguards. "Call the cops off," he said out of the side of his mouth. "And get me the fuck out of here."

THREE DEAD, SCORES INJURED IN NEWARK GHETTO RIOT OVER BILLIONAIRE'S GIFTS. "A bizarre philanthropic gesture ended in tragedy today as thousands of residents of Newark's Central Ward battled police and each other over a billionaire's hundred-dollar handouts."

I was lying on a cot in the emergency room of Frederick E. Douglass Memorial Hospital in a section thoughtfully reserved for the press, which was only proper since all my injuries had been caused by my colleagues.

"Three were killed and scores injured when Bascomb Blodgett IV, heir to the Blodgett banking and real estate fortune, entered this impoverished black ghetto with the avowed intention of giving away a million dollars to its residents as personal atonement for the 'great crimes' committed by his family."

The livid bruise on my forehead, which only hurt when I raised my eyebrows—a gesture I make too often anyway— had been caused by the elbow of a panicky cameraman. My trousers had been torn and legs scraped from shinbone to thigh hanging onto the back fender of Reva's limousine as it felt its stately way through the rampaging mob without me. A fleeing photographer had been kind enough to step on my back, forcing me to relinquish my hold and fall flat on my face, to be trampled seconds later by the entire "Eyewitness News" team.

"Blodgett had only distributed a few one hundred-dollar bills from a valise purported to contain a million dollars when the riot began. Moments before, a member of the Sensual Spades, the largest youth gang in the ward, numbering over a thousand members, had been rebuffed by feminist and television personality Athena Stuart, who was in Blodgett's entourage. The youth had returned with a contingent of hundreds of fellow gang members. Screaming, 'The Sensual Spades will not be denied,' they attacked Blodgett. In panic he overturned the money-laden suitcase, strewing packets of bills all over the street."

I'd managed to salvage three hundred-dollar bills out of the chaos that ensued when all that money hit the street. One bill had bought me an hour's refuge in a tenement apartment above the street. A hundred bucks for an hour, and I didn't get a woman to go with it. Another bill got me a ride on a pickup truck that some enterprising citizen had converted to a shuttle to the hospital for panicky reporters and wounded policemen. Those with broken limbs had to pay double because they took up twice the space. My third hundred had gone for a cot by a public phone and a dime to call my office. Talk about inflation. Newark made the Weimar Republic look like a piker.

"In the riot that followed, competing gangs fought police and National Guardsmen, braving mace and fire hoses to gather the hundred-dollar bills which carpeted the street.

"Mobs roamed the Central Ward all afternoon, breaking into stores, looting and burning. The damage was worse than that inflicted during the 1965 riots, according to police and local merchants.

"Police Commissioner Ernest Washington said the death toll might mount dramatically by nightfall as police reported sporadic incidents of violence and looting."

It hadn't exactly been a slow day. The subway fire had still been page one when I phoned in the Agamisou explosion. They had managed to hide that. "But how are you going to bury the destruction of Newark?" I screamed at Levinson.

"You're writing the whole goddamn paper today," he said. "I hope you're saving a copy for your mother."

"I'm saving a copy of my expense account for the Guinness Book of Records," I said.

"'I hope this will keep all amateur do-gooders out of our

city,' Mayor Henry Ellender said. 'We've had millions of dollars of property damage, not to mention the cost in human life. I'd like to ask Mr. Blodgett if he thinks it was all worth it.'

"Bascomb Blodgett IV could not be found to answer this question. Late this afternoon reporters were turned away from the Blodgett mansion in Short Hares, New Jersey, by a squad of Army rangers on training maneuvers there. Mr. Blodgett's whereabouts were not disclosed."

"You gotta give me something on this for tomorrow," Levinson moaned.

"I'm on sabbatical," I said. "Besides, you don't print what I give you anyway."

"Something to explain all this. A think piece on the kid. His background and associations."

"Reva St. James has all the background," I said.

"She won't write for the city side," Levinson said.

"Anyway, I don't know that much about him, and there's no way to find out."

"So ask Bessie Schildkraut," Levinson said.

"Give me a half hour," I said.

I hung up and began composing a little biography of Bascomb Blodgett IV. Luckily, the newspaper form is short. How many lies can you possibly get into two hundred and fifty words? I was amazed at how much I did know about Boomer, thanks to Reva.

I called back and dictated the story, then got Levinson on the line.

"I know our leader is too busy spiking stories to come to the phone, so just give him this message," I said. "If he doesn't print this Blodgett story in its entirety, I am going to blab to the *Times,* the *News* and the networks about Wilkins and Agamisou. . . ."

"Hold on," Levinson said. "He might just take a moment out from his busy schedule. . . ."

A second later Grissom was on the line. I had the feeling he had been listening all the time. "Got anything on for the evening?" he asked.

"Dinner with the pope, but I can cancel," I said.

"Why don't you come into the office and have a cocktail?" Grissom said. "We'll have a little talk."

"Oh, goody," I said. "A cocktail and a little talk. Can I wear my lavender frock?"

Grissom was working on his smile as I entered his office. At this point it looked like the rictus of a plague victim, but even that was an improvement.

"Hello, Josh," he said. He shook my hand with the dead porgy he kept up his sleeve. "Martini?"

"Five to one, please," I said. "Stirred with the blunt point of a three-H pencil . . ."

Grissom hollered into the intercom for a copyboy, and Ishkowitz came in.

"Go down to the liquor store on Water Street and get me a bottle of Cinzano vermouth," Grissom said.

"Right," Ishkowitz said. He backed out smiling and winking at me as if we shared some secret knowledge from which the rest of the world was excluded. Grissom watched this exit in astonishment.

"Every copyboy we get these days is a spastic," Grissom said. "It used to take them at least ten years in this business to get that way."

"It's the marijuana," I said. "Makes them paranoid."

"Could be," Grissom said. He took a bottle of Bombay gin out of his desk drawer. "Want a head start?"

"I'll take a sociable."

Grissom poured two little metallic drinks into paper cups. The famous conjugal snort, I remembered it well. Sneaked into a paper cup and chased with a shot of Binaca. The aperitif that prepared you for a dinner *en famille*. A little push into the uphill battle of the evening. They should make a whiskey called Old Momentum for such occasions.

Grissom raised his dixie cup. "To a pleasant summer in Hawaii," he toasted.

"I'll aloha to that," I said.

Grissom threw the gin down fast, hoping to bypass his scorched larynx. No such luck. Lukewarm gin in a paper cup wouldn't go down easy if you poured it on the rug. I sipped mine.

"I guess you want to know why we killed the Wilkins story," Grissom said.

"And the Agamisou story as well," I said. "Seems kind of pointless. Eventually, it's all going to come out."

"Not this time," Grissom said. "We've already got the obits set for these guys, and they both died in bed. . . ."

"But the families . . ."

"The families are in on it," Grissom said. "So are the cops, the corporations. This is the kind of cover-up that stays under the sheets."

"There's no such thing, and you know it," I said. "This thing will come out, and when it does we'll all look like jerks for trying to suppress it."

Grissom poured himself another shooter and freshened my dixie cup. "Would you believe it if I told you I was on your side?" he asked.

"Nope."

"Would you believe it if I told you that I resented this interference into the operation of my newspaper?"

"Nope."

"Good," Grissom said, obviously relieved. "Then I can tell you the truth. They won't tell me why, but they want all this stuff killed. I've got to call the corporate office in Cincinnati and read them every story. They're killing everything and sending up cover stories."

"Why?" I asked.

"No explanation," Grissom said. "Only, everybody's very serious about this. We're all going to be bought off. All of us. I'll probably get a big raise, and so will you. Plus because you're a mental case, they're throwing you the trip to Hawaii. What do they say, the squeaky wheel gets the most grease!"

"Only when it's on the Czarina's coach," I said. "Part two of famous Russian folk proverb. I've been squeaking around here for nine years and never got a squirt. . . ."

"Well, now you're in the big time. Ah, the vermouth," Grissom said as Ishkowitz entered with a bottle in a paper bag. "Get us some ice, too, from the machine by the commissary," Grissom looked in horror at the bottle he had just taken out of the bag. Its contents were bright red.

"This is sweet vermouth," he said.

"Yes, sir," said Ishkowitz, unaware of the venality of his purchase.

"What do you think I am, a twenty-dollar hooker?" Grissom snarled. The hemorrhage vein in his forehead was starting to pulse. A lovely violet flush was spreading through his neck toward his fluttering jaw muscles. My God, this might be it, the coronary devoutly to be wished for. Grissom threw the bottle at Ishkowitz.

"Get out of here, you goddamn pothead!" he shouted.

Ishkowitz found something to trip over but managed to exit. I rose hurriedly. When a man like Grissom gets mad enough to waste whiskey—any whiskey—it's time to leave.

"Wait a second," Grissom said, struggling for breath. "I just want you to know what you're up against. The details on the riot will stay in. Even the feature stuff on this kid Blodgett. But the other stories will never see the light of day."

"If I were half a man I'd get to the bottom of all this," I said.

"You would be half a man if you did," Grissom said. "And the better half would be in a sack on the bottom of the Gowanus Canal. Be smart, get yourself a ticket to Hawaii. I know you don't trust me. There's no reason why you should. I wasn't put on this earth to watch out for you. But I'm giving you good advice."

"And I'll take it," I said. "You'll excuse me if I don't say thank you. It's kind of hard after all these years."

"I understand," Grissom said.

It was six-thirty, the time when an afternoon paper goes into limbo. The last edition had been put out, and another eight hours would pass before they'd begin getting serious about the first one. The city room was almost deserted. A few reporters huddled under the crackling fluorescents finishing features, which, barring a major story, might live through a few editions in tomorrow's paper. A porter pushed a refuse can like a plow through the rows of empty seats, emptying trash baskets full of false starts, misspellings, memos, coffee containers. The wreckage of a day's journalism. It would be easy to get sentimental about the newspaper business, but luckily it's so corrupt you never get a chance.

Divorce isn't what it's cracked up to be.

Instead of breaking the conjugal knot, divorce tightens it around your neck.

I got divorced so I could have my weekends free; I haven't seen a childless Sunday since. A married man is allowed to sneak away for a night with the boys. A divorced man is on twenty-four-hour call; after all, you never know when the little tyke might turn blue and need a Heimlich. Joint custody is worse for the sex life than wedded bliss. At least the married man gets to fantasize! The divorced daddy doesn't have time. Sunday mornings, while the Saturday night pickups are getting to know each other over brunch, the divorced daddy is fumbling with his bachelor utensils, trying to scramble the eggs "the way Mommy makes them," and finally turning in despair to the sure things, Twinkies and YooHoos, watching guiltily as the light of his life gobbles this dissacharide poison. And on Sunday afternoon, while others are crawling into the sack to work off the bloody marys and *fines herbes,* divorced daddies are in the park, throwing sticks to dogs while small children watch, or vice versa.

I got divorced so I could have other women. There, I've spilled the dirty secret. While trapped in the toils of celibate conjugality, I dreamt of women in great and varied profusion. There was a sexual revolution going on right outside my door. Just call me Comrade.

But I soon discovered that legal separation makes you about as promiscuous as a Trappist monk. For one thing, the low-grade poverty of the alimony slave makes it impossible to employ that time-tested aphrodisiac—money. For another, one is advised by ex-wives, school psychologists and Uncle Tom daddies that women are simply off limits until the traumatized kiddies have "adjusted." Why, the sight of a strange hairpin in your digs would be enough to send "the child" off the deep end, so he should never be exposed to that "chippy" you're going around with until you've settled down to "something permanent." Why do divorced daddies have "chippies" while the mommies have "lovers"? Why do we have to settle down while Mom is allowed to consort with any number of unworthy Lotharios? (I think it's called "getting back your self-esteem.") I've already had to compromise my feeble powers of seduction, taking the 4 A.M. shift in saloons, making moves on free-floating wives, who are the only women willing to put up with my schedule. I'm constantly interrupting coitus to attend Open School Day, go to a special program at the planetarium or a highly recommended puppet show in some chilly Soho loft.

And then there's the guilt, another attribute of divorced daddyhood. Why mommies never feel guilty I'll never know; Daddy did leave for a reason, after all. And there's nothing new about the departing-daddy syndrome either. Fathers have been using any excuse to bolt from home and hearth since the invention of the cave. They've gone to sea, to war, to the office. They've gone down the Nile, up the Amazon, over to the deli for a corned beef sandwich. The history of Western civilization was made by daddies who wanted to get away for a while.

My own daddy worked six days a week and slept the seventh. Daddies were invisible on my block, except for the few summer Sundays when one of them would take a bunch of us kids to a doubleheader at Ebbets Field, park us in the bleachers and immediately disappear. My dad even went away for weekends with his buddies. He hated us and made no bones about it, but I don't remember him going around all hangdog and guilt-ridden. The kids were the ones who were supposed to feel guilty in those days. Guilty over bad marks, or bad language, or dirty fingernails. Guilty over all the sacrifices Dear Old Dad was making on our behalf.

And what about the aloof daddies of old? The guys like James Mills and Randolph Churchill, who came around long enough to bed the governess, whack sonny boy with a pointer and give him another two volumes of Cicero to memorize. They spent less time with their kids than even the most profligate divorced daddy. But, of course, *they* weren't divorced. *They* hadn't abandoned their families.

What is with this compulsory companionship? Would anyone in his right mind recommend that a thirty-four-year-old man spend fourteen hours exclusively in the company of a six-year-old boy? Only if he wanted to punish them both.

So at eight-thirty on a Saturday morning, when I should have been nudging some heavy-breathing female into concupiscence, I was sitting on the Fire Island ferry with my face in the salt spray, looking forward to a day in which I'd do so many mea culpas I might break my sternum.

The ferry was loaded with weekenders, their tote bags bulging with drugs. Rings and bracelets glittered; denim tightened around sloppy haunches; toenails of nightmarish hue stalked the deck; giant transistors raised a mushroom cloud of discomania over the Great South Bay.

Fire Island formed out of the mist, a forty-mile ribbon of beach, the flower of New York pluralism upon which every inane enthusiasm of the past twenty years flourished unfettered by common sense or convention. Every little hamlet had its *leitmotif.* A community of aristocratic homosexuals could lay cheek by jowl with an outpost for beer-guzzling firemen. There were the singles' towns, the dopers' enclaves; Parents Without Partners were represented, as were the Young Marrieds, the Group Therapy set; there were the joggers, the swappers, the fasters, the poppers. Every autumn the Atlantic foamed up in a great storm and took a few more inches off the shoreline as nature sought its own solution to urban blight. But even when the island had been worn down to a mere capillary of sand, its summer population would be larger than ever.

My ex-wife shared a cottage with two other ex-wives in the village of Ocean Spray, the largest settlement on the island, the one devoted to families, whole or fractured. As the ferry nuzzled the bulkhead I could see the sunburned wives and kiddies of the still-nuclear families waiting for the daddies, while the distaff of the split families were presumably rousting late-sleeping lovers and bribing the children into silence.

The main drag of Ocean Spray is lined with discos, clothing stores and surf 'n turf restaurants, which provide the main services for the community. I stepped over a few comatose teenagers and onto Sandpiper Lane. The morning hush was buried in the chatter of televisions coming from every child-infested bungalow on the lane.

My son was sitting on the porch, eating potato chips and watching "Mighty Mouse." His eyes were starting to glaze over, which meant he'd been at the tube since Rex Humbard. He didn't even look up as I entered. Such insouciance, and only six. I wondered if I should be proud.

"Hiya, Quentin." I kissed him on the top of his head. He has soft blond hair, which his mother refuses to cut, causing an occasional elderly woman to mistake him for a girl, which sends me into a rage but doesn't seem to bother him in the least. Of course, my son isn't really a child; a broken home and "Sesame Street" have seen to that. He has the furrowed brow and weary air of a disappointed old man. He refuses to be enthusiastic and seems to demand nothing but the numbing routine of childhood, relieved by moments of television and unsupervised play. He treats me casually, which is as it should be. I don't fit any standard definition of fatherhood. I'm not a stern, distant disciplinarian, a figure to be feared and emulated; not even a good old pal, a jolly Micawber, who can be loved if not respected. I am merely the guilty bringer of gifts, the overgrown, maladroit playmate who shows up several times a week to get yelled at by

Mommy and take him to the movies. I am that most treacherous animal—the adult male—that he is being remorselessly conditioned against on TV shows, which portray me as Dopey Dad, the blowhard who can't do anything right; by his mom, who paints me as an irresponsible, exploitative villain; even by the gentle yet pointed syllabus of nursery schools, which emphasize the struggle of women against male domination. I sometimes wonder if he knows that one day he will grow into the enemy. I wonder what kind of man he'll be. And I think I detect—in his quiet manipulations, his gingerly acquiescence to his mother, his offhanded condescension to me—the workings of an embryonic patriarch, who is easing through this period of organ inferiority toward the day when he will ascend to man's estate and immediately throw Mom and Dad into charnel homes for the elderly.

"Did you bring your bathing suit this time, Dad?" Quentin asked. I had forgotten it the last two visits and had been forced to roll up my trousers and waddle like a simpering Prufrock through the surf.

"Yes," I said, pulling down my pants to show him.

Quentin sighed. "Why don't you get a bag to carry your beach stuff?" he asked. He rose like a pained pensioner and returned a moment later with that hated instrument of torture, the Frisbee.

Playing Frisbee with a six-year-old is a zen experience. Six-year-olds cannot catch Frisbees; neither can they flip them with any accuracy. Thus, the adult must chase and retrieve his tosses as well as his catches; it's like trying to hear the sound of one hand clapping.

"It's a little windy for Frisbee," I said. "How about getting your ball and glove?"

"Mom says throwing the hardball is dangerous on the beach."

"So we'll hand it to each other," I said.

He trooped back into the house and returned with his Pete Rose Fielder's Special—thirty-seven fifty for a Little League model yet. We walked down the path to the beach

85

like strangers who just happened to be sharing the same stretch of pavement. At the beach he slipped his hand into mine, not as a gesture of filial affection, but to effect a change of course.

"Better go to the right, Dad."

"Why?"

"Mom's got her calisthenic group down there," he said. "No men allowed."

"What's wrong with watching some ladies jump up and down?"

"They're naked," Quentin explained patiently. "So men can't go there."

Puritan fury and prurient curiosity formed that good old witch-burning melange in me. "You mean your mother leaves you in front of the television without giving you a decent breakfast and goes off to traipse nude on the beach?"

Quentin stared at a boat out on the ocean, wishing he were on it, no doubt, heading as far away from his crazy parents as he could.

That's good, I thought. At least he won't be a mama's boy.

"I'll soon put a stop to this," I said, striding down the beach. "Wait here."

Yep, he might be a parricide, but he won't be no mama's boy.

One, two and stretch, one, two and stretch . . ."

Twenty militant behinds challenged the sun. Twenty breathless shrieks strained for the proper cadence. Twenty Fire Island matrons, puckers of childbirth and junk food flopping like unbuttoned sleeves, stood in nude formation on the beach.

I approached from the rear flank, as it were. Only the group leader saw me, and she continued the calisthenics as if nothing were happening. It was Athena Stuart, the *agente provocateuse* of Newark, doing squat jumps in the sand and looking straight at me over the heads of her awkward acolytes.

"You certainly get around," I said.

The ranks broke at the sound of a male voice. Some women dived for towels, others ran into the surf, covering their privates. Athena Stuart just stood there laughing, her hands on her hips.

"Josh, get out of here," my ex-wife said, hastily buttoning one of my work shirts.

"You know this man, Sandy?" Athena Stuart asked.

"He's my ex," she said.

"Then relax," Athena Stuart said. "If he's your ex, he's certainly seen you naked."

"Only by accident," I said.

"You bastard," she screeched. "You wouldn't know what to do with a naked woman. . . ."

"A thousand bucks I shelled out," I said. "Because you wanted to take 'the child' out of the city. And what happens? He gets brain damage from cathode rays and OD's on Red Dye Number Two while you play grab-ass with a bunch of dykes."

"You bastard," she said. This was a danger sign. When she repeats herself, it means she's about to launch a vicious physical attack.

"I'd like to see if you can last a couple of hours on Fire Island without dropping your pants," I said.

She began biting her thumbnail, looking wildly around for something to throw. Luckily there was only sand.

"This is interesting," said Athena Stuart. She walked right up to me, giving me a good look before continuing. Her body was a hermaphroditic battleground, knobs of male musculature clashing with delicate femininity. Her long, slim legs seemed frail sentries to the dubious treasure between them; but they ended abruptly in jutting hip bones, the coral reefs of her virtue, which would wound on contact. Her neck was narrow and tenderly veined, but it broadened into shoulders of appalling sinew. Her breasts were girlishly timid; a sprinkling of blond mane in the cleavage gave her a pastoral look. But those girlish bosoms hovered over ribs terraced with muscle—more angry bastions to storm. Her fingers were long and delicate, but the palms were grossly square. She leaned forward on the balls of her feet like a gymnast. Her pubic hair was brown and bushy. The pelvis thrust forward like an angry animal ready to strike.

"Here we are, twenty healthy women being terrorized by one"—she gave me an appraising look—"puny male. He wouldn't dare confront a group of men like this, would he?"

She got a resounding *"No"* from the ladies.

"Quite the little demagogue, aren't you?" I said.

She nodded an almost imperceptible acknowledgment. "He couldn't take one of us, let alone twenty," she said.

"Oh, yeah?" I sneered. "I can lick any woman on the beach—if the price is right."

"You know, in ancient Greece women had rituals called bacchanalia in which they ran wild and free," Athena said.

"Is that why Plato was gay, teacher?" I asked.

"Any man who intruded on their ritual was immediately torn limb from limb," Athena said.

"We should tear him limb from limb," my ex-wife snarled.

"What about the check-writing limb?" I said.

Athena Stuart winked at me. "You're in big trouble," she said.

"Tear him limb from limb," squeaked a blonde in a velour jump suit.

I looked at this crowd of advancing harpies. My ex-wife lingered on the fringe, biting her nails. "Somebody's gonna get hurt here," I said.

"You're gonna get hurt," a disturbingly deep voice responded.

I tried to move laterally, but they cut off my path. The only way I could go was back into the water. The surf licked coldly at my heels. A middle-aged woman with purple lips and huge, swaying breasts came out of the pack and splattered me with a handful of wet sand. It didn't hurt, but I got the point. These maniacs were going to rip my clothes off and torture me in front of my son, who was unconcernedly flipping a baseball in the air only a few hundred feet away. This was one trauma he'd never get over. And neither would I.

"This is definitely grounds for a reduction in alimony," I called to my wife.

"Oh, leave him alone," she said.

"He's bluffing," Blondie said. "We'll teach him. . . ."

"Leave him alone!" my ex-wife cried.

The women backed up, responding to the hysteria in her voice. I quickly leaped onto solid ground.

"There you go being ladylike again, Sandy," someone said.

I put about twenty feet between me and the bacchantes. "Try and catch me now," I shouted.

My ex-wife sputtered like a dying motor and rubbed her eyes. "Go away," she moaned. "Go away and leave me alone."

Typical. Her friends try to kill me, and she feels sorry for herself.

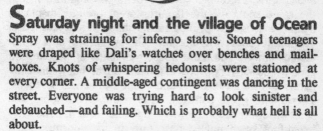

Saturday night and the village of Ocean Spray was straining for inferno status. Stoned teenagers were draped like Dali's watches over benches and mailboxes. Knots of whispering hedonists were stationed at every corner. A middle-aged contingent was dancing in the street. Everyone was trying hard to look sinister and debauched—and failing. Which is probably what hell is all about.

"Mr. Krales . . ." It was Ishkowitz, the adoring copyboy, feeding quarters into an ice machine as if it were a one-armed bandit. A Jewish mama's boy from the Deep South, built like a Bartlett pear with an expression of optimistic wonderment; the boy whose bubble was most likely to burst. The sun had seared him a bright, malign red from his squirrel cheeks to his fatted calves.

"Boy," he said, "what are you doing on Fire Island?"

"Trying to get off," I said.

Ishkowitz just couldn't get over me. "I'm staying at the Gruber house," he said.

"I'm supposed to know who that is, right?"

"Saul Gruber, the chairman of Plotcorp. I worked on a kibbutz last summer with his son Scott. He's got some spread out here. A pool, boathouse, a fifty-seven-foot ketch."

"What's all the ice for? Is Mr. Gruber having his appendix out?"

"No, it's a party."

"Is that what it is?"

Ishkowitz was cheerfully impervious to irony.

"You wanna come? It's just on the other side of the village. Gruber's a good guy to know."

"I know a lot of good guys to know already, Ishkowitz," I said, "and it hasn't done me any good. Lead on . . . lead on."

The Gruber compound was a five-minute walk out of the village, just far enough for the sea and the night to carpet over the racket. Silence and Gruber's gravel path began at the same spot. All the facilities were proudly displayed behind a hedgerow pruned in the shape of a picket fence. The tennis court was floodlit. The swimming pool shimmered tamely. The main house was made of wraparound glass windows. Very pretty in the moonlight, but it made my palms itch for a fungo bat and about a thousand baseballs. There were guest cottages, little white frame jobs. The boathouse was decorated with Japanese lanterns. The fifty-seven-foot ketch jingled peacefully in its moorings. How different from the Blodgetts. They hid their wealth behind a thousand acres of impenetrable foliage, guarded it with the might of the United States Army and gave no parties, getting their jollies in drafty strong rooms running gold coins through their gnarled fingers. They had the good grace to be tightfisted, suspicious . . . defensive.

"Ronald, there you are." A tan, round-faced man in faded jeans and tennis sneakers came through an arch in the hedges. He was so friendly, so unpretentious with his three-thousand-dollar gold chronometer on his hairy wrist. "We were just getting down to our last cube."

"I think I got every piece of ice on the island," Ishkowitz said. "Oh, and sir, this is Josh Krales, a friend of mine from the paper. . . ."

"Krales . . ." Gruber made a great show of running the name through his memory. "Any relation to Sandy Krales?"

"She's my ex-wife," I said.

"Well, I'm glad of that because she's here with another man." Gruber laughed and clutched my arm to show it was all in fun. "Mom," he called to a shrub, which straightened up and turned out to be an old woman who had picked up an empty pack of cigarettes from the walk.

"Look, Saul, how they just drop—wherever they're standing—something," she said.

"The gardener will clean up in the morning, Mom," Gruber said, smiling through his impatience. "This is Mr. Krales, Mom."

The old woman peered at me with maternal concern. I bowed deferentially, always a "nice boy" to the old ladies.

"Your wife is here with somebody else?" she asked in the querulous tone of the half-deaf.

"Ex-wife," I corrected loudly.

"Don't be angry with her," she said. She shrugged, nodded and shook her head. I understood exactly what she meant.

"Get yourself a drink, Mr. Krales," Gruber said. "Ronald will run you through the maze. I'm just showing my mother the new greenhouse."

Mama Gruber caught my eye and shrugged. What difference did it make if you had a greenhouse, a bluehouse even, if people didn't pick up after themselves? I shrugged, nodded and shook my head. We were getting along famously.

"C'mon," Ishkowitz said, reaching for my arm.

I sidestepped him. "Don't ever touch me unless it's to propel me from the path of a speeding truck."

"Boy, you're tough," Ishkowitz said. "What do I have to do to impress you?"

"Die heroically," I said.

Ishkowitz accepted this humbly and pulled his little red wagon down the path. Dwarf imitation streetlights twinkled at eye level. Little street signs hung from them—Suffolk Street, Norfolk, Essex, Rivington . . . a mini-topography of the Lower East Side.

"Mr. Gruber was born on Rivington Street," Ishkowitz explained. "He's very conscious of his roots."

I felt like burying a noogie deep in Ishkowitz's porous scalp. Reverence for the rich sets my teeth on edge, especially in the very young, who are supposed to be preaching their downfall. Of course, if Ishkowitz were one of those snotty, middle-class radicals, I'd hate him even more. The poor kid just couldn't win.

The path suddenly broadened into a floodlit lawn. At least a hundred decorous celebrants, all chic and gleaming from a day in the sun, arranged and rearranged themselves like the dancers in an endless minuet. The trick is to speak to the person in front of you and look at someone several yards away. If you looked at the person in front of you and spoke to someone several yards away, the country would soon be plunged into civil war.

This was no Kool-Aid and doughnut spread like Boomer Blodgett had put out. Saul Gruber had something to prove, and so did his buffet. The tables were laden with the kind of *haute cuisine* that goes bad as soon as you take off the Saran Wrap. A sturgeon in aspic was beginning to mummify, cement crusts were forming over the terrines and the brie was running off the table onto the lawn. A huge, pineappled ham lay in shreds on a silver serving dish. The skin on two shriveled turkeys flapped like a broken canopy. A man in a flowered apron over a white dinner jacket lisped orders at three weary Negro retainers.

Mindful of Mama Gruber's stricture, I threw my cigarette in a plastic trash can.

"Would you mind not dropping your butt in Mr. Gruber's special sangria?" the lisper in the dinner jacket called from the other end of the table.

"It won't do any harm," I said. "Cigarette ashes in alcohol are an aphrodisiac."

"Oh, goody. Let's dump a carton of Chesterfields in immediately." He fished the soggy cigarette out with a plastic oar. "Actually, with vodka, brandy, champagne and Cointreau plus fruit juices, I shouldn't think you'd need any outside help." He ladled some into a Dixie cup. "Here's lead in your pencil."

I gulped it down and almost choked on a melon ball. "Tastes like Kool-Aid," I said.

"Famous last words," he said, ladling me another.

I picked all the fruit out of it. "I don't like drinks I have to chew."

"Aren't you the lumberjack, go now," he said, giving me a little shove. "I don't want you standing near me when the aphro meets the disiac."

It was one of those parties filled with people you know, but have never spoken to.

There were the faces from press conferences and city agencies. The bright young political butterflies with the fixed smiles and the roving eyes. The administrative assistant, the speech writers, the city planners, fresh out of the prestige schools with advanced degrees in impressing their elders. It was fun to guess which of them would bankrupt his father running unsuccessfully for office; which would get caught with his finger in the till and have to break down in front of the TV cameras in order to get a suspended sentence; which would go gently into that dark office on Wall Street where he'd reconcile himself to making millions out of his ill-gotten connections.

There were my fellow freeloaders from the screenings, the

publication parties and the gallery openings. These were the hacks, the flacks and the self-promoters. The "new journalists" of the sixties, who now reviewed pop music for ladies' magazines. The women novelists, whose books abounded with pink champagne and purple phalluses while their conversation bristled with feminine barbs. In this era of the seven-figure belletrist, they were pathetic flops. They got the three-paragraph reviews, the slim paperback sales, the grade-B publicity on all-night phone-in radio shows and TV shots in Pittsburgh and Wilmington. The minor leaguers who blamed their failure on their integrity, when it was really the other way around.

I noticed a few professional Third Worlders, the no-constituency radicals supported by the Ford Foundation. A plainclothes security man trying to be unobtrusive in neon beachwear, was making sure that nobody pocketed the bonsai. All in all, a glamorous New York party in which the discussions were exclusively about other people's money, the men got drunk in the wink of an eye and the women were interested only in the cheese board.

My ex-wife was in the rock garden talking to a goon in a Baylor sweatshirt who had the biggest shoulders and smallest head I'd ever seen. She whispered hurriedly into his ear as I approached, and he stepped protectively in front of her.

"I've got a bone to pick with you," I said, keeping my distance.

"Oh, look," she said, trying to be airy; she likes to think our estrangement is taking place in the first act of a Noel Coward comedy. "It's the Horror of Party Beach."

"I don't like the way my son is being ignored," I said.

"Your twelve hours as a human being are up," she said. "You can go back to the zoo now."

"Listen . . ."

The goon moved so quickly I almost fainted from fright. He grabbed my hand and pumped a quart of juice out of it. "Are you Josh? I've been wanting to meet you." He had the kind of Texas twang that only sounded natural around words like *nigger* or *deregulation*.

"Winston, please," my ex-wife said. "Don't encourage him."

"Oh, now, Sandy, we can all be friends if we work at it."

"Group therapy has obviously come to the Sun Belt," I said. The goon looked around for a shotgun; it certainly didn't take much to make him lose his neighborliness.

"Ignore him, Sandy, and he'll become quietly extinct." The author of this advice emerged from behind a trellis with Saul Gruber. It was Athena Stuart in white jeans and a white undershirt, the kind with straps, which made her breasts look even more girlishly vulnerable.

"Stay out of this, lady," I said, hooking one of the straps under my finger and sliding it off her shoulder. She shuddered slightly, out of passion or revulsion. I couldn't tell. I never can. "I owe you a kick in the ass from this morning," I said, "and I'm not above giving it to you."

Gruber breathed through his nose a couple of times and raised his hand to make a speech, but Athena Stuart had a better way of dealing with me. Smiling, she flicked a finger and caught me on the bridge of the nose. It stung so much the tears welled up in my eyes. I growled and swung through the blur. I hit air and knew I was in trouble. A hand grabbed my belt, another came around behind my head. Suddenly I was airborne, and a moment later I had crash-landed in something wet. Ishkowitz peered regretfully at me from behind a shrub. The lisping caterer walked by, folding his apron. "I told you not to put your butt in Mr. Gruber's special sangria, didn't I?" he said.

~~~

Never make an ass of yourself on an island, and that goes for Staten and Manhattan as well as the more tropical varieties. Maybe it's the air currents or the general instability, but you just can't seem to outrun your mistakes on a land mass surrounded entirely by water. It hadn't taken me more than a minute to dry my besotted trousers in the bay breeze and slink out of the Gruber compound into the village. Yet every face I passed registered the hilarious knowledge of my mishap. By midnight I was sure the news would have drifted across Great South Bay to the mainland to become a permanent part of my legend. Why, it would probably end up being the lead paragraph of my obituary: "Josh Krales, who was hip-flipped into a trashcan full of sangria by a feminist at a beach party seventy years ago, died today. . . ." For a man who was so preoccupied with posterity, I wasn't doing much to ingratiate myself with it.

At midnight, the white hull of the *Fire Island Fury* emerged from the fog. We shuffled on like prisoners, the strikeouts of the weekend, the ones who hadn't been able to get even a bed for Saturday night, let alone somebody to sleep in it with them. There were no radios now, no raillery. I sat on the deck and watched the bow of the boat disappear into the gloom. What if this were death? If the captain were taking us outward bound to the hereafter? I didn't want to spend eternity with sticky trousers. I walked off the ferry onto the dimly lit dock waiting for the recording angel to intone my name.

"Going my way?"

Athena Stuart leaned out of the window of a sleek Mercedes sedan. At the wheel was Steve Spingold, a civil liberties attorney who took a lot of Fourth Amendment cases (dope dealers) and specialized in the First Amendment as well (pornographic film makers). A priest with finger waves was sitting in back between two of the most forbidding lesbians I'd ever seen.

"Looks like you've got a full house," I said.

She opened the door. "So I'll sit on your lap." She got out of the car and bowed. "Your throne awaits, sire."

"Maybe you'd better let me sit in the front," one of the lesbians growled.

"It's all right, Gregg," Athena said. "Mr. Krales won't molest me, will you, Mr. Krales?"

"Nothing could be further from my mind," I said, getting into the front seat.

Smiling, Athena lowered herself onto my lap. "How do you want to do this?"

"Just make yourself as uncomfortable as possible," I said.

"Why don't you just take the train, Krales?" Spingold said.

"I think I will," I said. I tried to get up, but Athena gently pushed me back against the seat. "He'll behave," she said.

Spingold gunned the motor, and the car lurched forward. Athena fell back against me, her arms around my neck. I had no choice, I had to slip my arm around her waist. She smelled of sweat and the salt sea. I counted every piece of golden stubble in her armpit.

"Have you met everybody?" she asked.

"Krales is the only reporter who can cover a trial without mentioning the defense attorney's name," Spingold said.

"I don't believe in false advertising," I said.

"Okay, you know Steve," Athena said. "In the back are Chris Toland and Gregg Pittman from the Sapphic Activist Group." The two lesbians rumbled like field artillery. "And," Athena continued, "Father Rick Munoz of the Gay Catholic Alliance."

"Very happy to meet you," the padre said. His hand felt like a day-old communion wafer. "Athena says you're a reporter. You know, we have a little church on Carmine Street, and we've been trying to get coverage in the straight press for the longest time. . . ."

Athena smiled and slid her rump right into my scrotum. "Mr. Krales's newspaper isn't interested in social change, Father Rick," she said. "Now if you had a good juicy homicide . . ."

"Which I'm sure they will," I said, trying to squirm free. "What's the name of your church, Our Lady of the Leather Cassock?"

Athena put her hand over my mouth. "Don't be rude," she said. "I'm sorry, Father Rick."

"Oh, I don't mind," the priest said with a laugh. "Our church is called Saint Sylvester's, if you're really interested. He's the patron saint of communicators, which includes journalists like yourself."

Athena slid her hand teasingly down the front of my shirt, sliding in to caress my nipples. With a guileless move, she managed to insinuate her right breast into my left nostril. I tried to snort it free. I was determined not to get horny. I'd insult the priest, arm-wrestle the lesbians, even grab the steering wheel if necessary and send the car careening into a ravine, but I would not give her the satisfaction of turning me down.

"I thought priests were supposed to be celibate," I said.

"Oh, that's a thing of the past," Father Rick said. "Now we teach togetherness of the flesh and spirit."

I writhed away from the right breast but got the left one right in the face as Athena reached innocently into the back seat to pat the padre's knee.

"Marry or burn," I snarled. "Didn't Saint Paul say that?"

"Yes, he did," said Father Rick, "and we interpret that to mean that human beings were meant to interact and interrelate with one another."

The flagship of my genitalia set out on a leisurely voyage along my thigh. In a moment or two it would make contact with the enemy hip.

Detumescence was my only hope. After all the times my champion had staggered like a drunken sailor, finally passing out before being piped aboard, all the times I had invented an excuse as limp as my condition and slunk away with my tail hardly between my legs—now, when I needed a little dose of inadequacy, I was prowess personified. Stiff as a subaltern, I inched forward to my doom.

"Another millionaire announced his intention to give money to the poor today," the radio announcer was saying.

"I'm going to smoke some dope if nobody minds," Athena said, leaning across me to get a reefer out of her bag.

"I'll join you, Athena," Father Rick said.

"Did you bring any of that hash, hon?" Gregg asked Chris.

"Don't you want to hear this?" I said, leaning forward to make the radio louder.

". . . Rob Ransome, millionaire sportsman, yacht racer and owner of the Topeka Tailspin soccer team, said today that he would distribute two million dollars in cash to the residents of the black ghetto of Topeka, Kansas. . . ."

"Anybody got a match?" Athena asked.

"Use the lighter," Spingold said.

"Will you people shut up for a second?" I said.

". . . Ransome said he felt the country wasn't doing enough for its poor. . . ."

"Just another chauvinist trying to ease his conscience," Chris said.

". . . Ransome, whose family fortune was made in real estate and retailing, announced the formation of a foundation. . . ."

"It looks like Boomer started a trend," Athena said. She passed the joint back. Everybody closed the windows, and in a minute the car was as steamy as a Turkish bath.

"Wouldn't it be nice if all those rich men started giving some of their money away?" Father Rick said.

"Wouldn't help a bit," I said. My lap had fallen asleep, but everything else was throbbingly alive. "The whole thing is ridiculous, and dangerous, too."

Athena tweaked my nose. "Oh, stop being such an old party pooper."

"Krales wants everybody to stay poor and miserable in the ghettos so he can write about the rats and the riots," Spingold said.

"We just had a little riot in Newark, asshole," I said.

"Look, Father Rick," Athena said. "Look at the cute faces he makes when he's angry."

"I can't see," Father Rick said. He leaned over into the front seat and peered into my face. "Oh, yes, I see now."

"Besides," I said, "I don't buy a Mercedes with the money I get defending drug dealers who contaminate these precious ghettos."

"That's it," Spingold said, swerved off the road and stopped on a shoulder. "You're walking home, Krales."

"Oh, c'mon, Steve," Athena said.

"We can't abandon a soul in torment," Father Rick chipped in.

"C'mon, Steve," Athena said. "Don't be so touchy."

"All right, Krales, where do you live?" Spingold asked.

"Seventy-second and Broadway will be fine," I said.

"You see," Athena said. "We're all going in the same direction."

"I know you are, Athena," Spingold said. "We're going for a drink. . . ."

Athena leaned back, pressing hard on my bruised but upright member, making sure it was still functioning before she burned other bridges. "Stevie, Stevie, you're so possessive."

"But I thought . . ."

"It's two o'clock in the morning," Athena said. "I've got a million things to do."

"Oh, shit," Spingold said. He took a tiny vial of cocaine out of his pocket, sprinkled some on his thumbnail and took a couple of ferocious sniffs. Then he wheeled the car savagely back onto the highway.

Chris and Gregg smiled broadly. They loved seeing a man put down. If they only knew what was happening on my lap.

Athena pulled my hair gently. "Say thank you to the man," she said. "You have a lot to be thankful for."

![decorative flourish]

Your place or mine?" Athena Stuart said.

We were standing on the corner of Seventy-second and Broadway. Spingold had just peeled away from us. His gay copilots had turned to watch, scandalized, from the rear window as it became apparent that we were an item.

"My apartment's a mess," I said, suddenly shy.

"I have company in my place," she said.

"We could go to a cheap midtown hotel," I suggested.

"Your place will be fine." She took my arm. "C'mon, I haven't had a piece of ass in weeks."

"You only love me for my body," I said.

Athena grabbed me from behind. I leaped and landed like

a wet chicken. "If you're checking for a hernia, I don't have one," I said.

She chuckled and moved her arm around my shoulder. "Do you know who's in my apartment? Boomer Blodgett. You be a good boy, and I'll get you an exclusive interview."

We kissed in front of an all-night delicatessen. I stared into Athena's gray eyes. She fidgeted and pushed me away. "Fluorescence is not the light for lovers," she said.

"You look fine," I said, taking her hand. A legless Korean accordion player serenaded us with "Moonlight Bay"; I tinkled a few coins at his feet. Up the block in front of the funeral home, a fat woman in black was lifting her veil to throw up on a car. Two ancient homosexuals were groping each other in the doorway of the bakery. Yes, it was definitely a night for love.

As we hit my lobby I knew we were in trouble. The super was there, and he never showed except for evictions, fires or suicides. "Elevators ain't workin'," he announced. "Nothing works in this heat."

"That better not be true," Athena whispered, squeezing my fingers.

"I live on the nineteenth floor," I said. "I'll be useless by the time we get up there."

"We can always take a break on a landing," she said. "I haven't come this far to be undone by an elevator."

I should have been flattered by this woman's compulsion to sleep with me. Instead, I found it highly suspect. I wouldn't walk up nineteen flights for the Dallas Cowgirls, let alone for one pushy feminist who had bewitched me into a state of reluctant priapism. I mean, walking upstairs with an erection beats anything the Gestapo could have dreamed up. I felt like one of Potosky's pygmies. Horizontal penises may be all the rage in the bush, but when you have to run for a bus they can be a terrible hindrance.

I was breathing hard by the time we reached my door. Except for a little sweat on the upper lip, Athena was in fine shape. "I used to run up and down the steps at the L.A. Coliseum," she said. "It's a good training technique."

Athena disappeared into the bathroom as soon as I got the lights on. She came out, holding her clothes. "Where do I dump these?"

"Anywhere you can see the floor," I said. "I told you this place was a disaster."

"Oh, stop bragging," Athena said. "Get into the woman's movement a little bit, and you'll see some dirty pads." She put her hands on her hips.

"Well . . ."

"Want to start with some squat jumps?" I asked.

Athena unbuttoned my shirt. "Don't be nervous," she said. "I know you're just an old-fashioned type of guy. Anxious, insecure . . ."

"That type of talk isn't calculated to calm me down."

"You'll be fine," she said, letting my pants drop around my shoes. "Jockey shorts." She snapped the elastic waistband. "Most of the men I know don't wear underwear."

"That's disgusting," I said.

She ran her finger down my rib cage. "A good body."

"Sleeping with me is a counter-revolutionary act, you know."

"I take off my politics with my clothes," she said. She got a good grip on me, and marched to the bed. "Now, c'mon. C'mon down here and fuck me."

It was the kind of lovemaking that kept me awake.

Not the standard marital tussle in which the object is to stay awake long enough to see it through. Not the one-night stand accomplished in the dark with eyes averted, bodies scarcely touching, leading immediately to a comatose state and a fierce hangover that conveniently wipes out memory. Not even the dainty coupling of young romantics; the decorous plunge, the protestations, the dream castles; the swain who dozes in his damsel's lap.

Sex as a soporific it wasn't. I didn't subside gratefully into postcoital tranquility but lay awake, listening to my heart pound long after it should have recovered its normal rhythm. I didn't look fondly upon my beloved but drew back in alarm. It seemed as if the woman in my bed was not the same person who had come into my apartment. As if some monstrous trick with changelings was being played on me.

It wasn't the kind of lovemaking I'd wish on anyone, least of all myself. It was like playing a slot machine. You do the same thing you've always done, but this time you hit the jackpot. For a moment you feel very grand and godlike. Then you're overwhelmed by the mystery of it all. Then, the unfairness.

We lay in bed, our thighs and fingers touching, and watched the dawn creep over the ceiling. Once she got up to part the filthy blinds and look out of the window. I smoked a cigarette. She sat at the foot of the bed and stared at me. We took turns patting each other down with a washcloth.

The city had kept docile and silent for us, but as the morning aged and the sun burned a grid on the bedroom floor, it could restrain itself no longer. Delivery trucks wheezed nineteen floors below. Irate voices floated up from the street. A clock radio in the next apartment erupted in hysterical jingles.

There was a purple bruise on her shoulder. I fingered it gently. "Did I do that?"

"Has there been someone else in this room?"

I pinched the bruise. She yelped like an injured puppy and pushed me away. "That hurts."

"Of course it hurts."

It was the kind of lovemaking that made me anxious. I paced the apartment while she slept. Painful childhood memories returned vividly. I recalled people and incidents I hadn't thought about for years. My father's friend who had been wounded in the Spanish Civil War. The old woman in the bus who pricked me with a long, bejeweled hatpin, screaming that I, a terrified eleven-year-old, was a "murderer of young girls." Like a sick drunk I vomited these

103

forgotten fragments. They came in no particular order, as if a long-padlocked closet had been forced open and the sundry possessions of another life had come tumbling out.

"It's going to be a scorcher," I told her.

My back itched with sweat. I lay back down in sheets chilly from our exertions. She nodded and murmured in her sleep. Her skin was cool. She smiled when I touched her and reached for my hand, bringing it to her lips. Women never stop dissembling, even in their sleep.

I had the kind of dreams you struggle to awaken from, reminding yourself all the while, "I'm sleeping, I'm sleeping." And not believing it. I was forced into going along on a stickup. We fled from furnished room to furnished room. I stumbled through a swamp into a mobile home. A girl came out of the bathroom. I could hear the toilet flushing. She shoved her crotch in my face. Then she led an old woman with leathery thighs to the bedside. My mother, too, she said. Then a smudgy blond girl with dirty feet. And my little sister, she said . . .

I awoke with the sun beating down on my face. The shower was running. Oh, Jesus, I thought, I'd better get her out of here before Sandy comes home. "Hurry up," I called. "Hurry up before my wife gets back."

Athena came out of the bathroom, toweling herself. "I thought you were divorced."

"Oh, Christ, I am," I said. "What a relief. I was just having a bad dream. What a relief."

She stood at the mirror, her hands clasped behind her head, her hair still wet from the shower. Her body had flowed into another mold. The shoulders had rounded; the flesh seemed so vulnerable now.

"You look completely different," I said.

"That's only because you know me better."

"No, no, you've changed yourself. Yesterday you were tough and stringy like a golf pro. Now you're the White Rock girl."

She jumped on the bed, pinning my arms. "The only

white rocks around here are between your legs, buster. That tough enough for you?"

I rolled her over easily. Sitting on her chest, I forced her arms back against the bedpost. "Your flipping days are over, my sweet."

"You men are so lucky," she said. "All you need is an erection to make you feel like conquerors." She struggled to rise, but I held her down.

"Well, I did conquer you, didn't I?" I said.

She tried to raise herself, but I planted my knee on her chest and pushed her back down. "I conquered you," I said. "Admit it."

"On one condition," she said, her face red with strain.

"What?"

"That you conquer me again."

She squinted through closed eyes as if trying to remember something. She traced numbers on my back, reaching eight before I slapped her lightly on the face. "You're a liar," I said. A minute later she bit savagely into my shoulder. Her body shook with such abandon that I became afraid. Then she traced the number nine.

"How housewifely of you to count your orgasms," I said.

"Can't help it if I'm an overachiever," she said.

Finally, it was the kind of lovemaking that depresses you.

"Well?" she asked.

"It was too good," I said.

"What does that mean?"

"That means it was so good it was bad."

"Well," she said, "I think we've made a major philosophical discovery."

"Too good is always bad," I said. "Somewhere along the way it transcends the merely good. . . ."

"Relax, will you!" She hugged me firmly around the shoulders as if to squeeze out all the *Weltschmerz*. "It'll be a lot better the next time."

"Better?" The word baffled me. It was as if I had suffered

105

the tiniest of strokes and lost the ability to comprehend comparatives. "If it's better it will be intolerable."

"Oh, Jesus," she said, squeezing harder, "you're such a romantic. Would it have been better if I hadn't had so much fun?"

"That would have helped a bit, yes."

The phone rang.

"At least you're honest," she said.

"Because then it wouldn't have been so intense for me," I said. "It would have been an ordinary night, and we could have had breakfast and forgotten all about it."

"Don't you ever answer the phone?"

"Nobody ever calls on Sunday. Must be a wrong number."

She picked up the phone and held it to my ear. "Mr. Krales, Mr. Krales." It was Ishkowitz.

"What the hell do you want?"

"Something terrible has happened, Mr. Krales," Ishkowitz said. "Mr. Gruber is dead."

He drowned himself," Ishkowitz said.

"Your friend Gruber drowned himself," I told Athena.

"Impossible," she said, putting her ear to the phone.

"Who found him?" I asked Ishkowitz.

"I did. I mean Scott and I," Ishkowitz said. "We were out for a walk on the beach, and we found his clothes neatly folded, his watch and wallet on top of his jeans. They were up on a dune just out of reach of the tide. About a hundred yards down, he was floating in the surf just off the shore. I gave him artificial respiration. A ton of water came out of him. But he was dead. It was awful, Mr. Krales . . . Scott really freaked out."

"Did you move the body?"

"We brought him into the house," Ishkowitz said. "Had

to get one of those stupid little red wagons. His arms and legs were hanging over the side. Mrs. Gruber came out of the house and saw it, and she fainted. She hit her head on the flagstone. There was blood all over the place. . . ."

"C'mon, Ishkowitz, relax," I said. "It wasn't your father."

"That's not the point. . . ."

"Sure, it is," I said. "It's unseemly to get worked up over the death of a casual acquaintance. It's taking the spotlight away from the real bereaved."

Athena shook her head. "You son of a bitch," she whispered.

"What makes you think it was suicide?" I asked. "Couldn't he have had a heart attack while out for a midnight swim?"

"He just wasn't the kind of guy to take off all his clothes and jump in the water at eleven o'clock at night."

Athena nodded in confirmation.

"So maybe it was murder," I said.

"But who'd want to kill Mr. Gruber?" Ishkowitz whined.

"Anybody who ever drank his sangria," I said. "Why would he want to kill himself?"

"He was in trouble," Ishkowitz said, lowering his voice. "Not so much him, you see, but his company. Plotcorp acquired secret interests in California lettuce and avocado farms last year. The ones where those three strikers were murdered. It was all going to come out. Plus that stuff about the gold mines in South Africa. Mr. Gruber was such a moral man. He was going to have to take the responsibility for the manipulations of his executives. But he didn't know anything about these acquisitions or the bribery."

"He knew about them, all right," I said. "He just didn't know that other people knew. Is that too abstruse for you?"

"I know you're a negative guy, Mr. Krales," Ishkowitz said. "But it's just not true in Mr. Gruber's case. He was a deeply religious man. . . ."

"So was Torquemada," I said. "Did you call the paper?"

"Oh, no," he said. "I mean, this is all inside stuff. I got it in the strictest confidence."

"That's known as an exclusive, Ishkowitz," I said. "Now see if you can worm a quote out of one of the less prostrate members of the family. . . ."

"I couldn't double-cross my friends."

"It's a lot easier than double-crossing your enemies," I said.

The operator cut in. "Mr. Krales, there's an emergency call for you."

"I thought nobody every called on Sunday," Athena said.

I promised to call Ishkowitz right back and hung up. A moment later the phone rang. It was Reva St. James.

"Is this Grand Central Boudoir, crossroads of a thousand broken hearts? Who's your queen for a day this morning?"

Athena put a finger to her lips and shook her head.

"Mary Fivefingers is the lucky lady, Reva," I said. "Come over and make it a threesome?"

"Vulgarity will not deter me, bubby. Not when I've got the cutest little item for your scrapbook."

"Saul Gruber just drowned himself on Fire Island," I said.

"I'm thrown," Reva said. "I'm crestfallen. I'm in shock. I'm fully recovered. How did you know that?"

"The question is, how did you?"

"What's this, the Norman Naive show? Little Reva's got every house slave in the Four Hundred on the payroll. Poor Saul played the guilt game and lost."

"What do you mean?" I asked.

"Rich man's roulette, bunny breath. Your money or your life. That's a pretty tough choice for guys like Gruber and Agamisou. Notice the linkage. Interested?"

"I'll read all about it in the Honolulu *Advertiser*," I said.

"Oh, fudge, you're making me give hints. How about . . ."

Reva cleared her throat and gave me her TV voice. "An angry Saul Gruber denies he's being blackmailed by the same radical group that has already forced two millionaires to redistribute some of their maxi-fortunes. . . ."

"Blackmailed?"

"Denial made about an hour before Saul was washed up," Reva said.

"I'm leaving tomorrow, Reva," I said.

"I can prove it," Reva said.

"I don't care. . . ."

"It'll only cost you a piece of Danish," she said. "Now, you've got a free night before you turn into a pineapple. Come over to my place, and I'll show you a little notebook that will make you break your surfboard into swizzle sticks."

"Reva . . ."

"And in case you stand me up, watch the obits for these initials: E. F. . . ."

"I have to hang up now," I said.

"Telephonus interruptus, huh, lover? Okay, drop in around ten. And don't forget the coffeecake. It's the least you can do."

Athena's neatly shorn head nestled between my legs. She did something with her tongue that made my spine go rigid. And it wasn't promise me an exclusive.

She waited until I asked her to stay, and then she left, pleading work and appointments, and swearing she'd be back. She was so desperate to escape that I fell asleep to make it easier for her.

When I awoke she was long gone. She made the bed neatly around me and swept the floor with two folded shirt cardboards. There were other obscure feminine touches. The towels in the bathroom were folded; my comb, razor and toothbrush were laid in formation on the sink. There was a note under my cigarettes.

"I don't know if you wash, eat or make your bed when you get up, but I'm sure you'll get around to your Camels," it read. "I've had my share of quickies, so I can tell the difference. This was different. It was scary. You were scared, too, and that's all to the good. There's a man I know and love very much who says that the more people do between themselves, the more they can do in social and political groups, the more nations will be able to accomplish. It's a great chain leading to a higher consciousness. And it starts with two. A couple. With us. This man says revolution is two to the millionth power. That the power of two sympathetic, feeling, telepathic individuals stretched to infinity is revolution. You remind me very much of that man. Ask me about him the next time I see you. . . ."

It wasn't exactly the kind of *billet doux* you'd want from a departing female. I stared at it for a long time before the chill began spreading over me. Then it made sense. After all, no sane broad will go all the way on the first date.

Reva's building had more security than the Chinese Embassy. It rose thirty-six floors over a long, potholed driveway, the modern equivalent of a moat. There was a sentry's booth in front of the building manned by a squinty old Irish doorman who looked as if he'd sell you the master keys for a six-pack. He gave me the bored once-over as I stopped to pass muster. "You gotta be announced."

A fat, black security cop dozed on a stool by the door. The lobby was bare and mirrored; no columns or sofas to hide the skulking miscreants. A bulky lad in a gray suit stood behind a desk by the elevators. He handed me a slip of paper with "Visitor's Pass" printed in ornate italics and my name penciled in on the dotted line. "Don't lose this, or we won't let you out of the building," he said.

About fifteen feet away, another burly chap in plainclothes checked my pass and got into the elevator with me.

"Off-duty cop?" I asked.

He patted himself down to see if his badge was showing. "Is it that obvious?" he asked unhappily.

"They don't hire ballerinas to guard buildings, do they?" I said.

The elevator stopped just before I got a nosebleed. I got off in a small foyer between two apartments. The door was open. I could smell the coffee.

Reva's apartment was done in Early Antarctica. A snow-white rug flowed to a floor-length mirror which showed how short my pants were. I didn't bother looking any higher but followed the white rug into an even whiter living room. An ivory baby grand dominated the room. Reva's blond coif was perched on a long white couch. A television in a white cabinet provided the only splash of color. Reva's show was on. "America's super zillionaires are rushing to outdo each other in a lunatic wave of philanthropy," Reva chirped.

"How cute to be so apropos," I said. "Which Reva is on tape?"

"More on what's behind this sudden wave of generosity next week," Reva was saying with her know-it-all smirk.

"You get a real kick out of yourself, don't you?" I asked.

She certainly seemed to. Reva was smiling from ear to ear, only she was doing it with her throat.

Her legs were drawn up neatly under her. She was wearing a white kimono with a slit that showed altogether too much of those poor stubby pins. There was a pretty oriental floral pattern embroidered on the top. It was a little hard to see it clearly because of all the blood and tissues that were flowing out of Reva's severed jugular.

There was an intercom on the wall with detailed instructions on how to get the precinct, the fire department, the security staff. There was even a little sheet issued by the police department on what to do if a burglar entered your apartment. "Stay calm," it advised.

"Stay calm?" somebody said. Then the same person let out a jagged shriek of mirth. I looked around the room. It was me. I was laughing. Laughing so hard I could hardly speak to the off-duty cop when he finally picked up. "You'd better come up here," I said. "There's been a little breach in security."

I looked around the apartment to see if the murderer might just be hiding behind a potted plant. Somebody had tracked bloody footprints all over the nice white rug. Clues. I followed the footprints around in circles until I realized that it was me. Oh, Jesus, I thought, Reva's really gonna kill me now.

The whole thing was pretty hysterical, so I sat down in front of the mirror and stared at my grinning face. What was

I worrying about? Even if I had seen three corpses in three days and had drunk the fourth one's sangria. It wasn't as if I were a carrier or something.

Somebody asked me if I was okay. "Why don't you ask the lady on the couch?" I said.

The young guy in the gray suit lifted me up by my armpits and waltzed me over to the couch where the off-duty cop stood there shaking his head. "Jesus Christ," he moaned. "How the fuck did this happen?"

"Neat job," the young sleuth said.

"They draw a dotted line first," I said. "Cut along the dotted line. Send in twenty-five throats and a boxtop, and you get a secret decoder ring."

"He's delirious," the young guy said. He let go of me, and I floated out to sea.

"We're gonna catch hell from Goldbloom," the cop said.

Oh, sure, there's always a Goldbloom around to give you hell when silly little gossip columnists from Brooklyn get their throats cut. He walks around shaking his head at the dried blood on the carpet. Asking a lot of pointed questions and not even listening to the answers. My knees went on strike, so I decided to sit things out on Reva's cool white carpet.

"Better call him," the young guy said.

That's right, fellas, call Goldbloom. I fumbled for a cigarette. "Take the matches away from that guy," the cop said.

"Clean out your lockers," I said, "You're through." Poor, silly, crass little Reva. She could have gone on writing that column for forty years. Nobody would have cared, nobody would have been hurt. Just go to the parties and the premieres; pick up the jokes from the press agents; get the snide stories from the vindictive friends; that's all you have to do, Reva. You'll make a nice living; and maybe when you're sixty you'll marry a nice guy, a little light in the loafers maybe, but you'll still be pure by then; and you'll do the grand-lady bit, and he'll be your escort. And it'll be a life. But don't go getting your throat cut because of some stupid story, Reva. My God, I mean, who's gonna play gin with Daddy in the kitchen on Friday nights? What'll Vito do with his limousine? We're all depending on you, Reva.

"We interrupt this program for a special report," the TV announcer said. You see, Reva, they cut your throat, and then they cut you off the air. "The Kansas National Guard was mobilized early tonight to restore order in Topeka after a millionaire sportsman dropped two million dollars in hundred-dollar bills over the city's black ghetto from a helicopter. At last report two were dead and thirty-six injured, including five policemen, as mobs of teenage looters swept the downtown area. . . ."

I crawled under the piano. It had thick, white sturdy legs like a middle-aged nurse. Sixty-nine with a baby grand. And who said Josh Krales wasn't decadent?

"Property damage was estimated in the millions. . . ."

"Jesus Christ, Mr. Goldbloom, I have no idea how it happened."

"Jesus Christ." I sat up so quickly I banged my head against the keyboard. "I forgot to bring the Danish."

Reva was bouncing like a marionette on a string. Somebody was playing chopsticks . . . badly.

"Stop the music," I shouted.

The music stopped, and I woke up under the piano looking at the biggest pair of shoes I'd ever seen.

"He's up," somebody said.

They weren't shoes, they were sailboats for midget wrestlers. I crawled under the bench to get a better look. Detective Silas Grey was sitting at the piano picking on the black keys.

"I thought you people were supposed to have rhythm," I said.

"Not me," he said. "I'm Irish."

"Don't let your boss hear that," I said.

A tiny, tasseled pair of moccasins joined the party. "You checking the brakes down there or what?"

It was Lieutenant John Duffy wearing a leisure suit. He had probably been in his finished basement when the call came in. "You oughta try *est,* Krales," he said. "Every time you go somewhere, somebody dies."

"What happened?" I asked, dragging myself out from under the piano.

"You fainted," Duffy said.

Reva was a ghastly crimson blur on the couch. A lab man crawled around her, scooping samples of hair and blood into glassine envelopes. A cop with a Rolliflex hopped around shooting Reva from a lot of different angles.

"What does he think he's doing, a layout for *Vogue?"* I said.

"You want him to rend his garments?" Duffy said. "Let's all sob so Mr. Krales will think the police department has a heart. How'd you blunder into this one, anyway?"

"Miss St. James invited me over to watch her show," I said.

"And when you walked in . . ."

"The TV was on, and she wasn't."

"How did you get so friendly with her all of a sudden?"

"We worked for the same paper."

"I work for the same city as the mayor, but he never invites me to his house."

"I'll talk it over with His Honor the next time we have tea," I said. "Now, if it's okay with you, I'd like to take a leak and wash my face."

Reva's bathroom looked as if it had been wrapped in cellophane. A tiny jet of air freshener was released like a perfumed fart every time the door opened. Golden fixtures gleamed in the porcelain bathtub. A map of the movie stars' homes in Beverly Hills had been papered onto the wall, so you could while away your evacuations looking for Raquel Welch's hacienda.

Duffy was going over the guest book in the living room

when I got back. He tossed me a dog-eared copy of the building directory. "See anybody you know?"

There were names from show business and the garment industry. A lot of absentee Hollywood types seemed to have Manhattan hideaways in the building.

"Everyone in this directory has been mentioned in Reva's column," I said.

"Anything bad enough to make them want to draw blood?"

I threw the directory back to him. "Only if she didn't spell their names right."

The two security guys scuffed sheepishly into the apartment, followed by a suede man with an eggplant tan, a lot of gold jangling around his wrists and a paper bag that he held between his fingers like a dead mouse. I would have bet a year's overtime it was Goldbloom.

"Any people enter the building who aren't in the book?" Duffy asked the security guys.

"Absolutely not," the young one said staunchly. "They're all written up, or they don't get in."

"I'd appreciate it if you weren't quite so proud of your operation," Duffy said. "I mean, you do have a dead tenant here."

Goldbloom took a kitchen knife with an ebony handle out of the paper bag. "One of my porters found this on the third-floor landing."

"So nice of you to bring it to my attention," Duffy snapped.

Grey arrived with a couple of baggies and wrapped the knife up.

"The blade's been wiped clean," Grey said. "There's some writing on the handle . . . Ginza Gourmet."

"That's Mr. Arowanna's restaurant," the young security guy said, eager to make points. "He's on the fifth floor."

"He's been in all night," the older one said. "Came in with a new broad."

"He's a real swordsman, the little Jap," the young guy said.

"A big blonde," the old one said. "Towered over him."

"Well, let's go talk to this samurai," Duffy said.

"Hold it," I said. Beautiful blondes meant only one thing to me these days. "Was she wearing a white dress?"

"Yeah."

"Did she giggle a lot?"

"She was feelin' no pain," the old guy said.

"You know this bimbo?" Duffy asked.

"We go to the same parties," I said, "but she always gets there a little ahead of me. You can take your time calling on Mr. Arowanna. I've got a feeling he's recently deceased. I only hope he's got a little sperm on his leg. Poor Reva didn't."

Mr. Arowanna had been slicing vegetables for tempura before he became the main course. He had been quite vigorously gutted and left to marinate on his kitchen floor. The giggly blonde was gone.

"So she picks up this guy in a saloon or something," Duffy said.

"Which means she had it all planned ahead of time," Grey said.

"He walks her by the vigilantes downstairs, and as soon as she gets in the house she takes his appendix out," Duffy said. "Then she goes upstairs and knocks at St. James's door."

"Thinking it's me, Reva lets her in," I said.

"Back up," Duffy said. "St. James knows this broad as well, otherwise she wouldn't have gone back to the TV like that."

"Unless the girl gave her a story about using the phone, or something," Grey said.

"Nah," Duffy said, "I like it better that St. James knew the broad."

"And the blonde knew me," I said.

"Why?" asked Duffy.

"She left the building between the time I arrived here and the time the lobby was empty because everybody was up here," I said. "Which means she killed Reva, went back down to the Jap's apartment and waited until ten. She kept calling downstairs, and when nobody answered she knew it was all clear. So she ran down the stairs, dropping the knife on the landing, through the lobby and out."

"She didn't have to know you," Duffy said. "All she had to know was that someone was coming to Reva's apartment at ten."

"And how did she know Reva was alone?" I asked. "She called from the saloon or the massage parlor or wherever she bagged Mr. Arowanna. She made an appointment with Reva. That's when she found out that Reva was alone and that I was coming."

"You're talkin' about a pretty cold, calculating killer," Grey said.

"I'm talking about a woman who could sleep with Alcibiades Agamisou and then put a bomb in his car the next morning."

"What?" Duffy said.

"This lady and I have already met," I said. "She was coming out of Agamisou's house before his car blew. She bopped me with her spiked heel."

"You're just guessing on that," Duffy said.

"You mean there's more than one blonde running around killing people?"

"There could be," Duffy said. He shook his head gloomily. "Take him upstairs and get a statement," he said. He looked around Arowanna's spacious apartment, at all the surfaces to be dusted for prints, searched for bits of hair or flesh, telltale pieces of thread, anything that might lead to that blonde. "This is another night I won't make it home. I hardly even remember what my kids look like."

"They look like the milkman," I said. "Feel better now?"

They were wheeling Reva out in a gray body bag when we got back to the apartment.

There was a nasty red splotch on Reva's couch. Luckily she wasn't alive to see what a mess she had made. I gave my statement to Grey and signed it. Then I called the paper. The phone rang forever. It was a slow summer Sunday night. Most of the population was nose-to-nose in railroads or bumper-to-bumper in traffic heading back to the city. Reva's TV was still on, and Topeka was still being sacked. National Guardsmen were standing in front of burnt-out stores, dodging rocks and insults. The governor of Kansas came on to denounce Ransome's "irresponsible, indulgent action." Levinson finally picked up the phone.

"You don't work here," he said. "I've got you penciled out for two months."

"I just wanted to apply for a new job," I said. "There's a vacancy in the gossip department."

Blondes have all the fun, but this was getting ridiculous. This lady was loping and giggling around the city in her white dress, snuffing millionaires, gossip columnists, maybe even mutilating teenagers in Spanish Harlem, for all I knew, and everybody seemed intent on covering up her crimes. Any second now, the whole thing was going to burst like a carbuncle, spreading poison all over the body politic. Some reporter would be very unpopular for a while, despised by his colleagues for not pooling information, punished by management for breaking a story they wanted buried, labeled a traitor, a fraud, an opportunist. . . . I was definitely the man for the job.

I went back to the *Event* city room. Copyboys were flying out of the wire room with bulletins on the Topeka riots and local stuff on Reva's murder.

"I might as well do the St. James piece," I told Levinson. "I was there."

"I don't like eyewitness journalism," Levinson said. "Give notes to one of our brain-damaged rewrite men. He'll get it all mixed up, and we'll have a normal newspaper story."

"Seymour," I said patiently. "You're shorthanded. The shit's hitting the fan all over the country. You know you'll be calling guys in soon, so I'll help you out." I felt I had to do something for the man I was about to traduce. "I'll even do the Gruber obit. This way you'll be free to keep guys on the breaking stuff."

"Breaking stuff!" Levinson threw a pile of AP bulletins at me. Sims Webster, president of Webster Coal, had announced that he was going to Pendleton, West Virginia, the site where his ancestors had first settled, to give two million dollars in cash to the residents. "I've found Christ," he said. "I've found new purpose in my life. I want to make restitution. . . ."

"The world is breaking," Levinson said. "There aren't enough people on this newspaper to cover what's happened in the last two hours."

"So I'll take Reva off your hands," I said. "And don't worry about my overtime. I'll get Grissom to clear it personally."

I went to a desk in the far corner of the city room and began making calls. While I chased around California trying to locate the attorney general, I typed out the St. James story:

"Syndicated gossip columnist Reva St. James was found stabbed to death in her luxury apartment last night. . . ."

The California A.G. was on the banquet circuit this evening. A guileless press man, who would soon be jobless as well, gave me his evening's itinerary. I just missed him at a B'nai B'rith sports lodge dinner and tracked him down at the annual barbecue of the "Don't Tread on Me Club," composed of the descendants of California's pioneers. He was in the middle of a speech and couldn't come to the phone. Meanwhile, I was writing on automatic pilot:

"Police were searching for a tall blond woman wearing a white evening dress, who had entered the building earlier that evening with prominent Japanese restaurateur Yuno Arowanna. Mr. Arowanna was stabbed to death in his kitchen shortly before Miss St. James was murdered, and police theorize that the blonde killed him, then ran up to Miss St. James's apartment and slashed her throat with the same knife she had used on Arowanna. . . ."

The attorney general wasn't too anxious to speak to a reporter for the New York *Event*. So when I called the annual dinner dance of the Association of Black Postal Workers, I identified myself as Henry Kissinger.

"The mystery blonde, whom police are beginning to refer to as 'Jacqueline the Ripper,' has also been implicated in the murder of Greek shipping magnate Alcibiades Agamisou, who was killed when a bomb exploded in his Rolls-Royce outside his East Side townhouse several days ago. . . ."

The A.G. was hoarse from all his oratory, but he had enough voice left to castigate me for misrepresenting myself. He clammed up, though, when I told him that I knew about the investigation into the activities of Gruber's company, Plotcorp, in the California avocado fields. Yes, he said, there was an inquiry going on into the illegal smuggling of Mexican laborers into California. Several deaths had occurred. Mr. Gruber had been informed, but by no means had the investigation entered the indictment stage.

"Miss St. James was working on an exposé of the epidemic of philanthropy among this country's richest men that has so far resulted in two riots, with the consequent loss of life and property . . ."

Consequent was such an unwieldy, unnewspaperly word; I could just see the copyreader wincing as he crossed it out.

Was it true, I asked the attorney general, that Plotcorp had actually leased trucks and hired overseers for this smuggling operation? That thousands of wetbacks had come to work as pickers on Plotcorp's "agrilomerates," a word coined by Gruber in his *Newsweek* cover interview.

"Miss St. James had hinted to colleagues on the New York *Event* that she was close to a break in this story. Police believe she may have been murdered to prevent her from making her information public."

The A.G. bridled at the word *wetback*. Much too strong

for a moderate politician like him. As for the "unfortunate fatalities," they had occurred somewhere on the road between Mexico and California, and had not been fully investigated. Mr. Gruber was absolutely not implicated in a personal sense.

I sent to the library for the clips on Saul Gruber. They came back in three bulging envelopes, a catalog of piety and good works that would have sent St. Francis back to his pigeons. He had the kind of rags-to-riches story you used to see in Yiddish musicals. Born in squalor on the Lower East Side of Manhattan (where else?), the sixth son of a pious man who sewed the fringe on prayer shawls to feed his family of twelve. Prayer-shawl fringing was never a good living, not even in the days of the five-cent bus ride, so little Saul hit the sweatshops to help out. And hit them even harder when Papa fell under a trolley on Delancey Street. Ten years and a hundred sweatshops later, Saul had his doctorate of law from Columbia. Then World War II, in which Saul rose through the ranks to become a full colonel and a hero of the Normandy invasion. He suffered a happy demotion to captain of industry when he built Plotcorp up from a manufacturer of corset stays to the biggest multinational textile firm in the world, doing what he did best—building sweatshops. Within the last five years, Plotcorp had been buying farmland all over the world. "Make 'em sweat in the fields as well as the shops" would have been a good company motto. You do business abroad, you bribe. I woke up the press guy at the Justice Department. How close to indictment were the bribery investigations against Plotcorp? I asked. The press guy was too sleepy to recognize a fishing expedition when he heard one and too shocked that I had uncovered a deep-cover investigation against one of the most generous contributors to the party in power. No, he said emphatically, the investigations in Guatemala and Ecuador were merely routine inquiries. And, he added, there had been absolutely no proof that Gruber was aware of Plotcorp's secret ownership of South African mining stock.

Gruber was a tree planter, a cornerstone layer, a wing

endower. He was a family man: thirty-five years married to Betty, his childhood sweetheart, a shy, smiling lady, fidgeting in her Mollie Parnis creations. "Ill at ease with her husband's high-powered friends," said one profile, "but always ready with a toothsome recipe for their wives." He had three kids, a pediatrician, an obstetrician and a proctologist. Well, you don't commit suicide because your family's a bore; you do it when you can't live with yourself anymore. And in my brief encounter with Saul Gruber, he had seemed like a man who could live very comfortably with any transgression in which he was not implicated.

I called Ishkowitz at the Gruber house. "Get me the names of some Plotcorp executives," I told him. "I'm in the process of assassinating the deceased's character, but it's still breathing."

"I can't do that to the family," Ishkowitz said. "They've had so much trouble in the past few days with these phone calls. . . ."

"What calls?" I asked.

"Somebody had dug up a lot of dirt," Ishkowitz said. "Mr. Gruber said it had to be political enemies because nobody could have known. They were calling him, sending him letters. This Guiltwagon thing. They wanted him to go down to his old neighborhood and give away a million bucks, I think, just like Blodgett and all the rest."

"And if he didn't?" I asked.

"I don't know. Mr. Gruber didn't seem to be afraid. Just angry. He gave us a lecture the other day about the persecution of the rich in this country."

"A cause we can all get behind," I said. "What would you say if I told you Gruber might have been murdered?"

"Gee, in a way that would make it easier on the family," Ishkowitz said.

"So get me those names," I said, putting a fresh sheet in the typewriter.

I wrote the Gruber obit straight until the last few paragraphs. Ishkowitz hadn't called back with the Plotcorp names, but I didn't really need them; I had the attorney general of California and the press man at the Justice Department to quote. I'd have to sit down when this was all over and figure out how many careers I was ruining. Counting my own, of course.

I hinted that Gruber might have killed himself because of the impending scandals that threatened his conglomerate. And then:

"Late last night the *Event* learned that Mr. Gruber had been receiving blackmail threats for the past few weeks. According to a close family friend, [bye-bye, Ishkowitz] they came from an unknown person who insisted that Mr. Gruber return to the neighborhood of his birth and distribute a million dollars to the populace. Mr. Gruber ridiculed the threats, but in the light of the violent deaths of Cyrus Wilkins, chairman of Global Paper, and Greek shipping magnate Alcibiades Agamisou, both of whom had received similar threats, police were investigating the possibility of foul play."

I strolled into the wire room. The machines were in a frenzy, disgorging reams on the Topeka riots. The death toll had risen to six. Snipers were attacking the National Guard. Black politicians were going hoarse denouncing everybody.

Reaction was flowing in from every part of the world. Tass said the riots were an illustration of the inability of the capitalist system to deal equitably with all its citizens. The New China News Agency said it was all a Soviet-inspired plot to undermine the rapport between the U.S. and China. In Rome the Red Brigades kneecapped a cosmetics millionaire as a warning "to all the privileged classes not to try to co-opt the proletariat with meaningless offerings." American embassies had been attacked in Damascus, Tripoli, New Delhi and Warsaw. The Guiltwagon was careening around the Global Village, kicking up a lot of dust.

At five in the morning Grissom came in to put the first edition to bed. He charged into the city room like a maddened hippo, scooped up all the stories—mine included—and slammed his office door. I read the out-of-town papers and dozed a little. At about five-thirty

Grissom's office door opened slowly, and he peeked out, his fat red face glowing like a traffic light. A moment later a hesitant copyboy tapped me on the shoulder. "The boss wants to see you."

Grissom was curled up in a little ball behind his desk. "I thought we had this all worked out," he said, biting through one Marlboro, then slowly, carefully, reaching for another. "I thought you were going to Hawaii."

"We did," I said, "but this blonde is starting to irritate me."

A few arteries arrived on Grissom's forehead.

"What blonde?" he asked, breathing heavily through his nose.

"Look," I said, "this story's going to explode. It's going to get harder to cover up all these murders. An arm or a leg will stick out from under the tarp. Some cute reporter will make a couple of phone calls. Krales's Law, Mr. Grissom. The more people who know a secret, the less of a secret it is."

Grissom nodded slowly, like a man listening to his doctor's orders. "I don't care who knows about this. Just as long as we aren't the ones who tell them. Is that so hard to understand?"

"But doesn't it make you mad that some jerk on another paper, or maybe even a TV station, will beat the *Event* on this story?"

Grissom shook his head with such vigor I thought his ears were going to fall off. "No, absolutely not," he said. "You wanna know what makes me mad? My nineteen-year-old daughter comes home from summer stock with some thirty-year-old pothead who eats with his fingers and tells me that all newspapermen are whores. Then she takes him upstairs to her room and says, 'Please don't disturb us. We'll be fucking.' That's what makes me mad. Also what makes me mad is having degenerate lunatics working for me who I can't get rid of because of some stupid fucking union." He was standing and shouting now. "But some homicidal bimbo butchering a bunch of millionaires—zero on the Richter scale. A big fat zero! I don't give a rusty fuck if she slashes right through Burke's Peerage. Okay, Krales? You got that, Krales?"

"Take it easy," I said.

"How come it's the people who aggravate you the most who always tell you to take it easy?" Grissom said. "Now, we're going to handle these stories like good little professionals. First, we'll let the world find out that millionaire philanthropist Saul Gruber accidentally drowned in a sudden riptide. Then maybe a few days after that we'll find out that it was really suicide. And then maybe that Mr. Gruber couldn't reconcile his religious upbringing with his corrupt business practices. As far as Miss St. James is concerned, she was killed by a prowler. We print a little fairy tale of an obit about the generous Mr. Gruber, with transcripts from the telegrams sent by Cardinal Cooke, Menachem Begin, Georgie Jessel. For Reva we show a thousand housewives, the kerchief-over-the-hair-curlers-with-the-dark-glasses type, all lining up to go to her funeral. That's how we're gonna play it, Krales, while I'm running this paper." He jammed my stories on a spike. "And if you don't want to play ball, you're out of the game."

The New York *Event* may be the last sweat-and-ink newspaper in America. It still hasn't automated, the requisite number of printers having thus far refused to die, retire or otherwise attrite (sic). Oh, maybe the stock tables are done by computer now, but the rest of the *Event* hits the streets pretty much the way it did when Aaron Burr was managing the news. The composing room is as dark and hot and noisy as the furnace room of an ancient steamship. Savage, sooty men scream out of the din. The linotype machines belong in the Museum of Natural History, next to the dinosaurs. The linotypers, rows and rows of virtuosi pecking delicately at their keyboards; the stolid compositors bending over their forms, juggling the type into columns; the proofreaders, stooped white-haired Bartlebys with green visors hunching over the proofs; the profane, beery stereotypers; the sullen, cliquish pressmen, eyes gleaming dangerously from blackened faces—they could all be stuffed and put in a museum to be gawked at by schoolchildren with picture tubes for eyes. The American Craftsman.

At seven o'clock the paper closed down, which meant you couldn't get any more stories into the first edition. It was quiet in the city room. Rewrite men stood stretching at their desks. The copyreaders who edited the stories and wrote the headlines sneaked out for coffee. Grissom was on the phone to Cincinnati, telling corporate HQ what was in the paper that day.

I had kept two extra copies of my stories. I folded and marked them up a little to make it look as if they'd been out through the editorial mill. Then I sauntered out to the composing room and caught up with Abe, the foreman, a septuagenarian with a cigar that was older than he was, or at least smelled that way.

"Abe, I've got two last-minute subs," I said.

He lifted his seeing glasses onto his forehead and took his reading glasses out of his apron pocket. "You got new heads coming?"

"Same heads. We'll make it easy on you."

This he didn't like. "How can you change a story without changing the headline?"

"Abe, since when are they paying you to be an editor?" I said, pushing him toward the linotype bank. "Just get the stories in."

"Sure, sure," Abe said, shuffling away. "I'll put my fastest boys on it."

It was the perfect crime. In the proof room, the Bartlebys, still wearing the cuff guards and tweed trousers of another era, labored over the proofs of every story that went into the paper. Out in the city room, the editors took desultory looks at the proofs. It was accepted that the first edition would be full of typos. Nobody really paid attention. Well, maybe

Grissom, but he was reading the proofs of the decoy stories, while the new ones were turning on the presses. Soon copies of the *Event* would be sailing out into the world telling the public that someone was killing our nation's most precious commodity—its millionaires. John Peter Zenger, move over. Josh Krales was making constitutional history.

I took the subway uptown. It was rush hour. People were using their morning papers as shields, cudgels, prods—anything but organs of enlightenment. The *Times* and *News* were a bore, featuring stuff the straphangers had already heard in their sleep on their clock radios. The riot in Topeka had spread to the Mexican neighborhood. A few more guys with unpronounceable names had been executed in unspeakable dictatorships. There was more blood, less oil. They'd seen it all on the "Today" show.

But hold on, people, I thought. Here're a couple of stories you didn't get from the talking heads. In a few hours you'll be rushing out to buy the *Event*. I'll give you something to pep up the coffee breaks and get the old imaginations in gear.

I stopped in at the Golden Fleece, a greasy spoon on Broadway. They gave me an empty cup floating on a saucer of black coffee, along with an ashtray containing a piece of bubble gum and a sputum sample. The clock on the wall read eight-ten. Back at the *Event* a yawning copyboy was on his way to the mailer's room, where the papers come off the conveyor belt and are packed for various routes. At about eight-twenty the copyboy would drop a stack of papers on Persky's desk and go back to deliver a few to Grissom. They'd take their time about reading them. There was a two-hour delay between the first two editions; plenty of time to look over the mornings and have another cup of coffee.

Eight-thirty. The papers had long since slid down another conveyor belt to the platform where they were loaded onto trucks, the first ones to go out being those on their way to Queens and points east. There was no way to stop them. Of course, the circulation man could call ahead to the dealers and tell them to hold the papers because some terrible mistake had been made, but then they'd sell them as collector's items at five bucks a copy. No, at this moment, while Persky went out to the john with the *Event* under his arm and Grissom reached for his third cup of coffee while scanning the front page, the truth—or my highly speculative version of it—was on its way to the masses.

Eight-forty. The phone was ringing as I got home. It didn't stop for three hours, but I wasn't perturbed. I'd get nervous when they started banging down the door.

They started banging down the door at eleven-thirty. It felt as if they were using a sledgehammer. Chunks of plaster fell from the ceiling as I eased up to the peephole for a look.

"Open the door, you bastard. I know you're in there."

It was a woman's voice. I opened the door. Jill Potosky stood there with a boot in her hand. "You bastard," she said, charging into my apartment. "You've had this since that subway thing, right?" She looked around my apartment. "This place is an utter pigsty." She slammed the boot into the wall. "Oh, I could kill myself for letting you get away with this. Oh, you're a big celebrity, aren't you? You caught the whole city with its pants down."

"What a wonderful image," I said. "And there's more where these little tidbits came from."

Potosky whipped a first edition of the *Event* out of her shoulder bag. "What's this about the violent deaths of Wilkins and Agamisou?"

"Just wait a minute," I said. "I once offered you a piece of this story. . . ."

"In return for a piece of ass," Potosky said. "All right, what do you want me to do?"

"Let's play strip press conference," I said. "For every question an article of clothing is shed . . . understand it's really catching on with lady sportswriters."

"You pig, you slime, you throwback," Potosky fumed. "I haven't got time to play footsie with you." She ripped the buttons off her tailored blouse and stepped out of her Calvin Klein jeans.

"I'll bet you're sorry now that you don't wear underwear," I said.

She stood there nude, except for her shoulder bag and her left boot. "How many answers does this get me?"

"There aren't enough questions," I said. "You know, you could learn to love me. . . ."

"Cut the crap. What happened to Wilkins and Agamisou?"

I sighed. Hell hath no fury like a career woman scorned. "They were murdered," I said.

"But they haven't even been reported dead yet," she said.

"See if you can get them on the phone," I said.

Suddenly the door flew off its hinges. Detective Silas Grey stepped over the dangling frame, followed by Lieutenant John Duffy.

"Leave it to New York's finest to kick in an open door," I said.

A few more detectives stepped through my splintered portal. "Look around," Duffy instructed them. "Find a misdemeanor." He waved a piece of paper in my face. "And if you wanna get liberal about it, this is a search warrant, plus I also have a warrant for your arrest as a material witness in the murders of Agamisou and Wilkins."

"Which you say never took place," I said.

"Nothin'," a detective called from my bedroom.

"Not a grain of marijuana, an overdue traffic ticket?" Duffy snarled. "Everybody's got somethin'."

The bell rang. Two red faces in gray suits peeked around the broken door frame, flashing their open wallets. "Agents Argyle and Stretch, Federal Bureau of Investigation."

"Leave it to the FBI to ring a doorbell with no door," I said.

"We would like to question you regarding your allegations in"—Agent Stretch drew a first edition of the *Event* out of a suede portfolio—"the New York *Event* that certain murders have taken place."

"Krales . . ." It was Grissom himself, Persky, Levinson and the *Event* legal department in tow. He kicked brutally at my demolished door as he stepped into the apartment.

"Leave it to my boss to kick a door when it's down," I said.

Grissom came toward me, brandishing the *Event* like a club.

"Didn't somebody say they wanted to put me in protective custody?" I asked, retreating.

"You treacherous son of a bitch," he said. "I'm going to fire you now. No union, court or act of God will protect you this time. I've got cause."

Athena Stuart stepped daintily over the door frame, holding a copy of the *Event*. Potosky, who had been perfectly willing to remain unclothed in front of a variety of irate men, now began hurling herself into her jeans.

"Hi, Jill," Athena said, giving her a casual look.

"Leave it to a feminist to notice the only naked woman in the room," I said.

"Can anybody join this little party?" Athena asked.

"No, I'm sorry," I said, "the guest list is restricted to people who are violating my constitutional rights. It's the new party theme for the season. Now, you have twenty-two amendments to choose from . . ."

"Pack your toothbrush, Krales," Duffy said.

Athena was wearing a white dress with a purple sash and a straw hat tied at the neck with a blue ribbon. "You look very pastoral," I said, making believe no one else was in the room.

"I was trying for a Seurat look."

"Seurat?" Potosky said. "That's a little bit out of character for you, isn't it?"

"September Morn is out of character for you, Jill," Athena said sweetly.

"There's a little matter of jurisdiction here, Lieutenant," Agent Argyle said.

GLITTERBURN

Detective Grey ducked under the door frame of my bedroom, smiling. "Jurisdiction?" he asked innocently. Which seemed to settle that matter.

Duffy twisted my hands behind my back and snapped the cuffs on me.

"You can't arrest me," I said. "I didn't do anything."

"You'll have to think of a better reason than that," he said.

"What are you doing here anyway?" Potosky asked Athena.

Duffy hustled me out of the apartment, making sure to bang my head against the wall.

"I came back to get my sweatband," Athena said.

"Doesn't anybody care that I'm being illegally arrested?" I cried as Duffy shoved me into the elevator.

"Is he good in bed?" Potosky asked.

The elevator door closed before I could hear Athena's answer.

Police brutality, false arrest," I screamed as Grey and Duffy dragged me through the lobby. Two close-cropped young men with matching leather jackets and earrings slithered through the door.

"Look," one of them said, "a man in handcuffs."

"God," sighed the other, "how lucky can you get?"

Grey slammed me in the back seat of a patrol car. Duffy came around from the other side. "Move over," he said, pushing my arm against the seat. The pain shot from my wrists to my shoulders and back again.

"This little miscarriage of justice is going to finish you, Duffy," I said.

"The guy's out of a job, hasn't got a friend in the world, is about to be charged with a coupla felonies and he tells me I'm finished," Duffy said.

"That's what you call *chutzpah*," Grey said, his pronunciation remarkably accurate.

I slid down a bit to ease the pain. "I don't understand why everybody's gotten so crazy about this story," I said. "People get murdered every day. Besides, the truth is bound to come out sooner or later."

"Well, maybe by then the epidemic will be over," Duffy said.

"I don't understand why reporters think it's so important for everybody to know everything all the time anyway," Grey said.

"Because it's their job," I said. "Would you let every third burglar get away?" An *Event* truck went barreling by and dropped a pile of papers in front of a corner newsstand. "I don't know why I'm wasting my breath on you thickheaded Cossacks anyway," I said. "The story's out now. Everybody in the country will be on it in an hour. There's nothing any of you can do now to squelch it."

"Don't make book on that," Duffy said.

They took me to the twentieth precinct and threw me in the detention pen with the day's catch. There was a toilet in the middle of the room, which nobody seemed disposed to use. A burly black chap wearing overalls over a bare chest stood by the door, checking out the new arrivals.

"I'm a dangerous psychotic," he said to me. "Got any cigarettes?"

I gave him the pack.

"Money?" he asked.

I found a few bucks in my pocket. He took the money with a serene nod. Now I knew why he wore overalls. You needed deep pockets in his line of work.

I stepped around a puddle of vomit and found a seat on a bench against the wall, next to an elderly man with a shock of gray hair and a courtly manner.

"Good morning, sir," he said, enveloping me in a noxious cloud of Ripple. The old man put his head on my shoulder and fell asleep. I tried to lift him, but his head weighed a ton. I didn't dare complain. Everyone in the place could easily beat me up, even the middle-aged crook in a madras jacket and a string tie who paced a small area, his jowls wobbling, grumbling to himself.

A Spanish lad with a glossy pompadour slid next to me. "Hey, baby, make room for Daddy," he said, sliding his thigh next to mine.

It seemed to be my day to be a sandwich. "I'm afraid we're a little crowded here. . . ." The old man snored percussively and fell onto my lap. I tried to ease his head off. "Maybe if I just . . ."

"Stay put, now," Valentino said. "I don't wanna have to chase you all over the goddamn pen." He grabbed my hand suddenly. "Whisper something in my ear. . . ." He squeezed. "C'mon, whisper. I like havin' chicks whisper in my ear." I was about to make a gender correction when I noticed he had *Love* tattooed on one set of knuckles and *Hate* on the other. "What do you want me to say?" I whispered in his ear.

He shuddered. "Makes me feel warm all over," he said. He caressed my palm with his index, a little trick to excite the girls that we had sworn by in high school. "You'll remember me when I see you at Rikers, won't you, baby?" he said. "My name is Ramon."

He patted my wrist and smiled. I tried to smile back. "Okay, Ramon," I said, patting the knuckle that had *Hate* on it.

I leaned against the wall, pillowed by a jagged piece of plaster, closed my eyes and waited for Ramon to go away, which he did after a few more minutes of hand-holding. I dozed through several shifts in the population of the pen. I sensed people moving around me, heard the clang of the pen door and was finally awakened by a vehement but nonviolent discussion that was taking place near me.

"I'm tellin' you they snuffed those two dudes."

My Spanish protector was whispering to a toothless, pasty-faced Irish kid in a brown T-shirt. They were crouching over what looked and smelled like a reefer.

"That's 'cause the dudes had the bread on 'em when they

was offed," the Irish kid said. His gestures and inflections were black. He had to have grown up hating blacks; now he aped them faithfully.

Ramon shook his head. "Well, this Gruber, he drowned himself."

"The paper said the police were investigating the possibility of foul play," the Irish kid said, quoting faithfully from my story.

"Oh, it's definitely murder," I said.

Ramon slapped me lightly on the leg. "Shut up, bitch. Speak when you're spoken to."

I looked around for some housework to do while the men continued their conversation.

"It's unfuckin' believable," the Irish kid said. "Some old dude with a million bucks in a suitcase."

"With bodyguards," Ramon reminded him.

"Hell, baby, I'll go to war for a million bucks," the Irish kid said. "I'll clean out every saloon in Sunnyside. I'll bring some heavy dudes down on this case." He leaned back to dream. "Score me a coupla magnums, a sawed-off, hell, I get me an M-sixty for this number."

"You'll get your shit blown away," Ramon said. "They'll be ready for you."

"Hey, man, but this ain't like hittin' no liquor store and hopin' the cat had a good day, you know," the Irish kid said. You just wait until the dude names the time and the place, and you get there first."

"The money's probably marked," Ramon said.

"No, man, this is charity for the ghetto brothers."

"Then it's counterfeit," Ramon said. "These rich people don't give nothin' away."

"A coupla million don't mean nothin' to these cats," the Irish kid said. "They get the publicity, and then they can go on rippin' the people off for another thirty years behind a move like this."

Ramon was suddenly gloomy. "Shit, there's guys sittin' in joints all over the country makin' plans like this," he said. "Two crews would end up tryin' to hit the same dude. We'd be wastin' each other, and the rich guy would just walk on out."

"Well, somebody's gonna make a score," the Irish kid said.

"Yeah, and they won't even have time to whack it up before everybody'll be offin' everybody else for a bigger piece," Ramon said. "That's what's wrong with this country." He reached up to pat my knee while he surveyed the crowded pen. "Too damn many crooks."

I never really got to enjoy my story. I mean, I had wrecked my life (and several others) to get it. The least they could have done was let me watch the avid readers grabbing the papers off the stands, squinting over them on the subways, stepping into puddles and bumping each other as they consumed every word. A newspaperman's euphoria is about as long as a butterfly's life span, which also happens to be about as long as it takes to get a writ of habeas corpus. The story and the butterfly would both be dead by the time the writ was ready.

I'd seen enough movies to know I was allowed one phone call. Only I didn't know who to call. Not that I could expect anyone to help me, but I didn't even know anybody who would turn me down. So I sat and enjoyed my small moment of notoriety among my fellow felons, who insisted first that I prove authorship of the stories by reciting them from memory while someone followed in a dog-eared copy of the *Event* that had been smuggled into the pen at great personal risk, along with alcohol, cocaine, marijuana, dirty pictures and a couple of hot Rolexes. Then, satisfied that they had a real celebrity in their midst, the inmates peppered me with questions about the murders, all expressing their admiration for the mysterious blonde.

"That blonde ain't no bitch," one of them said. "A bitch'll

get mad and cut you with a kitchen knife. But she can't plan nothin'. Bitches ain't got the kinda brains that can plan."

There was unanimous agreement on this point. To me it came as no less than a thunderclap of revelation.

"It's a dude in drag," the conclusion was.

"A CIA hit man. Wastin' all those millionaires before they can talk."

"Talk about what?"

"Whatever they been doin'. These people are always runnin' somethin' down."

After several hours I was a seasoned con. My swain, Ramon, had been taken to Central Booking, along with the man in the overalls, whose position I quickly assumed. I stood at the cell door and accosted a timorous little chap with a facial tic, who turned out to be the lookout for an Ecuadorian pickpocket team.

"Got any cigarettes?" I demanded.

I got a minute's worth of tic in about fifteen seconds and a pack of *Cabritos,* Peruvian cigarettes made of tobacco ends and the nail parings of diseased goats, which I then had to smoke with great élan.

Time passed quite agreeably in this windowless way station. After a while they wheeled in a snack, a cart loaded with jelly sandwiches and a rusty urn of cold tea. We fed ravenously on this repast; the guards let us eat all we wanted.

Things were so pleasant that I was just getting up enough nerve to use the toilet when Duffy came to the door of the pen.

"All right, Krales, honeymoon's over," Duffy said as the turnkey unlocked the door. "Hope you didn't make any lasting relationships."

"What are you going to do now?" I asked.

"Let you go," Duffy said, grabbing me under the arm in a special pressure point reserved for cops and lifting me three inches off the ground.

We went downstairs past the forlorn graffiti of thousands of prisoners scrawled on the peeling walls. Steve Spingold was standing at the desk, talking to the lieutenant.

"Well, Krales, you finally made the grade," he said.

"You're a civil liberties issue, a cause. Or at least some people think so."

"I thought I was going to be charged," I said to Duffy.

"Why waste the taxpayers' money?" Duffy said. He shoved me toward the door. "I don't think you'll be much of a threat to society after tonight."

"What's going on?" I asked Spingold as we left the station. "Everybody's switching gears on me."

"You're out, aren't you?" He paused at the door of his Mercedes. "I'd offer you a lift, but then you couldn't get run over by the bus I'm hoping will hit you."

It's a setup, I thought, as he peeled away. That blonde, that CIA man in drag, is going to kill me right here in the middle of the street. EVENT REPORTER SLAIN IN MUGGING ATTEMPT. That was how they'd get rid of me.

I weaved through the triple-parked patrol cars, expecting any second to hear that manic giggle, to catch a flash of that homicidal heel. Walk in the middle of the road, I told myself. Sing, draw attention to yourself, that's the classic method for safety on the streets. But Upper Broadway was jammed with people doing exactly the same thing: singing, ranting, making idiots of themselves. There wasn't a normal pedestrian to be seen; everybody was walking amok. A giggly blonde and a bleeding Jew would hardly turn a head on this berserkers' boulevard.

The lights were out in my lobby. I tripped over a bag lady who had set up a camp chair and three Hefty bags of garbage by the elevator.

"Get outta here," I screamed, kicking the chair out from under her. The elevator door opened, and a stream of pallid light caught me in the act. The passengers formed a single file and tried to ease by me.

"She tried to mug me," I explained feebly, while the old woman pawed the floor for a cigarette butt. "She's got a meat cleaver," I said. "As long as my arm. I've seen some of them with pistols, you know. One of them pulled an Uzi on me last Christmas Eve."

The lights were out on the nineteenth floor as well. The darkness was contoured with lurking shapes. "Sure," I said

137

aloud, "turn off all the lights. Make it easy for the CIA to get me. Have a goddamn blackout while you're at it."

I fumbled with my key. "Can't find the hole," I joked loudly. I swung viciously around in the darkness to make sure nobody was coming up behind me. "That's always been my problem."

My door swung back smoothly, opened from the outside. Candles glowed in the living room. It was a black mass. "Pretty kinky for civil servants," I said.

Athena floated out of the darkness, her face framed in the candlelight, disembodied, opaque.

"Hello, baby," she said. "Welcome home."

We made love by candlelight. Athena had placed the candles around the bed. ("A charmed circle," she said. "No one can harm us as long as these candles are burning.") We made love until they all burned down. Then she got more.

"I bought ten boxes," she said. "I was here when the lights blew."

"Doing what?" I asked.

"Getting your door fixed," she said. "Wait until you see the shiny brass hinges."

"Still playing housewife," I said.

"I'd rather play than be one," she said.

The candles made me nervous. I kept pulling the sheets back so the bed wouldn't catch fire. I'm not one for picnics on the grass; moonlight strolls; couplings on beaches, heaths or bosky dells. I'm a rootless cosmopolite. (Stalin had it right.) I prowl the urban sprawl, shrinking with a snarl of fear from the elements.

I was right to be afraid of the firelight. It changed her aspect. "Gray-eyed Athena," I whispered, but she went beyond the time when men could conjure epithets. The light sought out the hollows in her cheeks; it made her sad, submissive. There was nothing of the mocking feminist in her now; nor the track star. The candles spat gently, and the flames played their calligraphy on the bedroom wall. I felt the silence of prehistory, of great rustling rain forests, of women hovering dumbly at the edge of crackling fires.

"Candlelight does strange things to you," she said.

"I was just thinking the same thing about you," I said.

She took my chin in her strong hands and turned my head into the light. "Makes you look like an ancient Hebrew prophet," she said.

"Ancient Hebrews make a lot of profit," I said.

"Oh, be serious," she said. "You do. Your features are sharper. All this lovely hair"—she slid her palm slowly down my chest grazing my nipples, moving slowly to my groin—"that bony rib cage. You look like a righteous man, a man who would fast for days and then lead his followers into battle."

"And you look like an ancient Saxon maid. A seminude virgin bringing slabs of meat to hairy guys in bearskins."

"In what porno movie did you get that fantasy?" she laughed. "Saxon maids were as big and hairy as Saxon men."

"And Hebrew prophets were little dark guys with big noses, who looked like Armenian rug salesmen. I would say neither of us has a very transcendent imagination."

"Well, the man you remind me of is the closest thing to a prophet we have in this country," she said defensively. "You should be flattered. He's famous and very sexy. I used to sit in his classes with the ooze dripping down my leg."

"How graphic," I said, shocked at her sudden vulgarity.

"And I wasn't the only one," Athena said. "Helene's crazy about him. I never met a girl who wasn't."

"Who is this Semitic satyr?" I asked.

"Eliezer Fischer," she said.

"The famous Professor Fischer," I said. "Author of *Sexual Symbolism in Revolutionary Literature*."

"That was his Ph.D. dissertation," Athena said.

"He's a crud," I said. "I hate everything he stands for."

"Did you read *Orgasm and Revolution?*" she asked.

"Why should I? I haven't the slightest interest in either of those subjects."

"He's a Jewish boy from Brooklyn, just like you," she said.

"There are millions of Jewish boys from Brooklyn shooting their mouths off all over the country," I said.

"He looks just like you," she said.

"All Jewish boys from Brooklyn who shoot their mouths off look like me," I said.

"He's full of jokes and wisecracks," she said. "For a girl from Santa Barbara, California, it was an absolute epiphany just to meet him. . . ."

"Watch your language, now," I said.

"I'd never had ideas speeding so fast at me before," she said. "I sat in the freshman poli sci class, and in forty-five minutes every notion I had about the world had been destroyed. By the end of the term I'd been made over. . . ."

"I'll bet you had," I said.

"Oh, not that way." She shook her head nervously. "Jesus, I think I'd drop dead if he ever laid a hand on me. At this point it would be too intense."

"So you go around finding harmless surrogates like me," I said.

Athena rose over me, her face slipping into the shadows. "Such a vulnerable little boy," she said. She tried to push me back down on the bed.

I dug my fingers into the mattress and held on. "I just don't like being compared to people I don't like," I said. "Especially on such flimsy grounds."

"Oh, you're not that much alike," she said. "For one thing, he doesn't hate himself like you do."

"If he doesn't hate himself, he's only posing as a Jewish boy from Brooklyn."

"He's a very great man, Josh," she said. "You don't know him, and it's not fair to judge. I don't know one person who has met him who hasn't been touched by him. Whose life hasn't been completely changed. That's what revolution is about, too, you know."

Blue veins stretched tightly across her stomach. Shadows nestled in the hollows of her thighs. I slid down between her legs, cupped her buttocks and brought her like a goblet to my lips. If that didn't staunch the rhetoric, nothing would.

"Josh." She grabbed my neck and pushed me further into the labial cavern. I dug my knuckle into her anus. She jumped, then settled down on it with a vengeance. My feet dangled off the bed, tickled by the warmth of the candles. I nibbled an epidermal protrusion I took to be her clitoris; I can never find them unless they hang out like shirttails. She stiffened and pressed her thumbs into my scalp. Something was happening in the distance. The cavalry was riding to the rescue. The earth shook under the pounding of hooves. I bit harder, rolling that capillary-rich piece of flesh between my teeth. Pain? Pleasure? After a while the two just seemed to merge. Shove a finger up my ass, and you'd hear about it. Bite me in the groin, and I'd never sit in the same room with you again. But then I was a Hebrew prophet. What did I know?

Only that the phone was ringing. One of the news magazines, probably, or a network, or a wire service. I tried to struggle free, but she pushed me harder into the bed. My arms were pinned. The phone was ringing. There went my Pulitzer, my Fulbright, my ticket to Hawaii.

Never interfere with a woman who's waiting for the cavalry. I tried to slide my arm over. Just let me reach the phone and knock it off the hook. They won't hang up then. They might even send help.

"No," she cried.

"No, what?" I hollered into her deaf ear.

And then, thankfully, the troops thundered home. She screamed a welcome and rose a few inches to wave them in, then slid off me, sobbing like a policeman's widow.

"Don't answer it. . . ."

"I have to," I said. "It might be about my son. I have certain responsibilities. Hello," I shouted.

All was quite calm on the other end. Then I heard a shrill snicker as if a maiden lady were being goosed, not entirely against her will. "You're a flop, aren't you, Mr. Krales?"

I squinted into the darkness. Had someone else been in the room?

"You go to all this trouble to get your story before the public, and with a few phone calls they completely negate you. Discouraging, isn't it?"

"Who is this?" I demanded.

"I sense that I've called at an inopportune moment. You obviously haven't been following the progress, or should I say regress, of your own stories. You wouldn't be in the mood for love if you had. My name is Edward Foley. Sound familiar?"

"Should it?"

"If you read the business pages," he said a bit huffily. "If you read the late Miss St. James, the initials E. F. might ring a bell."

E. F. were the initials Reva had quoted to me. "You're the next candidate for the Guiltwagon, aren't you?"

"Yes, but I'm not jumping aboard, thank you, in spite of the efforts of the mass media and the United States government," Foley said. "I'm going to join forces with you."

"I don't need you," I said.

"Oh, really." I heard that unpleasant snicker again. "You'd better kick yourself out of bed and read some newspapers. When you're ready, I'm in the book. The only Foley on Sutton Place."

Athena lay with her face buried in the pillow, cringing as if awaiting an attack. A candle fizzed out. Then another one. The party was definitely over.

I got dressed and ran down to the newsstand on the corner. A gas main had exploded in the garment center, sending manhole covers whirling like killer Frisbees through the rush-hour streets. That was the page-one story in the final edition of the *Event*. In the lower right-hand corner there was a little black box headed RETRACTION. "The management of the New York *Event* regrets the bizarre chain of circumstances that led to the publication in today's first edition of a story filled with misconceptions and errors of fact. Clarification is on page three." That baroque prose could have issued only from the gin-soaked pen of Grissom himself. Most of page three was a point-by-point refutation of my stories. Police sources said a burglar was suspected in the murder of Reva St. James and denied the existence of the mystery blonde. The Wilkins family said Cyrus had died of a heart attack at a private hospital in Connecticut. Clytemnestra Agamisou said her father had passed away in his bedroom after spending a quiet night with the family. The Grubers denied vigorously that they had received blackmail threats. Both the Justice Department and the U.S. attorney in California denied that they were investigating Plotcorp or Gruber.

The front page of the *News* had a sheet-draped victim of what police were now calling the "Barrio Butcher." Inside, they ran an almost identical story, with a quote from Grissom that "Krales has been suspended from the *Event*. He has been an incompetent, insubordinate employee throughout his tenure and was only kept on by inanely stringent union regulations."

The *Times* was concerned with Afghani guerrillas and Japanese TV sets, but found time to denounce me on the editorial page. "The name Krales will soon become an eponym for inaccurate, misleading, sensational journalism," the *Times* railed. "Such gross distortions and personal axe grinding in daily journalism are very much the exception and not the rule."

I had been strictly a bush-league pariah before this. Now the whole world had closed ranks and booted me out. I had been banished to an air bubble just big enough to hold me. It seemed as if the people I passed in the street could neither see nor hear me.

Athena had lit fresh candles. I threw the papers down on the bed. "Did you know about this?"

"I didn't have the heart to tell you," she said. "I thought I wouldn't have to."

"Why are they doing this?" I said. "Why go to such

143

lengths? They must know that the whole story will be blown. They must!"

"I don't know," she said.

"But it's crazy," I said. "You see, you don't know how crazy it really is. I've bumped heads with the paper before on worse stuff than this. I just don't know what I did."

Athena reached out to me. The charmed circle of candles flickered. Within that circle lay bliss and forgetfulness. But candles went out, and bliss got repetitive. And newspapermen never forget. I switched on the clock radio. I was a glutton for punishment.

". . . in a gun battle that recalled the days of Dillinger and Bonnie and Clyde, the bodyguards of Sims Webster, president of Webster Coal, shot and killed eight would-be highwaymen, who ambushed them on the road to West Virginia late this afternoon," the newscaster said. "Webster was on his way to distribute two million dollars in cash to the residents of the poverty-stricken Appalachian region where his Scotch-Irish ancestors first settled after the Revolutionary War. According to West Virginia state troopers, the robbers were coal miners who had recently been laid off by Webster Coal in a cost-cutting drive. . . ."

"Maybe you ought to get away from here for a while," Athena said.

I picked up one of the candles, but my hand was shaking so much the flame went out. I reached under the bed for the phone book and found the Foley on Sutton Place. I had to grip the phone between my legs while I dialed. Foley took his time about answering.

"Mr. Krales?"

"Yes, Mr. Foley," I said. "I think I need you."

We'll make it at ten-thirty," Foley said. "Sorry it can't be earlier, but I have a dinner. CYO is making me its man of the year. Do you have a tape recorder?"

"No."

"What kind of reporter are you, anyway?"

"Oh, I just like to get the name right. Then I make everything else up."

"So I see," Foley said. "Well, you won't have to fabricate any of this story. I have a cassette. I'll begin my reminiscences now, and we can play them back over coffee. . . ."

"Uh, wait a minute, Mr. Foley," I said. "I'm not really sure I know who you are."

"Do you have access to your paper's morgue?" Foley said. "No, I suppose you don't. Well, I'll give you a quick pedigree and leave it to you to read between the lines. My great-grandfather came over from the old sod and settled in what is now Hell's Kitchen, Forty-fifth and Tenth. This is where our altruistic friends want me to make my donation, two million dollars' worth, right on Tenth Avenue."

"And you won't do it," I said.

"They think I will," Foley said, "but that's only because I don't want to suffer the fate of the other reluctant philanthropists. I'm counting on you to save my life and my money."

"Which comes first?"

"I'm a very wealthy man, Mr. Krales," Foley said. "My great-grandfather stayed long enough on Tenth Avenue to buy every vacant lot from Fifty-ninth Street to the Battery. My grandfather was a major stockholder in the Interborough subway line when it was private and later transferred most of his holdings to Con Edison. My father had a knack

145

for the market. He bought Coca-Cola during the Depression. I am the conservator of the family fortune. Very wealthy, very frugal, very vulnerable. And I have absolutely no sense of humor. I find flippancy in the face of catastrophe tedious and wasteful. May I expect you at ten-thirty?"

"Yes."

"Good. Get some sleep; you'll probably be up most of the night."

"Who was that?" Athena asked sleepily.

"Mr. Edward Foley," I said. "Looks like he's going to pull my chestnuts out of the fire before they're even roasted."

I slept until dusk and awoke with a rose clasped between my fingers as if I were a reposing corpse. It was a grisly parting gift from Athena. There was another note in my cigarettes which I was afraid to read, fearing more apocalyptic sentiments. "Sleep tight, you're a very lucky man," it said. "See you around midnight."

I went downstairs for a paper. The *News* was all worked up about a Saudi Arabian diplomat who was refusing to pay his parking tickets. The *Times* was leading with a Dallas oil man who was planning to distribute two million dollars in the Mexican slum ("boystowns," they're called in the Southwest) of El Paso. Newark had been declared a federal disaster area. The funerals of the eight men killed in the ambush on Sims Webster had been postponed when the funeral parlor was firebombed. The Urban League had demonstrated in front of Chase Manhattan Plaza, demanding that David Rockefeller contribute personally to the rebuilding of the South Bronx. An editorialist on the *Times* had his ear to the ground and his finger in the wind, and he still didn't know what position to take. He squirmed through the elephant grass of journalese, declaring that the "altruistic impulse in men had to be a good thing" and that "direct philanthropy" was "an attempt to confront the world on a one-to-one basis," but one could not entirely ignore the "dead, wounded and homeless that came in the wake of this sudden wave of generosity." The harried editorialist finally made port with the declaration that this "contrition should be channeled more carefully and crea-tively in the future" and limped off the Good Ship Malaprop for a little shore leave.

The *Event* was going the picture route. The eight dead bodies spread over an Appalachian highway. Headline: BONNIE AND CLYDE RISE AGAIN. Sims Webster posing with the inviolate valise. HE'LL TRY AGAIN ANOTHER DAY. An aerial photo of thirteen square blocks of devastation in downtown Topeka. TOPEKA, THE MORNING AFTER. Inside, there was nothing about my stories the day before, not even a further retraction. They thought they had shoveled the last spadeful of dirt over me, but I wasn't dead yet. Mr. Edward Foley, the CYO's man of the year, would roll back the rock.

Foley lived in an obscure enclave known as Turtle Bay, a quiet block of brownstones and carriage houses, which hid behind the ostentation of Sutton Place. His house crouched behind a looming thicket of unpruned hedges, surrounded by a high, black wrought-iron fence, its sharpened pickets strung with barbed wire. The house was dark and the gate was locked, but I could hear the screech of rock music coming from inside. I rang the bell by the gate. No answer. I leaned on the bell. It sounded as if Mr. Foley's kids were having a party.

Finally the front door swung open, and a teenaged punk sporting a cowboy hat and a black cape marched up to the gate.

"What the fuck do you want?"

"I have an appointment with Mr. Foley," I said. "Is he in?"

The kid pushed open the gate, and I got a faceful of wrought iron.

"Yeah, he's in," the kid said and brushed by me. I noticed a tattoo of a purple snake running down his arm. "Well, go ahead," the kid said, shoving me. "He's waiting for you." He swirled his cape around his shoulders and stomped off down the street on high black boots.

"Hey," I called. "Who are you?"

The kid stopped under a streetlight. His boots gleamed, his white face seemed featureless like some punk apparition.

"Who the fuck do you think I am, asshole?" he snarled and took off into the darkness toward York Avenue. He was moving so fast I expected him to turn into a bat and blot out the moonlight.

Two coach lanterns sparkled hospitably over Foley's door. There was a shiny silver knocker in the shape of Paul Revere on his horse. I banged Paul's silver head against the door. No one came. Then I tried my fist. I wanted to call out, but you just don't raise your voice in this part of town.

I picked my way through the shrubbery to the front window. I tapped politely. Then more assertively. The music seemed to be coming from inside that room. I banged on the frame. "Hey, Foley," I yelled. Nothing.

The window was overhung with black drapes, but there was a chink which let out a glimmer of light. I pressed my face against the glass and squinted through the narrow opening. A man was lying on the floor, his left leg folded under him. It could have been a yoga exercise, but with the loud music and my serendipitous rapport with corpses it seemed a bit more serious.

I picked my way through Foley's herbal camouflage, and found an aluminum garbage can. I rushed the window using the can as a battering ram. The window shattered, and my momentum carried me through the broken frame. Broken glass tinkled like a Japanese lantern on the back of my neck. I fought my way through the thick, black drapes, and poked my head into the room. What I saw made me crawl back the way I had come.

The man on the floor was sticking his tongue out at me, which was really uncalled for, considering all the trouble I had gone through to keep my appointment. Then again, it wasn't bad manners that caused the tongue to protrude, but a telephone wire that was knotted tightly around his neck.

It had to be Foley, unless of course I had broken into the wrong house, which would have come as a great relief, proving that people who didn't know me could also be murdered. That chubby, pink naked body looked like an elephantine infant on a bear rug. The wrists had been play-tied with a bathrobe sash; he could have easily kicked free of those bonds. Black pantyhose were wrapped tightly around the arms, pulling them at a painful angle behind the back; he wouldn't have been able to twist free so easily. As for the telephone wire around his neck, one could only assume he didn't want it as tight as it had gotten.

There was no blood, no sign of a struggle. Patti Smith was screaming on the turntable. I turned her off.

On the desk there was a photo of the late Cardinal Spellman with his arm around a plump young man. Foley in his younger days. A photo of a sour woman in a print dress with a high collar. Mom. A small cassette recorder with a few cassettes alongside. I put one on.

". . . to resume my narrative." I recognized Foley's voice from our phone conversation.

I took the tape out and turned it over.

"I will try to make this short and concise," Foley's voice said. "I am being blackmailed by an unknown but obviously very influential group of people. They want me to distribute two million dollars to the Hispanic population of the Hell's Kitchen area on the West Side. They have sent me circulars advising me to jump on the Guiltwagon, which I have ignored. . . ." There was a photo on the desk of a rail-thin little girl kneeling in front of a hut. It looked like a magazine ad for foster children.

"They have made threatening telephone calls, two of which I taped. The gist of the first call was that my private life would be exposed if I didn't make the payments. I got the candid snaps you are now looking at in the mail two days later. . . ." There was an envelope on the desk overflowing with snapshots on the floor by the desk.

"My, uh . . . private life is a matter of some concern to me, as you can see," Foley continued. Here he had a coughing spell which continued for such a long time that he turned off the machine until it passed. There were at least fifty photos in the envelope. The personnel was different, but the pose was the same. Foley with a tall black man whose head went right out of the frame, Foley with a muscular, tattooed man in his forties. Foley with a bald, thick-necked wrestler type.

"You see why I have left the room while you listened," Foley was saying. "I hope you aren't too repelled. I assume you've seen worse. Maybe even done it."

I'd seen worse. Still, I doubted I'd ever be able to eat a frankfurter again.

"These pictures were taken in a very exclusive male bordello," Foley's voice went on, "where men like me pay for absolute secrecy. I am a homosexual. . . ."

A tiny red button over the door was blinking. One of those infernal electric eyes that was connected to the private security service, the local precinct, the FBI, the National Security Council . . . I had probably tripped a silent alarm when I broke the window.

". . . an urge so strong it could not be resisted," Foley was saying.

At this moment an invasion force of cops, Pinkertons, Green Berets and John Duffy was probably speeding toward the house. And guess who they'd find? Old corpse-a-minute Krales, Mr. Bubonic Plague. REPORTER SLAIN FLEEING MURDER SCENE. Not tonight, he wouldn't be.

I picked up the recorder and the tapes, and stepped back over the drapes and the broken glass. The street was still quiet, but on York Avenue a police car rolled quietly around the corner, cutting its light. The two cops were stuffing slices of pizza in their mouths, expecting to find a minor burglary or maybe even a short circuit. A good deal of that pizza would soon be on the rug next to Foley's body, unless these boys had strong stomachs. Anybody who follows me around really ought to stay on a bland diet.

The fish-eye mirror in my elevator showed a man with swollen features, eyes bulging like a demented hyperthyroid. I checked the car out warily. There was nobody there but me.

It was still dark in the hall, but I could see someone in white pants sitting in front of my apartment.

"You're late." It was Athena. She rose to embrace me, but I stepped away. "What's the matter with you?"

"Let's get into the house first."

I was on the perforated edge of another faint. What a sissy I had turned out to be. Lose my job, trip over a couple of stiffs and my knees buckled on me every time. I switched on the light.

"Foley's dead," I said.

Athena put her hands protectively over my face. "Josh . . ."

"Some kid, a punk rocker. Made it look like a fag murder. He was dead when I got there."

She drew her hand away from my face. It was covered with blood. "You're all cut up," she said.

"Broken glass from the window," I said.

She led me into the bathroom. "Do you have any gauze or bandages?"

"Nothing but aspirin," I said. "I usually don't have to treat anything more drastic than a hangover."

I sat down on the toilet seat. A slow blue flame was spreading through my lungs. With every breath I felt a searing pain.

Athena touched my neck. Her fingers felt like razor blades. "You've got glass splinters. . . ." She held a towel under the hot water. "I'm going to have to get these out."

"He made these tapes for me," I said. "He was going to tell how he was being blackmailed. How none of this giveaway stuff was really voluntary. He even taped the blackmail phone call." The bathroom turned blue as Athena pressed a hot towel against my neck.

"Just hold still for a second," she said.

I ran out into the bedroom and got the recorder. "Better play this thing." I slammed a cassette into the recorder. There was the ominous crackle of static and shadow voices. It sounded like a telephone line gone dead. Then a nasal, mocking laugh, an adolescent bray. "It's all erased, asshole," the voice said. "You wanna hear how many dicks this creep sucked, go ahead, get your rocks off. . . ." And that was it. I put the other cassette back on.

". . . in boarding school," Foley was saying. "I followed this boy around for weeks. He tyrannized me, humiliated me in front of the other boys. . . ."

"Jesus, is that all there is?" I pushed the tape ahead. Dead air. "They erased everything," I said.

"They?" Athena said. "I thought you said it was one kid."

"I don't know who it was," I said.

"I'm going to have to take these splinters out," Athena said. "Do you have a tweezer?"

"If I had I wouldn't tell you," I said.

"Oh, never mind, Paco will take care of you. He's doctored himself so many times. . . ."

"Who's Paco?"

"A guy out at the beach. He'll help you. I guess you can wait for a couple of hours as long as the area's disinfected. . . ."

"Back up," I said. "What beach?"

"Malibu," Athena said. She looked at her watch. "We can just make a midnight plane if I call for a limo. Which I'd better do right now."

She walked into the bedroom and rummaged through her bag for her address book. Her white pants were streaked with my blood, but she didn't seem to notice. The first time I'd seen her she'd been bloody, too, after walking on the thorns in Boomer Blodgett's garden. She hadn't noticed then, either.

"What am I going to do in Malibu?" I asked.

"Hide, for one thing," Athena said. "I'm a little better at conspiracies than you are, and there's definitely one in the works right here. With you as the target."

"I'll have to call my family."

"We have phones in Malibu. Also a beach and sun and the best hideout you ever saw. You'll have time to get your head together and make plans. Professor Fischer will know what to do."

"Is he there?"

"Plus a lot of other very interesting people. You'll love Professor Fischer. . . . Oh, shit, I hate it when they pick up the phone and then put you on hold immediately." She turned and smiled at me. "You're going to love California, you know."

She had enough credit cards to play canasta. "Don't worry about the expense," she said. "I charge everything, even revolution."

I stared at her making notations in her appointment book with a flashlight pen.

"Are you serious?" I asked.

She didn't look up. "Of course."

"I just can't run away to California."

That got her attention.

"What are you going to do? Stay here and let them kill you?"

"Don't give me any of that counterculture paranoia. . . . Nobody's going to kill me."

"Oh, I love that," Athena said. "I can't wait until they come down on you. I guess you never read Professor Fischer's *The Fourth Dimension of Repression*. Government is as much a conspiracy as revolution is, and you're going to find that out the hard way."

"I'll sweat this one out right here. . . ."

"You know how easy it is to get rid of you now that you've been set up as a fraud and a failure? They can fake suicide. Come in here and hold you down and slit your wrists. Stick a funnel in your mouth and pour down three hundred seconals. Throw you out of the goddamn window. You think it's never been done before?"

"They can't cover this mess up," I insisted. "Too many people know about it."

"Okay, so it'll come out in a couple of years like Watergate and Cambodia, and who knows what else. Will you be around to cash in on your martyrdom? You'll be dead, honey! Or maybe you'll be doing fifteen to life for the murder of Edward Foley. The best thing for you to do is go underground for a while. . . ."

"Underground," I said. "Have I really come to that?"

"Some of the best people in this country are underground," Athena said. "You'll be in very good company."

I needed time to think, but Athena was on the phone booking a flight and calling for a limo. If I was going underground at least I was going first class.

Maybe Athena was right. They had suppressed my stories and defamed my character. A lot of people were dead because of this "Guiltwagon" thing. No reason for me to be immune.

"Athena," I said, "I know this is going to sound silly."

"What is it?" she asked impatiently.

"Do you think I'll get to see any movie stars?"

A squat, smiling Mexican was waiting for us at Los Angeles airport. "Paco," Athena screeched. She pushed her way through the crowd to embrace him. Heads turned. Everyone in California knew Athena.

The Mexican rose on his tiptoes to kiss Athena's cheek. Then he turned his radiant gaze upon me.

"This our new recruit?"

He had a smooth, sleek moonface and massive weight lifter's arms, but his hands were small and his grip gentle to the point of innuendo.

"We're gonna need a little of your bush medicine, Paco," Athena said. "Josh got all cut up jumping through a window."

"What happened, man, her husband come home too soon?"

"It was just one of those things I've always wanted to do."

"Uh huh." Paco looked me over warily. "Another weird dude from New York. I shot a weird dude from New York a coupla years ago."

He trotted ahead of us to the baggage carousel. "Old family retainer?" I asked.

"Paco was one of the Santa Rosa Eight, the guys who tried to sabotage the military installation in New Mexico. He escaped from Soledad a couple of years ago and robbed banks to stay alive until we contacted him."

"And now he steals valises. The man's rehabilitated. . . ."

Paco trotted out of the terminal with our bags under his arm. We followed him outside to a kelly-green Rolls.

"Oh, Helene sent the car for us," Athena said. "Wasn't that nice?"

I didn't want to get in. "The last time I saw a green Rolls, it blew up," I said.

"Gotta leave those psychedelics alone," Paco said.

"Anyway, this is a Bentley," Athena said. She hopped into the front seat. I chose the back to be as far from the explosion as possible. The upholstery was so hot I had to sit on the edge of the seat. "Put the top down, Paco," Athena said. "We'll give Josh the scenic tour."

"We're supposed to be underground," I reminded her.

She ignored me. "How's the weather been?"

"Smog alert." Paco's brown arms moved smoothly, turning the Bentley out into the orderly traffic as the top slowly descended. A real Rolls stopped behind us, and the driver, a teenage girl with a pair of sunglasses buried in her frizzy coif, waved us on.

A blonde in tennis whites jumped on the hood of a limo screaming, "Alan, Alan, over here." Chauffeurs sweating in black livery were pacing the terminal, holding cardboard signs with the names of their prospective passengers. Athena waved to a few admirers. I ducked under the seat. The way she was acting, we wouldn't make it out of the airport before I was arrested.

Paco lit up a joint. A fuzzy gust of marijuana blew back at me.

"Is that a good idea?" I said. "I mean, under the circumstances . . ."

Athena laughed and lunged headfirst into the back seat, landing in my lap. "Will you relax?" She tried to force the reefer into my mouth. "Bad karma gets more people arrested than anything else. Just don't give off the scent and you'll be cool, believe me. C'mon . . ." She stuck the reefer up my nose. "Take a toke, it'll loosen you up."

The marijuana seared my lungs. I writhed on the red-hot seat and had a five-minute cough.

Paco reached back and gently extricated the joint from between my fingers. "This dude is uptight," he said.

Athena slid her hand into my shirt. She touched my nipple, and I almost jumped out of the car. "Maybe we'll initiate you into the Freeway Club," she whispered in my ear. "That ought to calm you down."

I pushed her hand away. "What's the Freeway Club?"

"It's just having sex on the freeway. Gets really wild when a trucker passes. . . ."

I retreated to the other side of the car. "I can't have sex in moving cars. I don't know if I'm coming or going."

I slid away from her across the burning seat. The heat radiated steadily through the muddy morning clouds. The hush of the desert rose like a mountain around me. Everything was muted. Even the billboards seemed to whisper.

We drove down a boulevard of motels and chain restaurants, and turned onto a highway. Four blond girls roared by in an open jeep, barefoot teenagers in white shorts and halter tops, long hair flying, huge womanly breasts bouncing on narrow chests, sisters, probably, from one of those absurd American families that keeps Minute Maid and Tampax solvent. The jeep was brown, with racing stripes and tongues of orange flame painted on the doors. The girls turned in unison and flashed the peace sign before the sixteen-year-old at the wheel downshifted expertly and zoomed by, weaving through the traffic.

"What's the driving age in this state?" I asked.

"You don't wanna mess with these cowgirls, man," Paco said. "They drop a 'lude and hump you to death."

"Cowgirls?"

"That's what we call those little Anglo honeys," he said.

"Where I come from they're called *shiksas*," I said.

Paco checked me out in the rearview mirror. "Chickasaws? Look again, man, these chicks ain't Indians."

Every variety of American female was roaring by us. Not a type had been left out. Dusky blondes in pickups, glazed, defiant flower children. Dark-glassed Isadoras in Porsches dripping languid ashes out of their windows. Primly permed housewives boiling with secret lust; beestung secretaries expert in the quick weekend and the slow recrimination; horn-rimmed professionals with bottom-line breasts and coffee-break bellies. Women at the Wheel. The ultimate fantasy from an era when both women and automobiles were equally inaccessible. They had been carefully preserved on this time warp known as a freeway. Even the cars were there, the fifty-seven T-Birds, the forty-nine Packards, jeeps, Volkswagen bugs, Ford wagons, Impala convertibles, Corvettes.

"C'mon, get some sun," Athena said, yanking my shirt out of my pants. "You're as white as a fish's belly."

I resorted to my father's line. "Leave me alone, I'm thinking."

It didn't work. It never had.

"Stop thinking. Feel, just feel for a while." She threw me back against the seat and tugged at my belt.

"I'd rather think, thank you. This place is giving me culture shock. The cars, the women . . ."

"And for Chrissake, don't start with any of that East Coast analysis," she said, tearing at my zipper. "That's all verbiage. We put the verbiage in Hefty bags out here."

A red Ferrari roared by us. Athena ripped off her blouse and waved. The driver offered an insouciant salute out of his window and sped on.

"Pretty cool for a guy who's just seen a chick with her tits hanging out in the back seat of a Bentley," I said.

"My tits aren't so great," Athena said. "But if he'd seen

my ass!" She pulled off her pants and leaped on the seat, spreading her cheeks to the California sun.

I tried to pull her down, but that made it look like I was attacking her. "Is this the way people usually go into hiding?"

"A few hours ago you were ready to give yourself up, and now suddenly you're scared to get caught."

"Maybe these few minutes in California have revived my will to live."

"California is the wave of the future, man," Paco said solemnly.

"It's a blast from the past," I amended. "Cars and hairdos I haven't seen for twenty years. If I stay here long enough, I'll develop a cowlick. Communities of whiteheads will settle on my chin, my voice will crack. . . ."

Athena jumped up on my lap and clamped her hand over my mouth. "Swallow that lecture," she commanded.

I pushed her off me. You can beat me, rob me, take my wife, I'll offer no resistance. But don't try to shut me up.

"I've come back to the neverland of my youth. Cheap food, snazzy cars, sexy virgins who could only be had between the fingers. . . ."

Athena put her fingers to her ears and rolled on the floor of the car. "Shut up, will you shut up. . . ."

"How often I've said if I only knew then what I know now. Well, I know it. And then is now. Hooray for Hollywood. . . ."

"*Shit!*" Athena screeched. She pounded the seat. "You're hopeless."

"Maybe I'll just close my eyes and let this all wash over me. . . ."

"*Josh . . .*" Athena gasped and reddened, fighting for breath. She burrowed into my lap, shuddering in asthmatic spasms. Her eyes bulged fearfully. "Shut up, Josh," she rasped between wheezes. The veins in her forehead stood out in blue relief. There was a creak in her throat that sounded like death's door opening a crack.

I stroked her head. "Athena?" Her nails dug into my

thighs. "I've talked people to sleep in my time, but this is the first time anybody's gone into convulsions."

She moaned and dribbled on my pants. "I'll be okay," she rasped. "Just let me catch my breath."

In the front seat, Paco had a revelation. "You talk too much, man."

I thumped Athena on the back, the old wives' cure for a coughing fit. She raised her hand weakly. "No, no, don't do that. I'll be okay in a minute. . . ."

I tried apologizing. "I'm sorry if I upset you. Maybe it's all those murders, all the insanity in New York. I'm not much of a traveler. I get jet lag in an elevator. And I can see I won't be very good as a fugitive. I mean, I get palpitations when my Bloomingdale's card is overdue, so don't expect me to evade the police of three continents without blowing my cool. . . ."

"It'll be all right," Athena said, trying a few deep breaths.

"Maybe I just ought to go home." Suddenly those hot, slimy prisons and those hot, slimy prisoners didn't seem so bad.

Athena raised a hand to silence me. Her voice was muffled in my lap. "No, no, it'll smooth out."

"Maybe if you put your head between your legs instead of mine."

"No, I've had this before. . . ."

"Livin' in the fast lane," Paco commented smugly.

"I've been pretty freaked out the last couple of weeks, Josh, but now that we're home it'll be all right. . . ."

She hugged me tighter. For the first time since I'd known Athena, her embrace had become a clutch. My grandmother, in her immigrant savagery, had warned me once never to get involved with a woman who was poor, sick or crazy. I never seemed to meet any other kind.

"I guess my life is over," I said, flicking the reefer out onto the freeway.

Paco passed back another. "It ain't over until you're dead, baby. And then it's just beginning."

Sure. Here I was in a green Bentley with a nude feminist

in a coma on my lap, besotted with marijuana, having a metaphysical colloquy with a Mexican stickup man. If that didn't add up to a terminated existence, it was a good start.

We turned onto a four-lane highway. The Pacific Ocean sparkled beyond the windshield. A thin, sooty strip of beach ran all the way to the postcard-blue mountains at the horizon. Houses leaned precariously from porous cliffs on the landward side of the road. Squat bungalows hovered over the beach.

"This is Malibu," Paco announced.

"Where are the palm trees and the pounding surf?" I asked. It hadn't looked this way in the movie when Frederic March walked into the ocean. Or James Mason. Or Joan Crawford. It had seemed such a magnificent place for a sacrifice. In person the place was a disappointment. They would have been better off putting their heads in the oven.

Paco veered to the left, and a dirt road appeared in a scrubby cutoff, sloping down from the highway to provide a perfect hideout.

We drove to the last in a row of abandoned, boarded-up houses on the road. It was a faded blue cottage, reminiscent of the dilapidated bungalows in Rockaway Beach that I had vomited in as a child. A drab, dying shrub crawled through the front yard over the peeling picket fence. Water seeped out of a huge wooden vat. "What's that?" I asked Paco.

He looked at me as if I were a Martian. "A hot tub, man. What does it look like?"

Athena sat up and looked around, rubbing her eyes. Her face was white and clammy, her hair dark with sweat. "Oh, Jesus, are we here already?"

We parked next to a black Rolls. Athena stumbled out of the car. "I've got the fucking headache of the century."

"Maybe you ought to put your clothes on if we're going visiting," I suggested.

She gestured irritably and walked over to a shiny, antique panel truck. "Is he back from Sacramento already?"

"He came in last night," Paco said.

Athena wandered among the other cars, two brown

Mercedes and a bright red Ferrari. "Oh, shit, everybody else is here, too."

"Everybody," Paco said. "Zero hour."

Athena beckoned angrily. "Well, c'mon, Josh, don't make this any more difficult than it already is."

We entered through a hallway decorated with publicity stills of leading men of the thirties—Gable, Tracy, Cagney, Barrymore, right down to the lesser lights like George Brent and Wayne Morris. "Now this is more like it," I said. "Movie stars."

The hallway led to a sunken living room backlit by the sun. A bay window overlooked the ocean. Several people were sitting on a ragged couch. A black girl, one globular breast oozing out of a flannel bathrobe, was asleep in a wicker chair by the fireplace.

In the kitchen, a thin, dark man with a large head and a protruding Adam's apple was slicing a banana into a gigantic bowl of cereal. He looked up and rubbed the stubble on his cheeks as we entered, Paco leading, Athena crouching behind me, sheltering her nudity.

"Leave it to Athena to prepare a sensational entrance and then not have the courage to go through with it," he said.

Nobody moved a muscle or said a word. They just stared at the dark man with the slack-jawed attention reserved for flying saucers or religious miracles.

"Are we all too stoned to observe the amenities?" Athena said coldly.

"The naked wanton cries out for propriety," the dark man said.

"Athena wants her intro," said a blonde on the sofa. She eased out of a complicated tangle with a heavy-set, bearded man, who was either comatose or in a state of exaltation. "Heeere's Athena," she said with a flourish. "Want a little theme music, too?" The blonde wore a man's white shirt and a leopard-skin bikini bottom tucked into the cleft of her buttocks. Her toenails were painted crimson, a jade bracelet dripped off her wrist, a slash of rouge pushed her cheekbones into prominence—pretty elaborate makeup for a day just lounging around at the beach. She looked vaguely familiar, but I couldn't place the face . . . Of course, it was the blonde I'd seen with Athena at the Blodgett mansion. Helene Sanders, the TV star. It had been so long—at least two weeks.

"Well, you wanted to see stars," Athena said. "Now you've got a room full of them."

"Stars?" the dark man said. "Myths would be more like it, Athena. After all, stars are a dime a dozen in Malibu." He upended a box of raisins over his cereal. "I believe you know Helene already, Mr. Krales. . . ."

"We spent an afternoon in Newark together," Helene said. She turned quickly to Athena. "If we're going to do this in the nude . . ." She reached up to undo her shirt, and Athena was across the room in a bound, her hand looking gross and mannish as it closed over Helene's wrist. "We're not doing anything in the nude," she said, forcing Helene's hand down.

"Athena wants to be the only naked lady in the room," Helene said. "Okay, you got the part. Now go get dressed. . . ."

"Slip into a little calico dress with a bonnet," the dark man said. He pointed to the sleeping Negress. "You know Belda Bressard, I assume, being a well-informed man, Mr. Krales."

"The singer. My six-year-old son has her records."

"That was probably meant to be a putdown, but it's not. Children do keep you on the AM wavelength, don't they?"

The bearded man woke up. "AM is where it's at."

"This is Artie Peterson. No doubt you had his records when you were six years old."

A touch of teenage hero worship returned. Arthur Peterson had been the lead singer of The Lifeguards, the big group of my youth. I remembered him on "American

Bandstand" with his blazer and white bucks. I had slobbered his lyrics into the arctic ears of many a skittish baby sitter. He was probably responsible for my exhaustive familiarity with the brassieres of the early sixties. He had been a skinny, manic lad with a pompadour that took two epic dips. Later, on "Hullaballoo," his hair got longer, and he switched to boots and vests. His lyrics were still hummable, but only to a psychiatrist.

"Whatever happened to Artie Peterson?" Peterson said in a whiny singsong, which I realized was an imitation of my voice.

Helene sat daintily on his massive lap. "Oh Monica/Santa Monica/ if you really only knew/how I'm suffering over you."

"Don't sing that," Peterson said. He held his belly carefully as if it were a huge glass ball. "That song was a karmic rip-off." His little eyes gleamed with malice through the greasy thicket of his hair. "Didn't recognize me, did you?" he asked me.

"Artie is an established myth, wouldn't you agree, Mr. Krales?" the dark man asked. He pointed to a little blonde who was sitting in the lotus position on the window seat. "Fritzie over there isn't. . . ."

"I'm nobody," the little blonde chirped with a practiced pout, which she had probably been assured was quite adorable.

"Fritzie's fishing for compliments," the dark man said. "But nobody's taking the bait, so on to the final presentation. Me."

"Eliezer Fischer," I said.

"Correct."

We didn't shake hands. It wasn't going to be that kind of relationship.

"Is he the mass murderer you were talking about?" Fritzie asked.

Helene squinted dubiously at me. "He doesn't look the part."

"Neither did Eichmann," Fischer said. His voice had traces of the Brooklyn streets and the California lectern. His

Adam's apple jumped like a hooked fish whenever he spoke, and he had the kind of knowing smirk that you wanted to wipe off with a baseball bat. A heavy beard lay like beach tar on his face. He wore thongs and cutoff chinos, which flapped like burlap bags over his veined, sticklike legs. A soiled white shirt hung from his scrawny shoulders. He had the relentless tan of the true sun worshiper.

"Looking me over, Mr. Krales?" he asked. "What do you see?" He popped a huge spoonful of cereal into his mouth and attacked it, his strong, equine teeth gleaming. It sounded as if he were chewing concrete. "That must be pretty strong grass they gave you," he said.

Athena shook me anxiously. "Josh, Professor Fischer's talking to you."

"It's the grass, Athena, never mind." A trail of milk drooled out of the side of his mouth as he spoke. "I don't think it's Mr. Krales's normal demeanor to gape at people as if he were in some kind of trance."

Somewhere in the house a door slammed. "Are they here yet?" a man shouted. The blonde by the picture window ran across the room at the sound of the voice.

A man with about ten pounds of gold in assorted jujus hanging around his neck and a bulge in his bathing suit that would have done Nijinsky proud came into the room, leaving a trail of wet sand. He was followed by a fierce, bearded chap with a lot of hard flesh hanging off his belly and various predators tattooed on his arms, who jumped between us as if to prevent a fight. The Naugahyde man sniffed. "That's okay, Vinnie, he belongs." He sauntered over and gave Athena a sexless smack on the cheek, ignoring her nudity. "Hiya, lover. You were great on the Griffin show. Great plug for the book."

He turned smoothly away from Athena and choreographed himself over to me. "Lou Kalish," he said, without offering his hand. He smelled of sweat, salt water and some kind of cologne that probably cost a mint but smelled like my Aunt Bessie's toilet water. His belly rose in a half moon under flabby fat-boy breasts. "Typecasting, Athena," he said over his shoulder. "Pale, burned-out, needs a haircut, looks

like he slept in the wardrobe, always a good acting device."
He tapped me lightly. "You got the part, now go take a
shower." He turned to the tattooed guy who was still staring
fiercely at me. "Get that vial of blow out of my safari jacket
in the car. Want a wake-up call, Krales?"

"I think I'd rather sleep late. . . ."

"Sure, sure, nobody ever wants this shit, and then you
gotta use a blowtorch to get their noses away from it."

He nudged the black girl. She snarled in her sleep and
twisted away. "Watch how it wakes her up. That's my old
lady, the love of my life, in case you have any ideas. I mean,
in case you get off on cadavers. She's been in a nod for two
days." He leaned in confidentially, speaking to me as if we
were the only ones in the room. "Have you ever noticed that
when a chick's tired of you she just starts sleeping? Passive
aggression, my shrink calls it. Day and night they're going
with the downs, the 'ludes, the booze. You see, what they're
doing is hoping that if they sleep long enough you'll be gone
when they wake up. Only thing is, they don't want your
house or your car or your bread or your drugs to vanish. Oh,
no. Just you. Have you ever noticed that?"

"You're staring again, Mr. Krales," Fischer said.

Kalish tousled my hair. "You don't know who I am, do
you?" He sat down and patted my knee. "I'm a very rich
and important man in this town."

"You've got the part, Lou, save the monologue," Helene
said.

"I'm a philanthropist, Mr. Krales," Kalish said. "I make
millions of people happy and hundreds rich. In which sub
group would you like to enroll?"

"Oh, will you slam a door on it?" Athena said irritably.
"He's a producer, Josh."

Kalish sighed. "Have you ever noticed how women try to
minimize everything? Let me give you an example. There
are a hundred big stars within walking distance at this very
moment. That's right, here in Malibu. A hundred, maybe
two hundred big stars. Well, they'd all be here in a flash if I
called them. Every one of them from Redford to Gary
Coleman. You know why?"

"Because you make them happy," I said. "Or am I getting my sub groups confused?"

Kalish jumped up as if the chair were on fire. "He's putting me down, Athena. How come your dildos always put me down?"

"Flattery will get you nowhere, Mr. Kalish," I said.

Kalish pointed accusingly at me. "Did you see *Broken Homes?*"

"I lived it."

"The most important film in a generation, Rex Reed said. Shit, even if you had, you wouldn't know me. Civilians never look at the producer's name. Critics never pay any attention, either. The producer's only the Jew with the money. . . ."

"Didn't see that either," I said.

Vinnie came back with a little brown bottle. "The guy's putting you down, Lou," he said, glaring at me with hatred.

"Big news," Kalish said. "Vinnie's my bodyguard," he explained. "Mindguard, too. He'd kill anybody who even hurt my feelings."

I thought of Reva's chauffeur, another homicidally loyal servitor. Why do those who have someone to kill for them always wind up dead?

Kalish poured a mound of cocaine on the glass coffee table by the couch. "Mercks Pharmaceutical, the stuff they give you when they're amputating your eyeball. Costs my dentist fifty dollars an ounce. He charges me three thousand. God Bless America." He leaned over and nudged his sleeping girlfriend. "C'mon, Belda, breakfast time."

Belda's eyes clicked open like a Barbie doll's, and all I could see were the whites. Then she fell forward, and two dark pupils popped up like cherries in a slot machine.

"Better put her in the hot tub, Vinnie," Kalish said.

Vinnie lifted Belda out of the chair in one practiced motion.

"Is this girl going to die?" I asked, trying to keep my tone conversational.

Kalish shook more white powder onto the table. "Everybody dies. Remember that? Garfield's exit line in *Body and Soul*. Anyway, you call that living?" He looked out at the ocean with furrowed brow. "That's an exit line, too. Or was it, 'shut up and deal'?"

"Shut up and chop," Helene said.

Kalish took out his gold American Express card and divided the cocaine into neat lines. "So where do you hang out back in the city, Krales?"

"Will you do it already?" Helene said impatiently.

Vinnie handed Kalish a gold straw. He took a pachyderm snort and passed the straw to Helene. "I like to know where all these intellectuals hang out back there. Like when I'm in town, I follow the Tinsel Triangle. Know what that is? The Sherry to Elaine's to some New Wave disco in a warehouse, back to Elaine's to check in, you know, and home to the suite at the Sherry. The thing defies space, time and gravity. Like I have lunch with a guy in Tokyo, and fourteen hours later he shows up in Elaine's at the next table. So where do you hang out?"

The little blonde slid in next to me. "Oh, Lou, you never let anybody talk when you get wired." She took two dainty sniffs and handed me the straw, which was flecked with the snot of those who had participated. The powder burned up my nose and into my throat. My eyes began tearing.

The blonde licked her pinkie and applied it to my nostrils. "You've got to keep it wet."

"He does his best," Athena said from across the room.

There was a splash in the front yard. "There goes Belda," I said.

Fritzie giggled and tossed her plentiful blond hair in a groin-stabbing move. "Take another hit," she said fondly.

I steam-cleaned my nostrils for the second time. A smooth, cold sweat covered my body from ribs to armpits. I stared at a bent Camel that had magically appeared between my fingers. Fritzie produced a gold lighter. I touched her hand to steady it. It was like grabbing my own genitalia.

"Leave it to Fritzie," Fischer said, clicking the spoon against his teeth. "California's ambassador of good will."

Fritzie made that move with her hair again. "Well, I don't care how hip you are, it's always tough to get down with new people in a new place."

"Getting acclimated?" Athena asked caustically.

"You told me I'd see stars," I said.

"Bitch, bitch, bitch," she said. "I save his life, and he doesn't like the cast."

Helene flounced around, acting hurt. "I'm not a big enough star for him."

Kalish snatched the straw. "Lemme guess. You want movie stars, right? You want Henry Fonda, Jimmy Stewart, Ingrid Bergman. . . ."

"Yeah, I want stars."

"You see, I knew it." Kalish took another snort. "Schmuck." And another one. "Those are fossils, not stars. We call them the Late Show. You buy 'em for three hundred thousand. They're all sitting by the phone waiting for me to call. Helene's poster made more last year than all of them did in their careers." Kalish shook his head in weary contempt. "That's what's wrong with this business. The public is all civilians."

"Jimmy Stewart's a star," I said defiantly.

"Sure, sure, *It's a Wonderful Life, Winchester 73.* Well, a little picture I made called *The Pulsar Project,* which you may have heard of, did more business in Rhode Island than *Mr. Smith Goes to Washington* did in the whole forty-eight, okay, and you ask Mr. Stewart and Mr. Fonda if business isn't the name of the game."

Through the window I saw Vinnie come around from the side of the house, dragging Belda like a sack of flour onto the beach.

"Oh, shit, he's gonna dunk her in the surf," Kalish said.

"Is she dead yet?" I asked.

Kalish took another hurried snort. "She will be if I can wake her up long enough to kill her." He got up and ran out of the house.

"I never heard of *The Pulsar Project!*" I shouted after him.

Kalish answered me in a ghostly voice from somewhere in

168

the bowels of the house. "It grossed three hundred million. . . ." A door slammed, and I saw him running out onto the beach to help Vinnie get the inert Belda to her feet and drag her down to the ocean.

They were all looking at me. I felt I had to explain. "Movies only cost a quarter in those days."

Athena shivered. "Oh, please, Josh, don't make me sorry I brought you."

Fischer put the cereal down and stared at me with his bright, watchful rodent eyes. "You brought Mr. Krales because I told you to. And I'm very glad he's here."

"I'm going home," I said decisively.

"You can't," Athena said.

"Oh, yeah?" I got up to leave, but the floor slid out from under me. "It's an earthquake," I said.

"It's the cocaine," Fischer said.

I stumbled over to a battered leather armchair. My head was all blood and no brains. It felt as if the marrow had been drawn from my bones. "What did Sherlock Holmes see in this crap anyway?"

"Energy, Mr. Krales," Fischer said. "The trick is to make it help you concentrate on one specific task."

"I don't see you using it."

Fischer smiled indulgently. "My only task has been eating breakfast, and it wouldn't be too much help for that."

"Call me a cab," I said. "I'm going home."

"They'll kill you as soon as you get back," Athena said.

I lunged for the phone. "Okay, then I'm going to give myself up to the Los Angeles police."

Athena whipped the phone away from me. "Then we'll all get it for harboring a fugitive."

"It'll be good for your image." I swiped at the phone, but Athena stepped back.

"Paco," Fischer called sharply.

Paco came in from the kitchen with a newspaper. "Hey, man, you wanted to see some stars. Well, take a look." He threw the paper to me. It was the L.A. *Times.* The eight-column headline read: SEEK NEWSMAN IN MILLIONAIRE'S DEATH.

They had unearthed a photo of me. I was wearing a sports shirt, squinting into the camera with a big smile. It looked like one of those family snaps that I had snatched off the mantel when the bereaved wasn't looking, a photo that was never meant for the papers. Some enterprising reporter had gotten my ex-wife to open her album. They were going to a lot of trouble on this story.

"I guess I'm today's news," I said.

Athena looked at the picture. "They'd never recognize you from this."

"It was taken at least six years ago," I said. "I was a good boy then. I'd say cheese when you took my picture, change the Pampers, take out the garbage, drive my mother-in-law home."

The *Times* was running an AP story out of New York which began: "An all-points bulletin was issued yesterday for Josh Krales, 34, a former reporter for the New York *Event* who is wanted for questioning in the death of investment banker Edward Foley, 58, who was found strangled in his brownstone late Sunday night. . . ." I looked further through the story. "Krales had been suspended by the *Event* on the day of the murder for fabricating a story about a terrorist extortion ring. A police spokesman said Krales might have murdered Foley to create proof of the existence of such a ring. He speculated that Krales was trying to contrive a sensational story to advance his waning career and got caught in the act."

"They got my age wrong," I said.

Athena read the story over my shoulder. "They're making you the fall guy. Didn't I tell you?"

There was a sidebar on the front page. REPORTER'S COL-LEAGUES PUZZLED was the headline. "Friends and coworkers of reporter Josh Krales sat stunned in the *Event* city room today after learning of his possible involvement in the murder of investment banker Edward Foley.

"'Josh was never the most scrupulous reporter,' City Editor John Persky said, 'but I never would have thought he would resort to murder just to make a story stand up.'

"Executive Editor Warren Grissom expressed surprise at Krales's behavior. 'We knew he had a drinking problem and that his personal life was a little up in the air, but we never thought that his professionalism would be affected.'

"Krales's ex-wife was unavailable for comment, but a close friend of the family said that his conduct seemed the result of long months of frustration in his personal and professional life. 'Josh couldn't get it together,' he said. 'He was going downhill real fast, and I guess this whole plot was a last-ditch attempt to save himself.'"

The old nameless "friend-of-the-family" routine. I had used it often enough to know when it was being used on me. A reporter stuck for a neat ending had made this friend up and given him the last word. Why not? It was a slow day, and I was the only game in town.

I could see them all back at the paper. Grissom with his composed editorial expression, expatiating on my emotional condition to visiting newsmen. How they must have gloated over this. They couldn't fire me, couldn't bully me; they had to frame me for murder to get me off the job.

And the guy who had used that convenient anonymous designation "police spokesman" to bury me. Was it Duffy getting revenge? Or had that also been the creation of some rewrite man stuck for a good quote? I had invented a few "spokesmen" in my time, had even thrown in a few "spokespersons" to show how liberated I was.

"I'm being framed," I said. Two hours in Hollywood, and I was talking like a character in a B movie. I wondered how my ex-wife would explain all this to my son. "Your father is an escaped murderer and won't be by for his weekly visit." No, she would be oblique, cushion the blow. "Daddy is sick in the hospital." No, that would engender too much anxiety, unmerited sympathy. "We don't know where Daddy is, but you know he's kind of a little baby who can't think of anyone but himself. We love him, but we really shouldn't expect too much. . . ." On and on in such logorrheic Modern Mommy prose that the kid's eyes would glaze over, and he would forget I ever existed.

"I have to get in touch with my son," I said.

Fischer shook his head slowly and with great relish. "They're waiting for you to do that."

"You know they got your phone tapped," Paco said.

I tried to get up, but my extremities were numb. My mouth went dry. I knew I was in trouble: Paco was beginning to make sense to me.

"As soon as you pop up they're gonna waste you, my man. They're setting it up in the media right now. . . ."

"By tomorrow they'll have the whole country believing you're a homicidal maniac," Fischer said.

Helene pointed an Instamatic at me. "Look ferocious now."

"They'll have to kill you," Fischer said. "You're a threat to the Establishment."

"But the people who are killing all those millionaires are the threats," I said.

Fischer shrugged. "Maybe they're not. One thing's for sure: If they already know you're innocent, then their interest is not in letting you clear yourself but in keeping you guilty, and the best way to do that is kill you. Dead men can't defend themselves."

My throat was so dry I couldn't swallow. Now even Fischer sounded rational. I turned to Athena. It seemed absurd to ask a naked woman for career guidance, but I had no choice.

"That's why I brought you out here, Josh," she said gently. "You'll have to stay with us."

"But for how long?"

"For as long as it takes."

Helene knelt in front of me for another shot. "You've gone underground, Josh."

"You're going to have to reconceptualize your life," Fischer said with that irritating smile. "You're a revolutionary now. You're one of us."

How many revolutionaries do you think it would take to overthrow the government of the United States?" Fischer asked.

"About as many as could fit on the head of a pin," I replied. Paco was digging the glass slivers out of my hand with a pair of tweezers that he had sterilized with Fritzie's lighter. It felt as if I had a ball of fire at the end of my wrist. My arm throbbed all the way to the top of my head. Kalish had taken his painkillers out onto the beach, where he cavorted with Athena and the others over the prone body of his black girlfriend. I was spending my last hours on earth with a collection of drugged-out lunatics and was definitely not in the mood for any coffee-shop theorizing.

Fischer smiled. "Governments have been overthrown in the past, you know. Governments that were stronger and more repressive than ours. Why couldn't it happen here?"

"Because my mommy won't let it."

Paco chuckled and shook his head. "You a weird dude, you know." He raised a blood-flecked fragment of glass that he had just dug out of my palm. "If you got this in your neck, you would have been dead."

"Look at the French Revolution, look at the Bolsheviks," Fischer said.

"Is that them in the red bikinis?"

"Look at Khomeni," he persisted. "One senile old man, and he managed to topple the one state that nobody thought would ever fall. So why couldn't it happen here?"

"Let me take a wild guess," I said. "Nobody wants it to. . . ."

Fischer peeled an orange. "Paco, do you want to overthrow this government?"

Paco grunted and dug the tweezers into my hand. "Hey, man, I wanna put all those motherfuckers against the wall."

I felt a moan coming on and covered it in a rush of words.

"That settles it. As Paco goes, so goes the nation. The polls are closed; the results are in; "NBC News" declares Paco the winner. . . ."

"He's delirious," Paco said.

"Do you want a Percodan?" Fischer asked.

"What does that do?"

"Kills the pain."

"Leave the bottle."

"They're in the medicine chest upstairs, Paco."

Paco patted my shoulder. "I'll be right back."

"Bring down some of that dust, too," Fischer said. "Angel dust," he said to me. "They use it to tranquilize horses."

"Good, because I've got a rabid stallion gnawing at my hand."

Paco came back with a vial of pills. I didn't have a jigger of spit left to swallow it with, so he got me a glass of water. "How long will it take for this to work?" I asked.

Paco lit a joint. "This'll beat it to the punch."

The marijuana had a sweetish taste, like pipe tobacco. Paco urged the reefer on me for a second and third puff. I finally pushed it away when I felt a wave of nausea coming on. "What's in this, anyway?"

"Don't worry, it's organic," Fischer said.

"So's horseshit, but I wouldn't want to smoke it."

Paco pushed my head back. "Just relax, man, and let it take over."

I closed my eyes and immediately began falling down an elevator shaft made of smooth, shiny metal. There was a hollow ringing in my ears. I tried to steady myself, and my nails grated like chalk against the metallic surface. I was falling faster and faster. My brain would burst if this continued another second. With a mighty effort I opened my eyes. Out on the beach the sun had risen, bleaching all the color out of the day. Joggers and strollers had appeared. It seemed that quite a convivial group had gathered around Kalish. Paco's face seemed to have gotten rounder. That little reefer glowed between his fingers. I took another drag.

"Feeling better?" Fischer asked.

I closed my eyes again. I could see the cops going through my desk in the city room, making sour jokes at my expense. They were going to find that envelope of dirty pictures I'd bought at the Port Authority Bus Terminal. Another item to add to my indictment.

"Is the pain gone?" Fischer asked.

"Maybe." I didn't have to open my eyes to see his smartass I-told-you-so look.

"Maybe now you'll trust me a little more."

"Sure." It didn't matter much. My life was over. By the time these drugs wore off, I'd have gangrene. They'd cut off my arm up to the shoulder and bring me back to stand trial.

"Because when you think about it," Fischer said, "it's going to take a major social upheaval to save you. . . ."

I thought maybe a little iodine and some plastic surgery might do the trick.

Now something on the beach caught my eye. Athena had run down to a white-haired man in a blue jogging suit.

Fischer was speaking quietly and earnestly. "You must understand—I'm going to take over the world. As strange as that seems, you'll come to believe it in due time. Because you will have taken an active part in helping me."

"That's the strangest thing," I said.

"I know you think that now. . . ."

"We're sitting here talking about revolution, and Athena is down on the beach flirting with Johnny Carson."

"He lives a half-mile down," Paco said. "Comes jogging by here every day. Shit, Mary Tyler Moore lives next door."

"Mary Tyler Moore?" I turned to Fischer. "Does she know of your plans for world conquest?"

He was unflappable. "Maybe."

"Is she one of those who wants to overthrow the government? How about Carson? Who else lives around here?" I asked Paco.

"A lotta heavy people. Neil Diamond, Henry Winkler . . ."

"Henry Winkler! Oh, that's rich, that's marvelous. Is he in on your little scheme? Is he going to lead the troops down

Pennsylvania Avenue on his motorcycle? Will Mary Tyler Moore make brownies for everybody while they're out in the bush?"

Fischer still wouldn't provoke but sat there eating his orange. "People's thought patterns are so strange. The fact that I'm in these surroundings talking about such things destroys my credibility for you. But if I were back in New York in some sooty loft, preaching to a bunch of scruffy, limited unknowns . . ."

"If you were in New York, my friend, you'd be an outpatient living in a single-occupancy welfare hotel with a bottle of lithium and a weekly visit from a psychiatric social worker."

"Maybe," Fischer said, "but I'm living in California, where I'm a tenured professor in a large state university. Where I'm constantly quoted in newspapers and magazines, my books sell out and I go on public television to comment on world crises. I'm a celebrity, a guru. Every morning I walk into my brand-new sunny auditorium. That's right, auditorium, my classes were too big for the biggest lecture hall in the university. I look out on rows upon rows of amiable, middle-class kids sitting there waiting for the word, waiting to be converted. Every morning I twist political theory around like a licorice stick and come up with something that makes them gasp with adoration. I see through their heads to those unformed masses of silly putty. Not a convolution in the lot until I leave my footprints on those brains."

Suddenly I saw something familiar about him. "You look like a kid I knew in junior high. Used to pick his nose and eat it."

"I was very clean as a boy," Fischer said.

"No confessions, please."

He laughed and nodded to Paco, who came up with another one of those sweet-smelling reefers. "As long as you're in a festive mood . . ."

"I've had enough," I said and took an enormous drag. The smoke had hardly settled in my brain when I knew I'd made a mistake, the kind that makes you make a few more. I took two more hits, and the room went dark for a moment. A ball of cotton was slowly expanding in my head. I licked the crust off my lips with a dry, swollen tongue. My body was becoming gross. I could feel a thickening in my arms and shoulders. My hands were blunt, spatulate. It wasn't an unpleasant sensation. Now I knew how Mr. Hyde had felt. A sudden surge of brute strength. It seemed as if I could clench my fist and drive it through a brick wall if I wanted to.

"You're going to have to find a resemblance, a similarity, aren't you?" Fischer asked.

In my present state Fischer's head would be nothing more than a papier-mâché model. I could stick my thumbs in his temples; his head would crumple with a slight crackling sound.

"I guess it makes you both more comfortable with me," Fischer said. "You identify me as the misfit from the old neighborhood. The old egg-cream syndrome, I call it."

"Oh, do you?" I said, savoring the image of those beady little eyes popping out of his head like buttons.

"And it's so easy to predict. All I have to do is learn about the background of the person, and I'll know what pigeon-hole he's trying to force me into. You probably locate me in the City College, Trotskyite, work-shirt, folk-song trip from the fifties. . . ."

"No." I had finally realized who Fischer reminded me of.

"You see, you need the familiarity to fuel your contempt. If you really admit that I'm different, that I bear no resemblance to any cultural stereotype, then you might have to admit . . ."

"No!" The muscles in my forearm bulged amazingly. How nice it was to be this strong. How comforting.

"All right," Fischer said in soft, soothing tones.

I opened my eyes just long enough to look at him, to make sure I was right. "I had an uncle once," I said. "My father's brother. They said he had been shell-shocked at the Battle of the Bulge, and we had to be very quiet. Also, they said not to pay any attention to what he said. He had a room in a private house in Coney Island. Everybody in the family gave him money. When I was a teenager I would see him wandering around the beach with his camp chair, a copy of Sartre or Kierkegaard under his arm. He loved the sun and would lay spread-eagled on the sand for hours. Then he would trot down to the ocean, splash a little water on his neck and ankles, and then trot back up to his spot. A few years later I ran into him in Washington Square Park with an off-print of his poems, sitting on a bench surrounded by adoring young college girls. He was quite a celebrity in his day, my Uncle Max."

"And what happened to him?" Fischer asked.

"He got hit by a car on Canal Street. They read some of his poems at the funeral. My father took me into the bathroom and whispered, "He was a bum, and I'm glad he's dead. . . ."

"And you think I'm a bum, like your wastrel uncle," Fischer said.

"I think you remind me of a bum."

"Fair enough," he said. "Let me present my bona fides. You be the judge. Now, first of all, you probably think you were brought here by a series of tragic coincidences, but the truth of the matter is that your time had come. You were expanding out of your little world; it could no longer contain you. Something drastic would have happened if you didn't find your way here. You'd probably be dead. . . ."

Okay, now, just go over there, and tear him apart like a piece of wrapping paper.

"Everybody comes to me that way. *In extremis,* a state of total existential crisis . . ."

Roll him into little balls, and throw them onto the beach. Here Athena, catch your little guru before he blows away.

"That's how I found Athena. She was a student of mine. A track star. Jockette, I used to call her."

"Clever," I said, savoring the image of Fischer's crumpling skull.

"Helene was a harebrained little masochist living alone on a mountain of money."

"Which you have helped erode . . ."

He was too far into his homiletic to respond. "Arthur Peterson was a kind of washed-out flower child. He hadn't worked and wasn't about to. He was looking for something; you all are, whether you know it or not. Lou Kalish was a lost soul with fifty million dollars. All of them seem to find their way to me at the moment when they are at the brink of a great and probably fatal disaster."

"And what do you do for them?"

"I give them a purpose, a mission. Every second of their waking hours is infused with meaning now. They live with an intensity that only a dedicated revolutionary can know. That you will know if you give yourself a chance."

"Never!" I said with mock firmness. "Why, I wouldn't have gotten where I am today if I had given myself a chance."

Fischer nodded slowly, and then, with an unmistakable threat in his tone: "Are you really going to turn out to be a lost cause, Mr. Krales? I hope not."

"Well, let's just say that I'm going to wait until you get a few more recruits before I join up."

"That's easy enough. Are you up to taking a ride?"

"Where to?"

Fischer got up and stretched, his rib cage visible beneath his shirt.

"Just down the beach a bit to my training grounds. I want you to see the members of my Revolutionary Guard."

Brooklyn, Jewish, Red, that's how you see me, isn't it, Krales?" Fischer asked.

We had taken the pickup truck onto the highway. Fischer drove with zest, wrenching back the antique floor shift, letting the truck buck a little before changing gears. Paco had given me another reefer "for the trip." It occurred to me that I hadn't eaten for almost two days. There would be plenty of time for that after I had gotten away from these lunatics. It just proved how crazy they were that they would actually let me go off alone with Fischer. For when the moment was right, I was going to put my fist right through his face and silence his inane chatter once and for all. I would dump his broken body in a trash can and take the truck. Take it to . . .

"Actually, except for an accident of biology, I'm none of those things."

Take the truck, take the truck; the words ran through my head like a broken record. I couldn't get beyond them to where I was going to take it and what I was going to do when I got there. To the police? It would have to be the police. But they would charge me with kidnapping and murder, not to mention grand theft auto.

"I'm something completely different," Fischer said.

I clenched my fists so tightly my knuckles cracked. His stream-of-consciousness babble was interfering. I couldn't think. "Okay, so you're the lost Dauphin. You're Anastasia with a sex change. You're the Messiah come to Malibu beach. . . ."

"Let's just say I'm not who I seem to be, and it would be a fatal mistake to dismiss me. I lived the first thirty years of my life surrounded by people who tried to convince me I was like them. Parents, teachers, relatives, an ex-wife—relentlessly, implacably ordinary people, who thought they understood me. Just as you do."

"Oh, but *I do*," I said, so full of hatred my chest hurt. "You're a coffee-shop hustler. Greenwich Village used to be full of them. . . ."

"Did it ever occur to you that I'm a prophet?" Fischer asked. "There have been prophets, you know. There have been men who started with much less than I and went on to change society. Why can't I be one of them?"

We were on a deserted stretch of road, the beach on one side, some scrubby, vacant hills on the other. Now was the time.

"Well, I've got a prophecy to make," I said. "I'm going to piss in the glove compartment unless you pull over."

Fischer turned up a canyon road, and I limped out. I was too weak to stand and had to lean against a pole. My urine was colorless, the last evacuation of a dying body. It splashed like acid on the porous rock, dislodging little chunks. My arms trembled; my knees buckled; my head lolled on my neck. I was like a marionette with too much slack in its strings. And yet I felt strong enough to throttle Fischer, to drive my thumbs through his windpipe, to rip his ears off.

We drove further down the Pacific Coast Highway, past the stunted bungalows of the rich, the powdery-pink cliffs, the canyon roads shooting up in frightening perpendiculars. I felt sick and depleted. Whenever I closed my eyes, a tidal wave of nausea overwhelmed me.

Fischer chattered amiably on. "You see, when the revolution comes to this country—notice I say when, not if—it will begin here. Southern California is the farthest point in the evolution of man. Every culture is mutating in our direction. This is the future. By the time India arrives at this point, can you imagine what southern California will be like?"

"Like India, probably," I said.

Fischer patted my knee patronizingly. "That's known as circularity of thought. It occurs in people who can't see beyond the present. But history doesn't always work that way. There are periods of great innovation, and that's what is happening here. California is exploding, detaching from the rest of the country. And when the smoke clears and the rock cools, new forms will have been created." He thumped his chest. "We will have created them."

We drove out of the high-rent district into an area of motels, efficiency units and fast-food places. Behind it all lay the mountains, the ocean and the dead blue sky. I was like one of those flying-saucer aliens with the huge head and the tiny body. My energy was purely mental. I didn't have enough strength to light a cigarette. Fischer was perfectly safe with me.

"Where are we anyway?" I asked.

"Heading for Venice. Heading for the largest guerrilla training camp in the world."

The streets suddenly got narrower. We drove along a potholed avenue, past mildewed, yellow shacks and ancient garden apartments. There were boarded-up stores, old folks trembling on canes, weary young girls pushing strollers.

"Venice," Fischer announced. "Built to resemble the real Venice by an eccentric millionaire." He pointed out the domes, the arcades. "Every building was a carbon copy. The millionaire, of course, lived in the Doge's Palace."

A fat black lady wobbled out of a side street on roller skates.

"Thanks for the travelogue," I said. "But I came to see the revolution."

"And so you shall. Because, you see, for years Venice moldered away into a low-rent, vicious slum. It was a town of nursing homes, forgotten people. The hippies came in because the rents were cheap. The drug dealers, then the artists . . ."

"If you're trying to sell me a few lots, forget it. . . ."

"And all the while something was happening, something that no one, least of all the residents, was fully aware of," Fischer said. "A new breed was being produced here, a breed with absolutely no connection to any of the social, sexual, cultural or economic precedents that had gone before." Fischer's voice quavered with excitement. "They play the system like virtuosos, taking what they need, exploiting it, every facet of it. And when the system ceases to serve them, they will destroy it and create one of their own."

Fischer turned down a narrow, winding street and headed for the beach. "Coffee shops, Krales, you see?" he shouted. "How many Lenins and Trotskys and Bakunins are sitting here? They may have blond hair and blue eyes, they may be high on drugs, they may have no knowledge of history, but that ignorance is their biggest asset. When the time comes they won't hesitate, they won't be put off by the failed revolutions of the past. . . ."

Fischer stopped in front of a rickety ice-cream stand. A blond girl in overalls waved frantically. "Hi, Professor Fischer." He came back to the car with a huge vanilla ice-cream cone that was already beginning to melt. "C'mon, we're here."

I heard a low roar coming from the beach. "What's that, an air raid?" I called to Fischer. "Have the imperialist warplanes come to destroy your guerrillas?"

He laughed and turned down the street toward the beach. I stumbled and reached out for his arm, but he danced away. When he turned back, he had a perfect white ice-cream mustache. The cone was dripping onto his fingers. He licked at it feverishly. "Come on, Krales, come on, Brooklyn boy," he said and dashed down the street.

The roar became louder as we approached the beach. Then I realized what it was. On either side of the street two lines of bikers confronted each other, filling the air with noise and fumes. Blacks on one side, astride gleaming bikes with elongated silver handlebars and short front wheels. "Stretched" bikes spit-shined, gleaming with chrome and silver accessories, their riders dressed in boutique black leather. Across from them were the Hell's Angels, covered, like their squat serviceable machines, with dust from the road, barechested under worn leather vests, bearded and bloodshot, their hairy tattooed bellies drooping over their garrison belts. I staggered through this gauntlet after Fischer, covering my ears, convinced that the two groups would charge into each other. But they seemed content to rev and smirk.

"Are these your revolutionaries?" I hollered.

He laughed and led me onto a promenade by the beach where the roar of the motorcycles was replaced by the shriek of disco music. Hundreds of people were roller-skating on the boardwalk, mostly teenage girls in cutoffs or bikinis, some wearing bright-colored knee pads, their long hair flowing, dipping. They were California blondes, although I saw a few black girls with rouged cheeks and electric hair. There were boys, as long and blond as the girls, blacks with high socks and shorts halfway up their buttocks. They wore headsets or "bone fones," or were content to skate to the cacophony of the dueling "boxes," huge portable transistors, each blaring a different station or cassette. Some of the girls were bare to the waist, their T-shirts tied around their hips. They skated aimlessly up and down, passing booths where older folks—superannuated flower children, the men thin and sallow with their shoulder-length hair and Indian vests, the women blowsy in their granny dresses—sold dresses and dried fruit, hash pipes and accessories. Over on the beach about a hundred black musclemen, their torsos ballooning out of skimpy bathing suits, preened and flexed and strutted. A little further down, a group of ascetic, starved types in white robes huddled around a woman in red who was gently stroking a comatose man on a cot, trying to levitate him. The scent of marijuana and deodorant hung in the breezeless air.

"It's a freak show," I shouted to Fischer.

"Show me its equal anywhere in New York," he shouted back.

I pointed to the bare-breasted girls. "They wouldn't survive fifteen minutes in New York."

"Oh, don't flatter yourself," Fischer said. He squeezed my shoulder, his eyes bulging, his mouth working like a fish under water. "Go to Central Park next year, and you'll see girls like this totally nude. You'll see people copulating in the bushes. All those sinister New York criminals that you're so perversely proud of will just stand around and gape. They'll be just as intimidated by the future as you are."

The girls skated by in dizzying profusion, close enough to touch, incurious, unafraid. Frankensteins made up of equal parts of drugs, junk food and bent chromosomes.

"Six months after New York, it will be London," Fischer shouted. "Then Paris, Munich, Scandinavia, everywhere. There will be regiments of nude roller skaters; of body builders; bikers; beautiful, amoral, homicidal youth. It's the socialism of the senses, Krales."

"Utopian bullshit," I hollered. "They'll all be pushing brooms and baby carriages in five years."

"You don't see their power," Fischer said. "I'm going to harness it, use it. . . ."

These girls smiled when you met their eyes, then skated away. I knew I was high, that I wasn't thinking clearly, but it seemed that I could grab one of them before she skated past.

"Do you see it, Krales?" Fischer shouted, waving his arms.

I pushed him away. Lust was seeping into places it had never been; the tips of my fingers, the edges of my teeth. Lust becomes lethal when it goes where it doesn't belong. So it was the socialism of the senses. Did that include me? Those girls seemed so soft and available. I could span those silky midriffs, gnaw the flesh off those shoulders right to the bone, tear those bodies right to the innards. I was high, and I knew it. But I could feel my heart pounding louder than the din and the disco. The California air would be rent with cries of panic. Clumps of fine yellow hair would float above the fray.

Sure I was high, and I wasn't thinking clearly. I grabbed Fischer, sinking my fingers into his bony arms. Suddenly my strength was back. "I'm going to smoke that other joint," I said. My voice sounded pleasantly feral. "I'm going to smoke it now."

You're out of control, Krales," a bitter voice said. It was only me, alone in a strange bed, shivering, fully dressed under the blanket, my knees drawn up in the famous fetal crouch, talking to myself again.

"You're high on drugs like some irresponsible teenager."

"Oh, stop talking to myself," I answered.

"Oh, shut up."

"You shut up."

My voice sounded strange, as if it were being played back on a tape recorder. "What time is it?"

"What difference does that make?"

"Oh, shut up."

It was getting colder. The temperature drops very quickly in the West, desert weather and all that. The twilight stared through the window like a bloodshot eye. The beach was deserted. Lights were going on all over Malibu. I heard festive voices downstairs. There was a party going on. People were laughing. Maybe the nightmare was over.

"Okay," I said. "I'm not going to be high anymore. I'm going to pull myself together."

I stumbled out of the room, down a long corridor, and found my way into the bathroom. I hissed at myself in the medicine-chest mirror, "Just shut up for a minute, okay?" I didn't reply. Then I ran cold water over my wrists, but that was only good when I was drunk. This was some kind of esoteric dope. It had given me premature softening of the brain. I stuck my head under the shower. Frigid needles pinged off the back of my neck. "Have to harden up the old brainpan," I said. "Harden it up." But that wasn't where the problem was. There was an imp camped in my entrails with a satchelful of dumb ideas, memory fragments, violent impulses, all the mental debris of a wrecked life. He was feeding all this crap into me. I couldn't wash him out, couldn't think him away. I could only run to the hallway, to the light and the voices, down the creaking steps to the living room.

"Oh, shit!"

I was pretty sure I had said that, although it was hard to be sure in this roomful of people. They were all looking up as if they expected me to break into song, which was not unreasonable because I was standing there with my mouth open.

"Surprise," somebody sneered.

Some of the people who had bedeviled me in the last few weeks were here. Boomer the Bomber Blodgett was twitching on the sofa, picking his nose. Clytemnestra Agamisou, the temptress of the gazebo, was leaning over a red candle, lighting a cigarette. Athena, wearing a green party dress with a slit up to the thigh, was flirting with a man in a pin-striped suit. I knew the others were on their way: Duffy with a posse, Potosky with a photographer, my ex-wife with a process server. Everybody was invited to the party inside my dying brain.

Fischer came out of the kitchen, chomping on a carrot. "Here's our guest of honor."

"He's stoned out of his fucking head," Boomer said with a nervous giggle.

Athena approached with a moist smile. "Why don't you sit down for a second, Josh?"

I wheeled on Clytemnestra. "What are you doing here?"

She dipped her pinky in a glass of white wine and dabbed at her nose. "I just can't resist you, cutie pie." She was wearing a loose black-wool sweater over black tights that were pulled up so high I could count every hair in her crotch.

The guy in the pinstripes wore steel-rimmed glasses that glinted in the light. He had the kind of shrunken face you see in compulsive joggers; his lips pursed in a fastidious pout. He extended a long white hand, palm down, like a priest performing a benediction. "Guess it's only fair for the hatchet man to introduce himself. I'm Michael Jax, Mr. Krales. I'm the man who made you famous in California."

"He hasn't seen the story yet, Michael," Athena said.

"Oh, well, being an old war-horse, he might appreciate it." He took a few tearsheets out of a leather envelope at his feet and offered them to me. "I'm rather proud of this bit of media manipulation."

"You'd better sit down, Josh," Athena said.

It was from the L.A. *Times* again, a one-column bold insert in the body of a long story detailing my misadventures. The headline read: "LOWNDES BLASTS 'LUNATICS IN THE CITY ROOMS.'" The story began, "Governor Lowndes yesterday condemned the 'atmosphere of laxity and permissiveness that allows lunatics to run unfettered through the city rooms of our nation's newspapers. . . .'"

"Am I the unfettered lunatic?" I asked.

Jax nodded regretfully.

"And you're the fetter merchant."

"I'm Governor Lowndes's assistant for policy. I'm the architect of his master plan."

"To be president," Athena said.

"Every white man over thirty-five wants to be president, Athena. Dan Lowndes is aiming a lot higher than that."

"Dictator," she said.

"You're getting warmer."

I continued reading. "Many people have been gratuitously libeled by this man Krales, and by other reporters whose infractions may be less sensational but are just as serious," the story went on, quoting the governor at a Sacramento press conference.

"This is a textbook example of deflection, a little invention of my very own."

"Nobody's going to ask you what it is, Michael," Athena said. "So if you want us to know . . ."

"Deflection is the method by which an elected official imposes an unpopular view on the public. He does it through an issue that does not affect him. Now, with a primary coming up, we have to do something to muzzle the media, to discredit the press in the eyes of the public, and *voilà*, the Krales case comes along, proving that all reporters are psychopathic liars and murderers. Nothing personal, Mr. Krales."

I read the final graph of the story out loud. "'How long can we tolerate this perversion of the First Amendment?' the governor said. 'Isn't it time the press was held accountable for its actions?'"

"You see, we're trying to establish eponymic identity," Jax explained. "Now the name Krales becomes a buzz word for media malpractice. If we accuse NBC or the L.A. *Times* of indulging in Krales-like tactics, the public will know exactly what we mean."

"Oh, goody," I said. "I'm going to have a tactic named after me."

"I'm sure you understand," Jax said equably. "I acknowledge that we're burying you, but, after all, you did give us the shovel. . . . Actually, this will probably turn out a blessing in disguise. A few months in a psychiatric hospital, and you can emerge to write a book. *The Fall and Rise* kind of thing. Everyone loves a born-again lunatic. You'll come out smelling like a rose."

"You're really doing me a favor, and I don't realize it. Is that your line?"

Jax smiled blandly. "Not at all. I'm ruining your life, and I know it. I'm using you . . ."

"We're using you," Fischer amended gently.

"For what?"

Fischer spoke with the infinite patience of a saint. "Why, to take over the world. I already told you that."

"I'm sorry, I'm a slow study," I said. "You people are playing at revolution . . ."

"We're not playing," Fischer said soberly.

"We'll ignore that for the time being," I said. "You got me out here, set me up . . ."

Jax corrected me. "We didn't set you up, but merely took advantage of a situation you had created for yourself . . ."

I ignored that too. "Athena, you were part of it."

"I saved your life, Josh," she said. "One day you'll realize that."

It was all too clear. I was trapped in a beach house with a group of dangerously, deluded people. I had to get away from them, and back to New York where the crazies were readily identified by their shopping bags and general incoherence. If necessary I would plead guilty to everything and throw myself on the mercy of the court. How many murders were there? Four? Five? If I had a hanging judge I might get three years. That was better than spending the next few years smoking angel dust and eating wheat germ at this padded cell on the Pacific.

A flying leap through the picture window was the only answer. It was about a thirty-foot drop to the beach. I'd be in Mary Tyler Moore's house before they knew what happened. We'd have a nice cup of coffee in the kitchen with the wallpaper bricks. I'd tell her everything. I'd be saved. Hallelujah!

I inched craftily across the room. I needed only a few feet for a running start. Who did they say lived near here, Neil Diamond, Henry Winkler? They'd all come to my rescue. CONVOY OF STARS RACES TO REPORTER'S AID. And in *Variety*: TINSEL BIGGIES FLOCK TO FALLEN FLACK. If I could just get close enough to that window.

"Okay, everybody, Kalish the candy man is here!"

Wearing a Coca-Cola jumpsuit and a Yankee baseball cap, Lou Kalish came marching into the room at the head of a triumphal procession that included Helene, Artie, Paco, Vinnie, Fritzie, the whole gang, all showered and scented and coked to the gills. Lou took out a piece of wrapping paper that had been folded in the shape of a giant ravioli.

"Anybody need any help?" he asked, emptying a mound of white powder on the coffee table.

Paco casually intercepted me on my way to the window. "C'mon, bro, we're gonna party now. This shit is primo. . . ."

Kalish smoothed out the pile with trembling hands. "C'mon, Krales, feed your brain."

Fischer sat apart, nibbling on his carrot like a satanic rabbit, while the others huddled around the cocaine. Even Athena, her eyes alight with anticipation, joined the crowd. They pushed me over to the coffee table. They wanted to keep me drugged and docile. Fritzie stared at my crotch and licked her lips. It looked like Mary Tyler Moore would just have to keep the coffee hot.

The secession of California," Michael Jax said in a loud voice, "will be the first step."

That was a conversation stopper if I'd ever heard one. It got better.

"In very short order all the states that border on California—Arizona, Colorado and Nevada first, Wyoming and New Mexico to follow and Oregon last—will confederate with it. By plebiscite the citizens will reject the entity now known as the United States, refusing to support the morbid Northeast, the backward Middle-West, the barbaric South. A nation will be declared, not on the basis of race or politics, but culture. The unique cultural sensibility that we have developed in California."

Until this moment it had been a pretty good party. True, I was rather anxious to leave, but I always am. The purpose of a party is to find a complaisant female and go to another party closer to one's apartment. I had found the female, Clytemnestra Agamisou. She was titillating me with the story of her near defloration—"It was on my father's yacht. The purser took me into the galley. All I remember are his big, hairy forearms and the ouzo on his breath. They discovered us just as he had me bent across the table. The captain gouged out his eyes. Then they threw him overboard."—and everything was fine. Only my place was across the continent, and all exits were covered.

The excessive amounts of cocaine and alcohol I had consumed had made me poisonously hostile to my fellow revelers. Nothing new about that, either. Only I couldn't display my contempt, couldn't take French leave of these bores. I was trapped in this limbo, until something worse happened. They would kill me if I tried to escape. And even if I stayed put like a good little nihilist there was no telling what my hosts would do.

"Soon the world will be divided into new sovereignties based on more rational cultural and economic relationships," Jax was saying.

Not everyone was paying attention. Paco was telling prison stories to Francine. "He still had part of the broomstick up his ass. . . ."

And Boomer was twitching like an enraptured insect in front of Helene. "Everything is done wireless these days. The IRA's got it down to a science."

But Fischer shut them all up. "I think you're putting the cart before the horse, Michael," he said softly.

They all looked over at Jax who blinked nervously, reluctant to yield. "Well, I think it's a plausible scenario."

Fischer picked up a heavy metal ashtray and hefted it menacingly. "If I throw this ashtray through the window we all know what will happen, don't we?"

"It'll break," Boomer said gleefully.

"Very good," Fischer said. "Now what we don't know is what will happen afterwards. Will a new window be built?

Will it be bricked in? Will the whole house be gutted? We just don't know do we Michael?"

Jax looked like an infant with a Pamper full. "I think a certain amount of speculation is possible . . ."

Fischer shook his head until Jax's voice trailed off, then assumed his classroom pose, folding his arms, composing his features, Daddy repeating the obvious for his backward children. "We know how to destroy, and we know what the direct results of our destruction will be. What will rise from the ashes cannot be known. Marx would never have predicted Stalin. Hitler could never have even foreseen himself. No, Michael, the challenge we face, the task to which we must devote all of our energy and ingenuity is the complete and total destruction of society as it is now constituted. No stone, no norm, no morality must be left unturned. This is our service to future generations."

"Aimless destruction," I said. It was impossible to keep silent, even though silence and stealth were the only things that would get me out of this house.

"Destruction is an aim unto itself," Fischer said. "Look how the countries of Europe are being subtly changed by terrorism. The world, the collective psyche . . ."

"And you see nothing beyond that," I said. "No ideology to rise out of the void."

"Only abundance, Josh," Athena said patiently.

"An equitable redistribution of the world's resources," Helene chirped, making those agit prop sentiments seem comic with her Betty Boop delivery.

"When the revolution comes everybody will have a house in Malibu," I said. "Everybody will have all the champagne, cocaine and Solarcaine their little hearts desire, is that it?"

My irony escaped them. Instead, Helene looked to the future with a militant glance. "But first all the houses in Malibu will have to be burnt."

And Clitty continued the litany. "And the homeowners burned along with them.

I felt I had to speak. Only the sound of my own voice could keep me from going mad.

"You really think you're going to start a revolution in this country?"

"The revolution has already begun," Athena said.

"Anarchy is just around the corner," Jax said gleefully. "We're just giving it a little nudge."

"America is the biggest, fattest sitting duck in history," Fischer said. "With its free press and open institutions, it's an oligarchy with a guilty conscience."

I turned to Athena. "And you're going to lead the attack on the White House, I suppose."

She smiled, and shook her head.

"There won't be a White House. Washington will be a vacant lot before the people wake up to what has happened."

"Mr. Krales wants parades, insurrections, rebellions," Fischer said. "That's conscious revolution, which is years away. We're in a stage now where people don't realize they're in revolt. They don't understand that they are dismantling their own society. Every meliorative step they take is ending in disaster. . . ."

"Like the riots," Boomer said.

"Exactly." Fischer threw him a flash of professorial approval. "The society is turning on itself."

"Newark is burning, Topeka, West Virginia. These are not isolated incidents. America is burning. . . ."

"To the ground," Athena said.

"To the fucking ground," shrieked Boomer.

"And the firemen are burning with it," said Arthur Peterson. He strummed his guitar and said it again. Now it sounded like a lyric.

Fischer was standing now, shaking his fist, looking over my head to the fervent millions. Gone was the smug aphorist, the Coney Island smartass. The man was revealed in all his glory. It had to be obvious to even the blindest acolyte. He was a raving lunatic.

Fischer hopped like a maddened satyr to the fireplace. "It started in the sixties, with those black kids streaming through the streets of the cities, screaming, 'Burn, baby burn.' Oh, all of our liberal bureaucrats thought they could put out the fire with job-action programs and welfare. The capitalists thought they could ply the underclasses with cheap consumer luxuries, while the government encouraged drug use to dull their minds and bodies. It was hopeless, Krales. The end was near."

Athena and Helene dropped to the floor at Fischer's feet. They held hands like little girls in front of the TV, their faces suffused with his reflected glory. "I saw it all in 1966. I was an English instructor at Vassar, very popular." Fischer spoke with biting self-disdain. "The preorgasmic little girls loved my act. My similes: 'Communism and capitalism are two ways of singing the same melody out of tune' was one. Quite popular, quite ineffectual: The system loves to have harmless little fire breathers like me around. It gives the illusion of democracy, of dissent flourishing in a free society. But then, one weekend in Vermont, I took acid, and I saw it all. It was in sixty-eight, after Martin Luther King's assassination. The people were in revolt. I watched the riots on TV, whole cities burning, and I realized that it was just the beginning. There was a fire smoldering below the decks of the ship of state, a fire that would reach the bridge before anyone ever knew it was there. The country, the world was doomed."

"What other revelations did you have?" I asked, pretending to take it lightly. "Did you think you could fly?"

"The drugs freed me," Fischer said. "I never had to take them again. And I haven't. Not once since that weekend. Because everything I saw has come to pass. Every exploited class has begun to put the torch to America in its own way." Fischer lit a match and threw it into the fireplace on a pile of crumpled newspaper. "First, the working classes: They slow productivity, go out on longer and more damaging strikes, indulge in alcoholism and drug abuse, become malingering cynics. They sabotage their system, burn the hand that feeds them."

"Prole burn," Athena said.

A low yellow flame sputtered around the edge of the

newspapers. Fischer dropped another match into the fireplace. "White working-class youth turns its back on the work ethic and degenerates into drugs, violence, promiscuity. Motorcycle gangs, cults, anything, just to get away from that assembly line. Their country/western culture glorifies defiance, violence, egotism, unbridled sex. . . ."

"Your cheating heart/ will tell on you," I sang.

Fischer shouted over my voice. "Where are the auto workers of tomorrow, the bent backs and blunted minds that stoke the furnace? While their unions fight automation, they vacate the jobs that are held for them. The result? Empty factories. White, ethnic, illiterate, young . . ."

"Greaser burn," Athena said.

Wisps of smoke rose over the newspaper as the fire spread. "Blacks in the ghettos burn, kill and loot without ideology. They form a subculture of hedonistic terrorists, laying waste to their own environment, preying on their own people. They are the ultimate anarchists. They see no value in anything the world has to offer. They accept nothing that goes beyond the threshold of their bodies. Avenging angels, you might call them, subjecting everything to the cleansing power of the torch. Black burn."

Another match flared in his hand.

"And then there's baby burn. Teenagers from the middle classes burn their bodies and minds with drugs. Punks, zombies; apathetic, analphabetic nonproducers. Like the Buddhist monks in Saigon, they'd rather immolate themselves than live out their lives according to society's program.

"Crat burn, Mr. Krales," Fischer said, dropping another match in the fireplace as the newspaper began to crackle. "Do you know what that is? All the technocrats, bureaucrats, psychocrats; the middle-managers, the executives, wrecking the system they are supposed to maintain. Leaving their posts to seek fulfillment through group therapies, encounter groups, ego massage; the search for the self, turning away from the corporate ethic, disdaining everything they are trained to uphold.

"Every class in this country is actively sabotaging its own interests. Only one class has yet to light its torch, and the conflagration will be complete."

"And who might that be?" I asked.

"The stars, Krales," Fischer said, his eyes widening with the revelation. "The rich and powerful, the adored. Those who have the most to gain from the status quo and are the most competent to destroy it."

"The glitter people," Helene said eagerly.

"Yes," Fischer said. "It's glitterburn time, Helene, and glitterburn will make everything else seem like a smothered campfire. Imagine a group with the ideas, the mobility, the wherewithal to go anywhere, meet anyone, put any plan into operation. Connections, visibility, charisma—no guerrilla group ever had these in such abundance. Glitterburn is not confined to neighborhoods, subcultures or ethnic groups. It can't be doused with money, good works or repression."

"Invasion of the jet setters," I said. "Great idea for a movie, huh, Lou?"

Fischer raved on, unfazed.

"Look around this room, Mr. Krales. There's a very real possibility that everyone here will one day be invited to a reception in the White House. We could all be in a room with the President, forming an ever-tightening circle around him before the Secret Service even knew what was happening. . . ."

"We could tear him apart," Athena said quietly.

"Yeah, but why would you want to?" I said. "Why would you want to change anything? You people are sitting on top of the world. There is no society, no utopia anyone could imagine in which you'd be better off than you are right now."

"There's one," Kalish said behind me. "And that's the one we dominated. The one in which we had absolute power."

"Yeah, but that's impossible."

I felt Kalish's hand on my shoulder. "Fifteen years ago I told my schmuck friends in the Bronx that one day I'd be the biggest producer in Hollywood. They all laughed in my face.

Well, the rest is history." He breathed heavily; the morbid gasp of drug halitosis spread over me like a miasma. "Well, I'm telling you now. We're going to level this country. That's right, the people in this room. I give it maybe five years, Krales."

"This country is beyond redemption," Fischer said. "It will burn to the ground, and something new will rise from the ashes."

"That's the scenario," Jax said.

Kalish patted me on the head. "Jump on the bandwagon now, pal, before it leaves you behind."

***

The lights of Malibu blinked off as if on cue. A preview of Fischer's total destruction. Total blackness; I couldn't tell where the sky ended and the sea began.

But it was merely movie stars retiring early for their beauty sleep, so they would be full of piss and charisma when they arose at six.

Movie stars had spartan schedules; only revolutionaries could afford to loll around until all hours, stupefied and incoherent. Movie stars had to make sense; only academics with advanced degrees could get away with all this obscure drivel. Thank God for movie stars!

Kalish shook the last few grains of white powder out of what had seemed to be a bottomless vial. That signaled the end of the party. The roller coaster stopped and everyone stumbled off, dizzy and disoriented, the euphoria drained from their faces. Pale and sullen they sat in silence, until Kalish threw a set of keys across the room to Vinnie.

"Go out and get the spare stash in the trunk," he said.

And everyone cheered up again. Boomer squatted in front of the fireplace, mumbling to himself. Helene and Clitty huddled in the corner hissing like Macbeth's witches. Peterson strummed his guitar dreamily. Athena and Fischer stood by the window speaking in vehement undertones.

Occasionally, Fischer would turn toward someone in the room. More often than not I was the target of his strange, cold look.

They excluded me from this round of festivities, let me slink into a corner. Ignored me completely. It was only a few feet to the door, but Vinnie was posted on a stool in the hall and he wasn't taking his eyes off me. I could always hurtle through the picture window, a broken leg and glass fragments in my eyeball seemed quite mild compared to what Fischer had in store for me. But Paco sat in the ledge, staring across the room at me. I had nowhere to go.

I was doomed, and too tired to care. It had been days since I'd slept or eaten or heard a kind word. Even if they left me a clear path I'd be too weak to make it to the door. Why didn't they just kill me now? What were they waiting for?

I closed my eyes and saw the beach at Fire Island. My son was playing at the shore, clapping delightedly as the wavelets broke over his feet. His lips were swollen, his head bulbous like some creature from a flying saucer. Everything was very slow. The sky broke into blue ripples as I passed out.

I awoke with a shiver in Athena's bedroom. I had slept just long enough for morning to cut a slit in the horizon. Shafts of golden light snaked across the dark expanse of ocean, but then gloom settled over the day. The sun, like any other Hollywood starlet, had been given a few minutes to do its stuff before old gray dawn picked up its option.

A gust rattled the window pane. Downstairs, people were speaking in whispers. Chairs scraped along the floor. It was too quiet. No hectoring from Fischer, no laughs, just an occasional whisper. There was something going on.

"Laser."

The word oozed out at the tail end of a moan. It rang a bell somewhere. I stopped to ransack what was left of my memory. Not a clue.

I rolled off the bed and crawled out of the bedroom along the hall to the top of the stairs. I inched down, placing my foot flat on the steps so they wouldn't creak until I had a clear view of the living room.

They had taken the cushions off the sofa and spread them on the floor. With all the furniture moved out of the way there was plenty of room for an orgy.

Kalish was in a corner with the still-comatose Belda. He had her against the wall, her legs over his shoulders. An absolutely torturous position; he'd never get a Jewish girl to do that. Clitty was nodding on a beach blanket, her cartoon breasts grazing the beard of Artie Peterson, who dozed in her lap. Boomer clung like a lizard to the hearth.

Fischer reclined like a sheik on three pillows.

Two nude blondes with their backs to me attended him. His hands clasped behind his head, he watched with a dreamy smile as the two murmuring girls stroked his thighs. His penis rested on his swollen testicles like a snake sunning itself on a rock. He closed his eyes and stretched with feline contentment. "My little assassins," he said softly, reaching around with both hands to knead their shoulders.

The blondes were new to me. Were they imports for the orgy? Part of the regiment of rollerskaters, Venice contingent? Long, obviously dacron tresses cascaded over their shoulders. One of them was tall and slender, with broad shoulders and long legs that seemed to travel all the way up to her neck. She turned. It was Athena. Athena in a blonde wig.

Athena in a blond wig, planting a lingering kiss on Fischer's stringy neck.

And the smaller blonde, the one tracing figure eights on his chest, slyly flicking his nipples with a crimson fingernail, that was Helene.

I watched them through the banister like a little boy eavesdropping on his parents' party. Athena had said she'd never touch him; that it would be too intense if she did. Well, what would happen now that she was about to fellate him? Would it drive her mad?

"Lazer . . ."

That word. It was the diminutive for Eliezer, Fischer's first name, a very Yiddish locution that sounded strange coming out of the mouth of a California blonde. He had probably told her at one of their earlier trysts, "My mother used to call me Lazer." And she had fastened onto it as proof of their special intimacy, so that in moments of loneliness or stress she could always think of him, of that little pet name they shared.

Athena came up for air, arching her back to Fischer's ministrations. I wondered if she'd been this delirious in our lovemaking. I had always been too delirious to notice.

"Lazer."

It was like a hypnotic chant. She turned langorously. Her eyes fluttered open like a Barbie doll's, and looked right at me. They were bright blue, not like Athena's at all but like that blonde on Fifth Avenue who had cold-cocked me with her shoe. But that blonde had just giggled crazily. This one talked. Just like that girl on the stretcher, the Puerto Rican girl with the long dark hair and the opaque black eyes, the one who had disappeared from the hospital. The one who'd said it, writhing and coughing, while Cyrus Wilkins died beside her.

"Laser."

Spell that with a "z," and there was the answer. She was Athena, and so was the blonde. Athena was all those girls. Everywoman, that was her name. Athena, my love. Athena, the assassin.

My memory spun backwards like a film in reverse. Out of this house to the airport, the plane, the townhouse in Turtle Bay, Reva St. James's white living room, Lieutenant Duffy's disbelieving squint. I had to get back to the very first moment of our acquaintance, but the mnemonic reel slowed on those scenes, still so warm in my recollection that I relieved the sensations that had accompanied them. Athena's tomboy body striding across the bare floor of my bedroom. Athena's strong fingers squeezing my shoulders, her chin digging painfully into my chest, the cords standing out on her neck as she struggled for pleasure.

I slid gingerly up the stairs. Her eyes had fallen upon me, but she had shown no sign of recognition, blind with passion as she was.

"Lazer!"

It was quite familiar. That sudden shriek of my name, her head thrown back, the flesh pulled stark against her cheekbones. (Why do passionate women always look as if they're suffering?) She had always shut her eyes tightly at that moment, the better, I now realized, to catch that fleeting image, the real trigger of her ecstasy.

"Lazer."

Again . . . That name mocked me as I sneaked back into the bedroom. Oh, Krales, you pathetic asshole. You would fall in love with a homicidal maniac and be cuckolded by a megalomaniac. You, who wrote the book on casual sex and its consequences. You thought you knew it all, but you let this psychotic put it over on you, didn't you? The Krafft-Ebing of the inner city. Wandering around like a love sick kid. Dumb bastard, if you hadn't learned by now . . . Each man is killed by the thing he loves.

But she was such a good actress.

It was such a great performance; I guess she'd had plenty of practice. A smart woman in the loveless world learns how to squeeze pleasure out of any encounter. To shut her eyes, throw her head back and think of . . .

Lazer.

With me it was easy. From the very first time she saw me, that day outside the subway when she lay in her Hispanic incarnation, coughing on a stretcher and mistook me for him, it was easy. She could be comforted by what were to her untutored Anglo-Saxon eyes the hundreds of resemblances we bore each other. And when I touched her she could sink into fantasy and think of him.

I closed the bedroom door. My teeth were chattering. From the cold, I assured myself, not from the sheer terror of knowing I had been sleeping with a murderess. Oh, no, that didn't bother me in the least.

I put my ear to the floor. This was the quietest orgy I'd ever heard. Maybe they were prowling the house, knives drawn, ready to cut me into bite-sized pieces for Fischer's brunch.

There were no footsteps on the stairs, no whispers in the

hall. Maybe one of those Hollywood-type guns—a .357 Magnum or a sawed-off shotgun—was trained on the door ready to blow my brains out in slow motion.

I tiptoed to the window. It was a thirty-foot drop onto the hard sand. If I survived the jump, I could crawl over to Mary Tyler Moore's house. She'd protect me.

But would she believe me? Would anybody believe that Athena Stuart, the darling of the woman's movement, had careened around the country in exotic disguises, murdering millionaires? Especially when the source was an unkempt weirdo who had planted all those phony stories and had murdered Edward Foley to back them up. Fischer had tightened the noose on me. It was either stay in the house and be killed, or escape and be committed.

I crawled out on the windowsill, trying to get up the nerve to jump.

"Hey, asshole!"

I ducked and rolled off the window down onto the floor. Black boots tapped impatiently. A black cape swirled around white legs. It was that punk who had brushed by me in the dark outside Foley's house.

"Where do you think you're goin'?"

The cape dropped. Long blond hair came tumbling free. There was a white dress. The Fifth Avenue blonde advanced on me, cutting savage strokes in the air with a carving knife. The wig floated down on the floor beside me. The dress came over her head in one fluid movement—women are such dexterous disrobers—and sailed onto the bed.

Athena stood before me wearing only a T-shirt that said USC TRACK. She twirled the knife like a cheerleader's baton.

"C'mon, cutie pie," she said, "join the party."

Are you mad?" she asked playfully. "Don't be mad."

They had sent her up here to seduce me, then kill me the way she had done to all the others. Just like a black-widow spider. The idea was frightening but oddly fascinating. She looked so good with the dawn washing over her.

I fingered the white dress. "Does your mother know you don't wear panties with this dress?"

"If I keep my legs crossed nobody will know."

"But you don't keep your legs crossed."

She danced by me and flopped on the bed with her legs raised. "I will if you tell me. I'll do anything you say."

There was something thick and painful between my legs. Not the enchanted wand of love, but a log, dry and leaden, the bark peeling in spots, twigs sticking up. I threw the wig and the white dress onto the bed.

"Your dress is wrinkled," I said.

"That's all right. It's a break-away frock just made to be torn off in a fit of passion. That's our little secret, you know. We wear these nice white virginal garments like that complicated bridal stuff with all the veils." She whipped around in the gloom. "We mince around hoping to irritate some maddened male into ripping it all off. The longer a woman takes to get dressed and made up, the quicker she wants all that crap just torn to shreds. The lipstick smeared, the pantyhose stretched out of shape, the dress ripped, the hair falling. We're all such darling little masochists. Daddy's little girl despoiled and . . ."

"You killed all those people," I said.

"I know, Daddy," she said in a little girl's voice. "I was bad."

I said it again in disbelief. "You killed all those people. You and your friends . . ."

"Hold it, bozo, I get top billing on this. I did it alone." She laughed dryly. "You don't think Miss Helene would get any blood on her lily whites; or Clitty, the vulva that engulfed Chicago. Boomer likes to do things by remote control. And Michael Jax, well, he's a good man with the flow charts, but I'm the enforcer. I'm Eliezer Fischer's avenging angel. Hurricane Athena, he calls me. I've caused as much loss of life and property as a natural disaster."

The knife glittered on the bed only a few feet away. "How did you kill Cyrus Wilkins?" I asked.

"Good old Cyrus," she said. "He thought I was an office temp. Got me in the conference room so fast I didn't have time to ditch my steno pad. I had the hair, the dark contact lenses, the slight accent. It was a masterful job. But, of course, I had to do him first. Smelly old bastard with big lumpy balls. It was weird, but I kept thinking, "After this I'm going to kidnap you, you filthy old bastard. . . ."

"Why?"

"Because he wouldn't give us the money, wouldn't jump on the old Guiltwagon, so we decided to kidnap him."

"Why?"

"To throw a scare into the idle rich, to get press coverage, create a revolutionary situation, pit class against class. Lazer says it takes only four or five dedicated people to plunge the whole system into chaos." Without turning, she pointed toward the bed. "Take the blade, baby. Put it to my throat. I love it. It's only fantasy for you anyway. You'll never use it."

I grabbed the knife. "Don't be sure." It was cold and strangely unwieldy. The idea that I might be using a knife for something other than slicing bread made it seem unfamiliar.

"You're a lover, not a fighter, sweetie. You should kill me, but you won't. You can't even kill to save yourself, face it. Do you think you could have wired a plastic explosive around that old man's chest? Boomer made it up with a remote-control unit. I laid it on him while he was still huffing and puffing with his pants around his knees. 'Guiltwagon,' I said, and he almost dropped dead. I got palpitations from it."

Her voice had become strident, as if a devil had possessed her. "He had put on all this extra security; bodyguards, electric eyes, the whole pizza. I just patted his little pink scalp and showed him the whiz button, so he knew what would happen if he got cute, and I marched him right through the office past the guards, the alarms, everything, right into the subway, because that's the only way to travel during rush hour. Lazer taught me that. He's a real New Yorker."

"Where were you going to take him?"

"To Clitty's house, right on Fifth Avenue. Beautiful, huh? Kidnap a billionaire and stash him in another billionaire's house. Up on the fourth floor where nobody but Clitty ever went. And the fuckin' train caught on fire." She laughed loud enough to wake up every pillhead in California. "All of a sudden the train stops, and black smoke starts pouring in, and me with this asthmatic condition I've had since I was a bucktoothed little girl. I start coughing. My dirty old man starts screaming, 'Help, help, I'm being kidnapped.' Everybody else is running for the door. People are fainting, and me, I'm dying. I'm sure of it. I can't let old Cy blow the whole scene, can I? Of course not, so I press the little button, and *BAFOOM*, like when you blow up a paper bag. Nobody heard it, nobody saw poor old Cy pitch forward and me collapse on top of him. I was coughing so hard. I knew I was dying, but I didn't care, as long as I'd covered our tracks. . . ."

She was rocking back and forth in delirious reminiscence. I could do it now; twist her head back and hit her in the back. Just like in all those war movies.

"Out I went," she said. "And the next thing I knew, there was this empty roaring in my head, and when I opened my eyes Lazer was standing in front of me."

"Only it wasn't Lazer," I said, gripping the knife handle.

She turned. "It was you, you sexy bastard. You stared right down at me, got a real good look. But the next time you saw me I was a stranger to you. Now, tell me that's not talent. I became a blond bombshell. Another woman entirely. Tell me I haven't got what it takes. Mr. Agamisou thought

I was fan . . . tastic. Clitty introduced me as her friend
Karen from California. Don't you love the name?"

"You mean she knew you were going to kill her father?"
Keep her talking, that was the idea. Keep her talking while I
built up the nerve.

"She couldn't wait. She wanted to videotape the seduction. Instead, we let her go downstairs with Boomer while he
planted the bomb. I played the Homecoming Queen for
Alcibiades, the squeamish little postdeb. Icky, icky poo;
believe me, that whole family is disgustingly oversexed. It
was like bathing in Elmer's Glue. But it made it almost fun
because I knew that while the old Greek was drooling over
my shoulder blades, Boomer was wiring his car. And then
when I rushed down into the street it was you." There it was,
that insane, high-pitched giggle; only now it was out of
control, and she had to gulp and wheeze to catch her breath.
"Jesus, did you make me paranoid. I thought you were a
cop, that we were under surveillance with thousands of FBI
men dressed as joggers and garbage men. I knew that Rolls
was about to blow, and here you were, running right toward
me. . . ."

"You looked like something out of a wet dream," I said.

"Well, I was. I mean, I put you to sleep, didn't I? And then
dashed off into the park as the car went . . . BAFOOM—
and I knew everybody would be distracted enough to let me
get away." She turned and swooped suddenly. I hardly had
time to get the knife into striking position before she was on
the floor beside me, her hand on my wrist, brushing my
forehead with parched lips. "I thought I'd seen the last of
you, my darling," she said. "Thought you were out of my life
forever then, but you kept turning up like a bad penny. I
almost dropped dead when I saw you at Boomer's that day. I
took Clitty and Helene into the gazebo and told them you
had to go. Clitty wanted to fuck you to death, the little slut,
but that would have taken days, knowing you."

"Thank you."

"So we decided to nail you during the riot."

"You knew there'd be a riot?"

"Lazer did. He's predicted everything right to a tee so far.

Hasn't been wrong yet, and won't be. We're going all the way
with him. . . ."

"That day on the beach in Fire Island," I said. "You really
thought those women were going to kill me?"

"A girl can dream, can't she? I didn't care by then. I knew
you hadn't recognized me. There was no urgency, it could
happen anytime. Besides, you were kinda cute. . . ."

"But you did kill Gruber. . . ."

"Saul took me for a walk on the beach. He told me he
loved me, offered me an apartment in the city. Of course, he
couldn't leave his wife, not right away, but Jesus, he said,
what a couple we would make. Can you imagine? The *Times*
would do a spread on our house. *New York Magazine* would
cover our parties. The ultimate 'in' couple of all times. Poor
Saul. I enticed him out into the surf. Call me Circe. He went
down on his knees. Such a good boy, so considerate and
eager to please. 'Guiltwagon,' I said and then pushed his
head under. It takes a long time to drown somebody. I never
knew that, did you? With waves crashing symphonically
around us, I held his head under. Saul was the cuddly type. I
just couldn't keep my hands off him."

"And Reva . . ."

"She got hold of Boomer's notebook with all our target
names and addresses. She had to go, Josh."

"And that Japanese guy along with her."

"Improvise, you know. I had to get into that building
without being recognized. So I picked up the obliging
Oriental. It was quick, Josh, if that's what's bothering you.
He was so proud of his kitchen: the food processor; six-
burner stove; butcher block; the cutlery; oh, yes, a wonderful
carving knife. I tried it out on him. Just wonderful. Then I
went upstairs. Poor Reva, she was waiting for you. 'Surprise,' I said. 'It's his better half.' Well, I was by then, wasn't
I? We were a pretty torrid item back then, as I remember."

"I was on the hit list, too, wasn't I?" I asked.

"Oh, way down at the bottom. Other names kept coming
up. . . ."

"Like Ed Foley?"

"That was my finest hour. Only one thing would get that

old pansy out of his fortress in Turtle Bay, and it wasn't a blonde from California. I created this little punk hustler character; the cape, the boots, the decal tattoos, even worked up a kind of blue-collar Brooklyn voice for the occasion. Chicken salad, they call it. I strutted up and down on the street for three nights. Finally, he couldn't stand it any longer. He sent the bodyguards home, poked out the electric eye. He was taping a message to you in his study. 'Wait outside,' he says, treating me like a trick. 'Fuck you,' I said. Don't you just love the voice? He did, poor bastard. Ten minutes later, he's crawling around in the altogether, kissing my boots. He even loved it when I wound that extension cord around his neck. I guess somewhere along the way he stopped liking it. You know, you get this squeamish tickle in your groin when it's just for fun, but what a thrill it must have been when he realized he was going to die."

Keep it light and amiable. Just two old friends catching up. "Why?" I asked. "Why did you do all this? I mean I know that's a stupid question . . ."

"I told you, baby. We want to change the world. A group of dedicated people can work wonders. Look what we've done already. A couple of notes, a few phone calls, a little selective assassination to keep the fat cats in line, and *BINGO!* America is burning. It's worked out even better than we thought. They put a publicity blackout on our little action."

"That's why I couldn't get my stories into the paper," I said.

"That's why you got framed when you did. The rich know how vulnerable they are. They didn't want to start a trend, so it was hush-hush until they cleared it up. Which made it even better for us, because now it looked like these million-aires were catching the guilt fever from each other. It made the whole thing seem even crazier."

"Okay, say it's working," I said. "So there are a lot of dead bodies and burned buildings around the country. You still haven't told me why you did it. What is there in this life that so offends you? Especially you, Athena; you're living in the best of all possible worlds."

"I'll tell you the story of my life, Joshie," she said and put her lips to my ear. I shuddered as she began to whisper.

"I'm Athena Stuart. I'm a star. Got a dirty little cause? Call me; I'll be there with my air-travel card in one hand and my standard speech—substitute relevant names, dates and issues—in the other. Abortion, women's rights, some down-trodden minority here, a defense fund there, an environmental issue or two, maybe some good old-fashioned police brutality. I fly around the country, lighting in polyester hotels, speaking in drafty gyms and meeting people who can lip-synch my aphorisms, they've heard them so many times; or sitting under the sputtering lights of a local TV station, debating some straw man while the neighborhood personality tries to show me how big-time he really is. I can go on writing my great polemics, bestsellers, every one. It's easy now. I have snooty graduate students doing all the work for me anyway. They know my positions better than I do. Everybody knows what Athena Stuart thinks on a given issue. And they love me for it because I reinforce their own good opinion of themselves. Sure, I can keep this up until I lose my looks, and what with face-lifts and exercise, who knows when that will be? Oh, yeah, it's a great life. First class coast to coast, limo at the airport, champagne in the bridal suite, cocktails with the elite, repartee bouncing off the walls, flashbulbs popping. . . . Disco dissidents strike at dawn. What a bore! What a mind-disintegrating bore!"

"So give it up," I said.

"And what would you have me do, pray tell? Retire to a cabin in the Rockies and become a Lady Writer? Cliterature, Lazer calls it. Dip your clit in ink, and do another gloss on the old fable of the Canary in the Coal Mine. It's a hustle, baby, just another way of getting rich telling them what they think they already know."

What had I been thinking all these months? The walks in the park, the deep postcoital communings. I had trembled like a child in her embrace. I'd fought sleep just to stare at her sleeping form. My cynical heart had melted and smeared like a piece of cheap chocolate. And for what? Another shallow sophomore in love with her professor.

Athena sprawled on my chest. Her nipples were like pebbles.

"So what's left for a girl, huh, lover?" She sang softly in my ear: "Here comes the bride/All dressed in white." She burrowed under my arm.

"I stink," I said, suddenly bashful.

"Like any good marriage," she said, nuzzling my armpit. She slid her fingers between my clammy thighs. . . . I closed my legs like a timid virgin.

"What's the matter, baby?"

"It's shrunken and wrinkled," I said.

"But that's the correct condition for the marital member." She reached into my pants, and her hand closed around it. "Cold and damp like a dead bird," she said.

"I don't perform well under stress," I said.

"And that's when a girl has to be at her very best," she said. "Close your eyes, and just imagine. A little Tudor house on ten wooded acres. A station wagon, exposed brick and me under the poison ivy. Cookbooks, wine racks and wicker hampers. We'd be the cunning couple, all right. You'd get a little lovable lead in the ass, and I'd swell up like a blowfish and extrude little Joshies along the gravel driveway. You'd stagger home from a four-hour lunch to find me swaddled in suede, straddling the butcher block. After dinner you'd tie me to the Cuisenart, and I'd shout the names of exotic foods while you violated me. Ever the frugal homemaker, I'd make lampshades out of my cellulite. You'd tiptoe around the baby-sitter, waving your shrunken head until she succumbed from an overdose of quaaludes. We'd live crappily ever after until burglars shot us in our beds."

I felt a sudden pain in my chest. Every breath was a stab wound. Droplets of sweat rolled off my forehead like rats leaving a sinking ship.

Athena loosened her stranglehold on my genitals. "Am I depressing you, Joshie?"

"I always knew I would be nagged to death by some insane woman," I said, "but I hoped it would come after the prostate operation."

"Oh, don't worry about death, baby. Lazer says death is a small price to pay for real social change."

"Not when it's your own."

"Oh, but you're not gonna die, baby," she cooed. "I'd never let anybody do anything to you. You're gonna come along on Momma's little operation with her today."

I tried to slide out from under her embrace. "Can I take a rain check? I'm not very good at disguises."

"You're coming along as your very own self," Athena said. "Lazer wants you to come and participate. He says you'll be very useful."

"Maybe if I just stayed here and whipped up a nice batch of fudge brownies . . ."

"It'll be fun, Joshie," Athena coaxed. "I promise. We're going to a little party at the Beverly Hills Hotel, just a little cocktail party."

"Well, that doesn't sound too bad," I said. "As long as we're out of this house."

"It'll be great, Joshie." She sounded like a mother talking her kid into a tetanus shot. "We'll go to the party, have some drinks and cheese and crackers."

"Will there be any onion dip?" I asked.

"Guacamole, love. This is California, you know."

"Movie stars?"

"Better than that. Tomorrow at a press conference in the Beverly Hills Hotel, Governor Dan Lowndes will announce the formation of a new political coalition made up of radical movements from every segment of American life. The disenfranchised, the dispossessed, the oppressed will now be truly united."

Her voice trembled with sarcastic eloquence. "Professor Eliezer Fischer will mount the rostrum and urge Dan Lowndes to run for president of the United States. Lowndes will demur. Do you know your Shakespeare, Josh? 'Thrice he offers the crown, thrice it is refused'?"

"Julius Caesar."

"And everybody knows what happened to him. Everybody but the politicians, the naïve little darlings. Governor Lowndes, unable to still the cheering multitudes, will acquiesce and declare his candidacy. The era of the New Politics will begin," she paused dramatically, "and end in the same moment. The presidential campaign of Dan Lowndes, the white hope of the liberals, will begin and end as well."

"I don't get it," I said.

"It's very simple." Athena's voice was soothing now. "We'll eat a little, have a few drinks, listen to a few speeches and then we'll blow up the governor."

Only in America could a handful of misfits wreak such havoc. Only in the land of the free where a credit card, a driver's license and a little spare change made you a revolutionary. In Russia you needed a passport to go to the grocery store. Here you could travel around leaving mayhem in your wake, as long as your Visa card was paid up. These frivolous jet setters had taken their cocktail party melange of conquest, orgasm and snobbery, turned it into an ideology, and loosed it on the unsuspecting world. They had left cities in smoking ruins, caused billions in damage, killed hundreds and driven a wedge between the classes. In other words, they had accomplished everything they had set out to do. This was the army of the new order, a rogue's gallery of pyros, nymphos, dipsos and megalos. And they would strike again, causing more death and disorder. They would get perilously close to their goal of anarchy and upheaval.

There was only one person who could stop them before they killed again. One person who stood between them and more bloodshed. But, at the moment, he had his hands full, trying to thwart the advances of one amorous murderess.

Athena wanted to make love. Here on the cold, wooden floor after confessing that she was a sadistic killer, she suddenly got romantic. She yanked at my belt while I fought back like a virtuous housewife.

"What are you doing?" I whispered vehemently.

"Taking off your pants," she giggled. "And your politics."

Shivering, feeble from lack of food and sleep, addled by drugs, my trousers around my knees, I was not the staunchest defender of the free world.

Athena stared carnally down at me. "Is there anything cuter than a guy with his dingus waving?"

"It's not a dingus," I said with as much outraged dignity as I could muster.

She swarmed all over me. "Stick it in, Josh."

Oh, no, she wouldn't get me that way. "I know it's silly," I said, trying to push her away, "but I'm just not in the mood."

"Oh, c'mon, don't be a tease. . . ."

"I'm not, honest. It's just that the idea of blowing the governor up isn't much of a turn-on to me. Now, if you were talking about decapitating the pope, well, maybe . . ."

She managed to get her knee onto my chest. "You know you want to . . ."

I didn't want to, not with old black-widow Athena. Afterglow to this girl meant killing your mate. I didn't want to be lying there, with traces of sperm and spittle along my thigh, just like Cyrus Wilkins, Alcibiades Agamisou, Saul Gruber and poor old Ed Foley.

She wrapped her legs around me and tried to roll me over. "Stick it in, Josh," she hissed. There was no foreplay, no whims, no preludes. A nerve in my back twitched wildly like a warning light. "Help, sex maniac," I said. So this was how it happened in back seats, empty apartments and wooded areas—how come we always used that phrase, "The victim's half-nude body was found in a wooded area"?

Athena's clammy hand drifted down my belly. "Josh," she murmured with a triumphant smile. Suddenly I didn't care. The future didn't extend beyond the next few minutes. I squeezed Athena's buttocks and tried to pull her down onto me.

"It won't work," she said. "I'm dry as a bone."

"Wait." I slid my tongue down her body. Her skin was like sandpaper. Her pubic hair crackled like parched brush, burning the meat off my lips. I was sweating from every pore, yet there wasn't a drop of moisture on my tongue.

"It's the dope," she said.

I lifted her under the arms and threw her over on her back. We gasped in each other's faces.

"Maybe the missionaries can help," I said.

I mounted her. It was like violating a box of shredded wheat.

"There's no room at the inn," she said.

"Then I'll sleep in the stable."

We were stuck. It was like trying to take off a Band-Aid. She crouched on her hands and knees. I moistened her with the sweat from my flanks. She shoved her face into the mattress and shrieked. It was hopeless.

The door flew open. Helene and Clitty, dressed for the afternoon in purple velour jumpsuits, marched in.

"C'mon, honeymooners," Helene said, slapping my behind. "Battle stations."

Fischer paced impatiently in the living room as we descended. He was wearing a dark business suit, nicely tailored to his scrawny body. His black shoes were shined, and the sharp creases in his pants bespoke careful pressing. Kalish was wearing black leather pants and a black silk shirt open to the navel, from which his hairless belly swelled obscenely. Vinnie and Paco were strapping automatics to their ankles. Artie Peterson, festooned with beads and flowers, looking with his beard and ponytail as if he'd been trapped in a time warp, gazed out at the ocean with a stoned, blissful smile. Athena had slipped away and changed into a white dress and wide-brimmed straw hat. She looked like any man's dream of the perfect suburban wife. You could stare into those blue eyes for hours and never guess they were windows on a murderous soul.

Fischer squinted intently at me. "You seem a trifle subdued, Mr. Krales."

"It isn't one of my better days," I allowed. "Actually, I expected to be dead by now."

Fischer cracked his knuckles, one by one, which gave me another reason to hate him. "We're not going to kill you, my friend. Not if you cooperate. You can stay alive indefinitely if you cooperate. Athena likes you."

"I think we make a nice couple," Athena said, taking my arm.

"Reporters aren't very good at conspiracies," I said. "They have this compulsion to reveal . . ."

"That would be fatal for you," Fischer said.

Boomer came in, wiping his hands on his pants. He was his own sloppy self. Good old Boomer. At least there were some things I could still count on.

"It's ready," he said and retired to a corner to pick his nose.

"Then we can go," Fischer said. "Michael is already at the hotel, locking everything in."

"Poor Michael," Helene said with a crocodile sigh.

"He won't feel a thing," Athena said with a trace of disappointment. I inched away from her.

"Let's review it one more time," Fischer said. "We arrive in three cars. Lou and the girls take the Rolls. Vinnie, you and Paco will take Mr. Krales in the brown Mercedes and I'll come a few minutes later in the pickup truck. We'll meet in the lobby and greet enthusiastically as if after a long absence. Then into the banquet room. Arthur, meanwhile, will have set up his instruments at the back of the dais. Boomer will maneuver the booby-trapped amplifier as close to the podium as possible. Be careful not to make it look out of place, Boomer, or some smart security man might investigate."

"I know what I'm doing," Boomer sniveled. "You wait until that thing blows."

"We're all looking forward to it, Boomer," Fischer said.

"You're a genius, kid," Kalish said. "You would have been another Edison if you hadn't been born rich."

"Don't bullshit me, Lou," Boomer snarled, waving his tiny fist.

Kalish made a great show of being hurt. "I tell the kid he's a genius, and he jumps on my case."

And I stood there thinking: *These stoned-out, squabbling brats are going to blow up the governor of California. Maybe it is the end of the world.*

And Fischer looked sternly at his troops. "Let's try not to bicker among ourselves, shall we? We'll need all our energy for the operation."

Kalish poured a pile of cocaine on the coffee table. "I'm willing to snort and make up."

"Let's go on with this," Fischer said curtly. They all looked over at him, cowed and attentive. "Now, the problem we face is getting on and off the platform. The governor's speech will have two parts. One, in which he announces the formation of a new radical coalition that will revolutionize national politics and then goes on to present his new appointees. Two, when he announces his bid for the presidency. Now, the governor likes the spotlight so we're going to oblige him by vacating the platform. Michael will remain, flitting in and out of camera range. I guess he'll have a split second to regret his ambitions. Anyone else who wants a little of the governor's reflected glory will stay on—and get more than they bargained for. All of us, of course, will be in our seats at the back of the auditorium by then."

"You'd better be," Boomer warned. "I've got ten pounds of plastic explosive in that amp. That fuckin' platform's gonna go to the moon."

Fischer nodded with satisfaction and continued: "We have sent three letters to the governor, asking him to get on the Guiltwagon and give away a million dollars of his personal fortune to the black community in Oakland where his family began their real estate empire. Up to now he has ignored us, but Michael Jax has convinced him to mention us in his speech today and express his defiance of terrorists and cheap extortionists like us. At the moment when he makes his disdainful reference to the 'Guiltwagoneers,' Boomer will activate the sonar equipment."

Boomer proudly held up a little electronic gadget. "It's just a tuning fork," he said. "I've got it set to the sound frequency of the E-major chord on a guitar. The fuse mechanism in the amplifier is set to the same frequency. The sound waves will activate the fuse. . . ."

"How long will it take for the amp to go?" Athena asked.

"From the time I start pushin' the vibes, a couple seconds at the most," Boomer said. "So everybody better be away from there, man, because this sucker's gonna blow."

"What happens to Jax?" I asked.

Athena shrugged and turned away.

"I thought he was one of you?"

"He is," Fischer said. "Michael thinks that a sniper—actually, Vinnie or Paco to be exact—is going to shoot the governor. It's unfortunate, but we need him up on that platform. Lowndes and his security people would get suspicious."

"He'll never know what hit him, Josh," Athena said by way of consolation. "One second he'll be alive, and the next he'll just cease to exist. His universe will just go black. You can't call that murder."

"What can you call it?"

"An easy way out," Vinnie said.

"I'd die that way anytime," Athena said. "I'd do it happily."

"And what about me, what's my little function in all of this?"

Fischer held his arms out to me. "Just see and be seen like the star you are. We want to place you at the scene. There'll be press, TV, and somehow your handsome face will appear on film. We want the police to know you were there."

"You want me implicated."

"You're one of us now, Josh," Athena said. "You won't regret it."

"You're going to frame me," I said to Fischer.

He stepped back instinctively, and I felt Paco's deceptively light touch on my arm.

"Take it easy, bro. Don't blow your cool."

"And what if I don't go along with it?" I asked. "What if I don't buy your glitterburn or your revolution?"

Fischer raised his eyebrows at my innocence. "Isn't that obvious? Do I have to tell you?"

"You'll kill me right here."

"There, you see, I knew I didn't have to tell you."

"The kid's a quick study," Kalish said.

"Good, then he'll understand. It's really very simple. You'll be photographed, implicated. We're framing you, Krales; you got that right. But if you promise to work with us, we'll protect you. You'll vanish into thin air, and they won't find you."

Kalish looked up from the cocaine and snickered. "Do you realize we're going to blow up ten million dollars' worth of talent today? All those rock stars and actors who'll wanna get their picture taken with the governor. Jesus, the agents are all gonna be in mourning on Monday."

Fischer waved his finger at me like the twisted pedant he really was. "And remember, the sooner we succeed, the sooner you'll be rehabilitated."

"You mean when the revolution takes power?" I asked, trying to hide my disbelief.

"Exactly. Why, you'll be something of a hero then."

"When we ride down Hollywood Boulevard in a motor-cade," I said.

Fischer looked sharply at me, presumably about to order my summary execution when Athena stepped forward.

"Let me talk to him," Athena pleaded.

Fischer consulted his watch, no longer the guru; now the general planning a campaign, the little boy who had used other people's money and gullibility to give shape to his psychotic fantasies.

"We have to leave in five minutes, Athena," Fischer said.

"I just want a few seconds," she said, drawing me out into the hallway where the leading men smiled glossily down on our tête-à-tête.

"Come with us, Josh," she said, squeezing my arm. "Come with an open mind."

"Do I have a choice? If I don't keep my mind open, Vinnie will open my head."

She shook her head hopelessly. "You just refuse to understand. If you give him a chance, you'll see. Look at me! I'm alive for the first time. You have to give yourself up to him, body and soul, to know what that really means. But once you do, you'll never turn back. You'll feel things like you never did before. Everything will be so intense; your senses and perceptions will be on another level. You'll taste food, experience the physical world. You'll get high, Josh, higher than anybody. Look at me, Josh. I get off now like I never did. You've seen it, you've been with me. It's him. He made me free, and now I want to take you into that freedom. Please let me . . . please."

A publicity still of Humphrey Bogart was right behind me. Bogey . . . Taken early in his career when he was playing "Tennis, anyone?" juveniles with the ascot and the rouged cheekbones and the pretty smile. Everything in place, but those cold, mistrustful eyes. "Don't believe her, kid," those eyes were saying. "She's gonna kill you."

"Okay," I said, "I'll give it a chance."

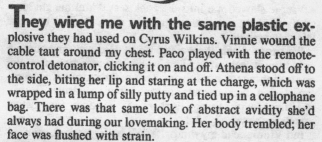

They wired me with the same plastic explosive they had used on Cyrus Wilkins. Vinnie wound the cable taut around my chest. Paco played with the remote-control detonator, clicking it on and off. Athena stood off to the side, biting her lip and staring at the charge, which was wrapped in a lump of silly putty and tied up in a cellophane bag. There was that same look of abstract avidity she'd always had during our lovemaking. Her body trembled; her face was flushed with strain.

Outside, a motor started.

"Athena," Helene called.

She darted forward and pressed her lips against my forehead. "I'll see you in a little while," she whispered. "We'll celebrate."

"Do me a favor," I said to Paco after she had gone. "Don't let Athena get her hands on that little gizmo."

He chuckled. "She likes to kick ass, don't she? Yeah, bro, I know what you mean."

Vinnie wired the battery pack to my back. I was all set now, a walking time bomb. They dragged me out to the car. Everyone had gone. Paco squinted up at the muddy sky. "It'll burn off in a couple hours."

"Should be a good beach day," Vinnie said.

"We'll be able to cop some rays when we get back," said Paco.

They made me put my shirt on and slipped my jacket over my shoulders. I winced at the accumulation of tobacco and body odor on my clothing. "Couldn't I clean up a little?"

Paco stepped back and examined me with a critical eye. "You look just like a dude on the lam to me."

"I didn't take a shower for three months when I crashed out of Joliet," Vinnie said.

Paco patted me sympathetically. "You gotta look good for the cameras, my man. Gotta look like you might be desperate enough to blow the governor away."

"Nobody's going to fall for that."

"Shit, they're already makin' you Public Enemy Number One."

Vinnie shoved me into the back seat. "You oughta stop worryin' about your image and just hope you live through this day, asshole."

We drove down the Pacific Coast Highway and turned onto Sunset Boulevard. True to Paco's prediction, the sun was beginning to burn the drear out of the morning. Joggers, cyclists and skateboarders appeared on the roadside. The air was thick with flying Frisbees. If I could just catch somebody's eye.

But Vinnie read my mind. "You'd better be cool, man. If you start a hassle, we got orders to ice you on the spot."

I groped gingerly around the plastic charge on my chest.

But Paco read my mind. He turned and showed me a switchblade. "It might be a little messy, you know. We might have to change the seat covers. But it'll be real quiet, and we won't blow the whole car up with us in it."

"In other words, motherfucker," Vinnie hissed viciously, "we got you covered."

"So when we get to the hotel, stay close to me," Paco said. "Don't start wanderin' away 'cause I'll get nervous and push that little button. Don't try to give anybody any signals. Don't do nothin' that'll make me the least bit suspicious, you see, because nobody will say nothin' if I jack you up."

"I could sure screw up your little plan if I decided to yell for help," I said.

"You wanna die for a dude you never met, go right ahead," Paco said. "I ain't gonna worry about it."

"He ain't gonna die for nobody," Vinnie said contemptuously. "He's gonna do exactly what we tell him, just like a little pussycat, ain't you, Krales?"

"Meow, meow," I said. That battery pack was biting into my back. The little blob of putty on my chest weighed a ton. I had seen what it could do. One flick of the switch, and there would be a hole big enough to back a Mercedes through. And they were going to flick it, too. There was no reason to keep me alive. They were conning me, just the way they had conned Michael Jax. Get me photographed, place me at the scene, then one little puff of smoke when the big bang comes. Drag me up by the dais; no one will notice in all the confusion. It will look as though I had been hoisted by my own petard. The perfect crime. Another of Professor Fischer's little triumphs.

The knowledge that I had about an hour to live made me tranquil and philosophical. There's nothing like a healthy dose of futility to dispel anxiety. I was a dead man, and there was nothing I could do about it. The last word I would hear would be "Guiltwagon," which would put me in a class with a lot of dead billionaires—what a way to make the big time! If this gadget belonged to the Pentagon it probably wouldn't go off, but old 4-F Boomer was a competent little fiend. Unless Paco had a sudden seizure, I was going to ride the lightning with the Governor. Kalish could add sixty-nine cents to the ten million dollars' worth of human flesh that was going to sizzle today.

Ahead, the Beverly Hills rippled like a huge pink birthday cake in the smog. There was a traffic jam in front of the hotel. Valet parking attendants, Mexicans feverish to please or else they would be sent across the border in the trunk of a car, the way they had come in, scampered from car to car, mollifying the impatient revolutionaries in their late model jobs. If the underclass was still this servile in California, then Fischer's revolution had a long way to go.

People stopped to peek in the car, then rushed by before I could make eye contact. They were looking for stars; a guy with a bomb on his sternum didn't even rate a hello.

Paco opened the door and took me by the arm. "Be real cool, bro," he whispered in my ear.

The TV press had come out in force with its mobile units, bullying technicians and reporters as groomed and cosmetized as store window mannequins. This was the ideal TV news event: a one sentence story with a lot of famous people for audience appeal. The reporters stared into the bulging eye of the video camera, reveling in their puny punditry.

"Governor Lowndes's call for a coalition of radical groups has been responded to by the largest collection of certified lunatic fringers ever gathered outside the cuckoo's nest," one reporter was saying.

In front of the entrance, under a banner reading LIBERATION DAY, another was wisecracking: "Indians used to have their powwows on this very spot, and today a powwow of another kind is taking place as Governor Dan Lowndes tries to mold . . ."

"Is that where the powwows took place?" a girl with a clipboard asked.

A bald man with cigar ash on his jacket shook his head. "He's got it mixed up with the Hollywood Bowl. I told him Hollywood Bowl is where they had all the powwows, but he wouldn't listen. Now everybody in America is gonna think the Indians had powwows at the Beverly Hills Hotel."

In the lobby another TV type, positioned in the midst of a milling crowd of crazies, smirked: "Call it a freak show, call it the birth of a new political movement, Governor Lowndes has definitely gotten the turnout he wanted."

"Josh," someone called.

"Just keep movin'," Paco said, steering me through the lobby toward a banquet room.

It was hard going through this crowd of crazies, ethnics, limousine liberals, chic radicals, Hollywood types in Guccis and tank tops, hard-eyed incendiaries scanning the crowd, reporters panning for quotes while the desk clerks stared aghast at the torrent of aberrant humanity chewing up the carpet. Where were the infiltrators, the cops from the Red Squads, the undercovers, the informants? Where were the Feds who would recognize my much publicized face and arrest me?

"Josh . . ."

Potosky was fighting her way through the crowd. I almost sobbed with relief. Good old stool pigeon Potosky; she'd turn me in just to get the story. She'd never let me out of her sight. Good old rotten, selfish Potosky.

I tried to plant myself to await her arrival but was caught up in the surge of history. Paco shoved me ahead. "Get rid of that bitch," he said.

I braced myself against him. "You gonna blow me up around all these people?" I whispered harshly. "You'll never get away."

Paco let me see the detonator. "I'll worry about myself, man. You just keep thinkin' about this."

"Josh, for Chrissake." Potosky was upon us, ducking elbows and wisecracks, holding onto my shoulder, glancing around nervously. "What the hell are you doing here?"

"I'm having brunch at the Polo Lounge."

"You're crazy. Don't you know this place is full of cops?" All of a sudden she was on my side. I had to antagonize her.

"I don't care who's here, Jill. I don't care about anyone anymore. I've joined the movement. I'm out of the closet. . . ."

"What are you raving about?"

"Glitterburn, guiltwagon—remember those words, Potosky. . . . Remember them when we put you up against the wall."

Paco shoved me ahead, but Potosky held onto my sleeve. "Keep your voice down, and hide your face," she said. "They might shoot you on sight."

"I'm invulnerable, don't you understand?" I shouted in her face. "No one can hurt me now. No one can stop us. Go ahead, call the cops, it won't do you any good. Go ahead, I dare you."

Potosky fished in her pocketbook for a card. "Here," she said, dropping it in my pocket, "the number of our L.A. bureau. Call me later, and for God's sake, take care of yourself." She turned and began to wedge her way through the crowd.

"Potosky," I called forlornly. She was my last chance.

She turned with her finger to her lips. "Don't worry, I'll cover for you."

"Potosky," I wailed. Every day of her life she'd been a selfish bitch, and she had to pick this moment to become a good sport. That was it, an omen. I had been lured out here by a woman who pretended to love me and let down a woman who was supposed to hate me. Was there any logic left in this world?

Paco shoved me into the ballroom, past a sign warning: OCCUPANCY BY MORE THAN FIFTEEN HUNDRED PERSONS IS PROHIBITED. There were at least three times as many in attendance, and more thronging in. They had removed the white tablecloths and centerpieces, putting bridge chairs on the tables to accommodate the overflow. The last time I'd seen so many people jammed together was when they had come streaming out of the Times Square subway station. Athena had been there for that calamity as well. She had only killed one person that day but was going to make up for it now. Of the scores pressing close to the dais for a better look at their heroes, perhaps fifteen would be killed when Artie's amp went off; another dozen or so would be maimed; and you'd get the stragglers—the ones who hung on, the family keeping an anxious vigil, and finally succumbed after a few days just when the story was getting stale. You could figure at least three trampled to death in the crush after the explosion when all these world changers stampeded for the exits; about fifty more injured from flying glass, splinters, collapsing chandeliers, etc. And don't forget shrapnel. Boomer's bomb would turn that amp into an antipersonnel bomb, little pieces of shrapnel rocketing at white heat right into the crowd. There was a catastrophe in the making. And only I could stop it.

But I would have to sacrifice myself. I would have to give the alarm, grapple with Paco, force him to blow me up. They knew that and were counting on my cowardice. In the face of my good sense, of my understanding that they could kill me anytime now that I had walked in the path of three TV cameras and had been photographed a hundred times in the crowd, they were hoping that I would be craven enough to wait, praying for a miracle or a reprieve; that I would let scores of people die to save my own life. That's how little they thought of me. That's how perceptive they were.

Gay, gay, gay, is there any other way?" A band of cheerful young boys in strapless undershirts asked that musical question.

"It's my body and I'll die if I want to," replied a motley collection of middle-aged ladies in tweeds and paisleys, holding aloft a banner that identified them as the RIGHT-TO-DEATH MOVEMENT, RTD ON YOUR BALLOT.

Other groups responded with theme songs until cacophony reigned. Other signs were raised, slogans shouted. Every conceivable radical group in the country seemed to be represented, and it looked as if a few had been invented for the occasion. There were old leftists, new leftists, plus a group calling itself The New New Left and waving a banner that read ENTREPRENURIAL SOCIALISM, EVERY MAN A PROFITEER. Trotskyists, anarchists, red flags, black flags, the puce flag of the HOMOSEXUAL MONARCHIST PARTY, WHAT THIS COUNTRY NEEDS IS A REIGNING QUEEN. The delegation of The Mississippi Communist Party, membership in which seemed the best way of committing suicide outside of putting a shotgun in your mouth, was trying to drawl the "Internationale" in Russian. The Black Army for Liberation and Development, whose members had shaved their heads, presumably in honor of their acronym, was rapping out its message disco style—"Oh, we're the black rebels and we've come to say/We're gonna bring the power structure down today."

The ethnic lobby showed an especial fondness for compound roots. I saw Afrofornians, Newyoricans, Idahopis and three youths with handlebar mustaches waving a banner for the Vermontenegrins. The assault wave of new arrivals deposited Paco and me in a corner, hard by a group of solidly built men wearing work shirts and jeans with burlap hoods over their heads. Their banner read: ESCAPED CONVICTS' BENEVOLENT SOCIETY. WHO WILL REPRESENT THE UNREPRESENTABLE? They sat very quietly facing the dais, but I could see their eyes roaming behind the hoods. "Don't you guys have a theme song?" I asked one of them. He didn't answer.

"I'm on the lam, too," I said. An idea was beginning to germinate. "You got a spare bag around?"

The eyes rested upon me for a while. Was I wrong, or did they seem to light with recognition? The hood I was speaking to leaned back and spoke to another incognito. More eyes shifted onto me.

Paco grabbed my arm roughly. Vinnie was battling his way through the crowd to get to us.

I struggled and said loudly: "Hey, man, I wanna stay here with my brothers."

A few more hoods whipped around in my direction. "It's cool, bro," a muffled voice said. "We got an agreement with the governor's people. They called the man off us for this rally."

Vinnie stumbled into me. There was a bulge in his pocket, and it wasn't because he was glad to see me. He looked up nervously at the escaped cons. "I don't want to be anywhere near these dudes," he said quietly to Paco.

Paco tried to pull me away, but there was nowhere to go. We were walled in by the masses. Oh, the soulful, malleable masses.

The celebs were beginning to filter onto the dais, through a private entrance, of course. The crowd cheered every new arrival: the rock stars, the actors, the sports stars. What a revolution! They'd have to print their manifesto in *People* magazine.

"Yo, Belda," I screamed as Belda Bressard shuffled on, with Kalish a few discreet paces behind in case she started to go. It must have taken a sand dune of cocaine to prop her up. She smiled wanly at the cheering crowd and lurched for the microphone. She thought it was a concert. Kalish grabbed her before she started singing.

"Yo, Lou," I shouted.

Vinnie elbowed me in the ribs. "Shut up. . . ."

"Careful, bro, you want me to go off?"

One of the escaped cons tapped Paco on the shoulder. "Your boy can stay with us if he wants. We're protected."

Paco ignored him and growled to Vinnie. "Let's get over to the exit. I don't like this."

The crowd was whistling and stamping its feet. With every new star, a roar went up and didn't subside. More people were streaming into the hall. "There's gonna be a panic like you've never seen when that amp blows," I whispered to Paco. But he had gotten the message and was plowing through the overweight minions of the Committee for Group Marriage, getting polyester burns on his forearms.

I turned quickly to the escaped con behind me and whispered: "He's a cop. They're both cops. They busted me in the lobby. . . ."

Vinnie came back from a fruitless mission through the thickening crowd. "The door is blocked off," he shouted.

"Let's get over by the wall," Paco shouted back.

Fischer and Athena walked out onto the dais, and the crowd went wild. They waved and smiled, relaxed, confident, the charisma just glowing out of them.

The escaped cons were in conference, but I managed to pluck one of them by the sleeve. "It's a trap," I whispered.

Now the governor's advance men and bodyguards came out on the dais, silk-suited cops and pols. They didn't like this group; they didn't like it at all. Jax was among them, carrying a black attaché case. Maybe he was wired, too.

The hoods were all together in a tight little huddle.

"C'mon," Vinnie said, pushing me toward a slight hole in the ranks of the Illegal Aliens for a Free Society. But the hole closed as Governor Lowndes came out. Fischer and Athena took their seats, and the gov strolled into the spotlight, wearing a white suit that his image-research people had probably told him would give immediate crowd identification with purity, sincerity, all the great political virtues. He raised his arms to the screaming crowd, turning slightly to say something to Michael Jax, something like, "You see how they love me?" Oh, yeah, they loved him. Wait until his little white suit was stained with blood. If you loved the candidate, you'll adore the martyr. Wait until his flag-shrouded coffin was driven in an open hearse down Hollywood Boulevard. What a cortege! What an outpouring!

Lowndes stepped to the microphone, his arms still outstretched, his smile getting a bit strained. Away from the pile of musical impedimenta behind the chairs, a little black amp stood alone at the edge of the platform like the ugly duckling. Artie Peterson was lumbering down the steps as if his bladder were bursting. On the other side Athena and Fischer, still smiling and waving, were retreating with more aplomb. To look at them you'd never guess they were escaping from a soon-to-be demolished banquet hall. But Artie gave the game away.

There had obviously been a change of schedule. They were going to do it now, with Kalish and Clitty still sitting up there; with Michael Jax smiling thinly, thinking he had plenty of time to get out of the line of fire. They had thrown us all a curve. They were cleaning house. Kalish and Clitty, the expendables; Jax, the disposable infiltrator; plus about a dozen illuminati, several of whom must have gotten Guiltwagon messages. At this very moment Boomer was somewhere in that crowd, tuning up his electrical pitch pipe, waiting for Fischer and Athena to work their way off the platform. As long as they stayed up there, we were all safe.

"Fischer, Fischer," I shouted. "We want Fischer." A few heads turned toward me. Paco began fighting his way back through the crowd to shut me up.

"Fischer's the man we came to see," I shouted. "We want Fischer . . . Fischer . . . Fischer."

Some people in the crowd picked up the chant. "Fischer, Fischer . . . we want Fischer."

"Get off the platform, Lowndes," I screamed. "No politicians today."

"No politicians, no politicians," the people shouted. Demagoguery was fun, and easy, too. It was a shame that I couldn't take over the world. Maybe some other day.

"Fischer, Fischer, we want Fischer. . . ."

They were stamping, cheering, chanting. Thousands of voices raised in unison. They drew strength from each other. The building shook. Lowndes turned from the microphone and beckoned Fischer and Athena back onto the platform. The back of his neck reddened. His politician's paranoia had to be telling him that Fischer had planned this spontaneous outburst. Fischer ducked and grinned and shook his head, modest and self-effacing. This was the governor's day, and he didn't want to steal the spotlight. But the governor's gesture became more insistent. Get up here, you conniving bastard! They won't shut up until you do.

"Excuse me, excuse me." I put my head down and tried to butt my way through the crowd. I was shoved back and caught a few elbows in the face.

"Krales!" Vinnie popped out of the crowd only a few feet away and lunged for me. I retreated desperately. "Excuse me, excuse me. . . ."

One of the hooded convicts grabbed Vinnie from behind and whispered something that made him stiffen and turn slowly. Paco was standing with three of the hooded men, his eyes popping as if he'd just had the biggest surprise of his life. He fell forward a bit and was caught around the waist. I saw the glint of a knife. Vinnie was moving carefully toward the convicts. He didn't even look back, didn't vow vengeance. He didn't know what had hit him.

Fischer had the microphone. He was smiling, clasping his hands like a champion. "I'll come back," he promised the crowd.

"Please let me through," I said, pushing at the broad backs of the Committee for Lesbian Rights. A stocky woman turned and grabbed me by the throat. "Will you get lost?"

And then I realized. I was a human bulldozer. I could clear a path for myself easily. What do you give a man with a bomb on his chest? Anything he wants.

I stepped away and ripped open my shirt. "I'm wired," I said cordially—I could afford to be nice. "I'm going to go off in thirty seconds."

"I've got a lot to say," Fischer told the crowd, "but so does the governor, and I'd like to yield to him . . ."

"Where do you want to go?" the shrinking lesbian asked.

I smiled and pointed toward the dais. "If you'll excuse me."

She clawed at her comrades. "Let him through. Get out of his way."

"Get the governor off the platform," I shrieked.

People turned to object, but the message had preceded me. "He's got a bomb on his back . . . he's wired . . . don't touch him."

My section of the room parted like the Red Sea while everyone else was still stomping and chanting. I tried to navigate toward the middle of the hall. "Get the governor off the platform," I shouted, my voice breaking.

I could hear the cries of alarm behind me. People were racing for the door. Panic was about to set in, but I would be untouched and untrammeled. My progress toward the dais was becoming more serene by the second.

"Governor Lowndes is in danger. . . ."

I heard the sound of shattering glass. The smart ones were going through the window. Suddenly I had a clear path to the platform. I waved and shouted hoarsely. Athena and Fischer were staring at me, waiting for Paco's little puff of smoke. "It's not going to come, Athena," I said. "Governor, get out of there."

Two plainclothesmen leaped off the platform, dropping to one knee in the combat position. I ripped off my shirt. "Don't shoot, I'm carrying plastic explosive." They put their pistols up and looked around in confusion. It had suddenly gotten quiet; all I could hear was the sound of people scurrying for the exits like mice in the wall.

"That amplifier has ten pounds of plastic explosive in it, Governor Lowndes," I announced. "They wanted to blow you to kingdom come. . . ."

The governor scampered off the platform and through a door being held for him. He was gone, Jax running after him. Everyone else had fled. There was a panicky cluster at the side door. Only Athena and Fischer remained, staring down in amazement.

I surveyed the room and saw Boomer cringing in a corner in the back. "Him," I shouted, pointing accusingly. "He has the detonator. Bascomb Blodgett." The cops moved cautiously toward him.

"It's over, Athena," I said. "You won't kill anymore. Tell them everything."

Athena tapped the mike with her fingernail. "Testing, testing." And then she emitted that insane little giggle, the one that always preceded some kind of horrible homicide.

"Athena," I shouted desperately. "Fischer, it's over. Be sensible. Get her to give up, Fischer."

Athena walked to the amplifier, her heels clicking assertively in the silence.

"Put your hands on your head, Krales," one of the cops shouted.

"Raise 'em slow," another warned.

I obeyed. "Look, I'm not the one you have to worry about. . . ."

"Don't turn around, Krales!" The voice was shrill, frantic. I could imagine a finger trembling on the trigger. Outside, I heard shouts and sirens as the governor's convoy sped away.

Athena took Artie's guitar off the stand and plugged it into the amp. She looked over at Fischer who was standing, arms sagging, head bent, staring dead-eyed like a senile old man. "Lazer," she said sharply.

His head jerked up.

"Lazer," she said, her voice a hypnotic command.

He walked slowly to her, holding his hands out for comfort. Athena was smiling proudly as if this were her wedding day. She picked up the guitar and strummed. One shimmering electronic chord rang out in the stillness. The guitar clattered to the floor as they embraced. The chord hung like a frozen echo in the air, giving me enough time to wonder if it was an E-major, decide that it was and then speculate casually on whether or not my little attachment was tuned to E-major and what a great story this was going to make before the chord and my headlines were drowned in a roar that brought the house down. The floor trembled. A chandelier crashed a few feet away from me. Chairs and tables hurtled by, sawdust fell from the ceiling in a fine drizzle. I somersaulted backwards and skidded across the floor for a few days until I finally came to rest on top of a fat, whimpering redheaded man. And I squeezed the folds of his belly until the noise stopped.

People were moaning, crawling, feeling themselves for critical wounds. Everybody was in shock but me. Hell, I'd been that way for three days now. This was just more of the same for me.

I sat up and nudged my redheaded roommate. "Look at this place. Aren't you sorry you missed this party?"

There was nothing left of Athena and Fischer but two blackened scarecrows, still tangled in embrace, their clothing hanging in tatters. As I watched, their charred remains disengaged and floated slowly to the ground like pieces of burned newspaper.

"Well, if that's true love," I said, "I'll definitely take the other kind."

And, just to be a good sport, I fainted.

It was an earthquake. That was the first thing everybody thought. Some Beverly Hills hippie who had tarried overlong in the sauna saw the east wing of the hotel crumbling and decided the San Andreas Fault had cracked its way to Sunset Boulevard. The man who has everything still lacks a Richter Scale, so he called the wire services, the networks, the police and his agent in that order. By the time somebody thought to consult the Earthquake Research Center, the story was out. It was a slow news day, so it didn't matter if it were true or not; every paper and station in the state jumped all over it. THIS TIME IT'S THE REAL THING, trumpeted a Fresno daily. Highways going north were jammed as people fled the fragmenting fault. There was a spate of desperation homicides as people settled grudges at the last minute. It was later estimated that thousands of infants were conceived that day; how many were given the right to life was another question. The earthquake panic continued long after police had released the real explanation of events. But most of the editors were content to let the earthquake run and sell papers with the "glitterburners" the next day.

Besides, there was a lot of explaining to do. For most of the day, the only story the police had was what I had babbled to the paramedics when they found me wandering through the rubble. It would have taken a leap of faith to accept the ranting of an incoherent fugitive wanted for murder. Luckily, at that moment an equally incoherent Boomer was shrieking the same story in another hospital room. The odds against two madmen coming up with the same fantasy are astronomical, so police consulted Jax and Kalish. Fischer had forgotten to inculcate a code of silence in his adherents, and when they discovered they had been his targets as well, the floodgates burst. The confessions came out in torrents, with huge blobs of mea culpas mixed in. "I was hypnotized," Kalish told the cops. "The man had some mystical power over me," sobbed Clitty. "Athena made me do it," Helene said. "Athena was behind everything." By mid-afternoon, while the district attorney was trying to figure out what to charge them with, they were all out on bail and making career moves. Kalish had made a book deal for Clitty and was negotiating a mini-series for Helene, based on her life as a terrorist. Artie Peterson had enrolled in a drug program and had gotten his hair cut. Boomer, escorted by a flying wedge of trustees, was taken to an exclusive sanitarium in Santa Barbara and put on a steady diet of thorazine and electric shock; this time they were determined to make the lobotomy complete. Jax had been spirited from the L.A. County Jail by a phalanx of highway patrolmen, and taken to parts unknown. Later in the day, the governor's office issued a statement attributing Jax's temporary breakdown to "overwork and pressure." The governor was plea bargaining for a man who had plotted to kill him. Jax knew too much to be punished, so the next best thing was forgiveness. For the scores of dead and wounded, the burning cities, their insane fantasies of world domination, they were all going to come out of this covered with glitter. Except for Paco and Vinnie, who were found dead of stab wounds under a collapsed fire wall.

Within hours, the tidying-up operation began. Governor Lowndes went on TV to tell the people that it wasn't an earthquake they had endured, but, more ominously, an attempt on his life thwarted by a reporter from the New York *Event*, who had been on secret assignment with this all-star terrorist group. Thus was I rehabilitated with one glib politician's falsehood. And sedated when I complained.

While I slept, a composite drawing of Athena with a blond wig and blue contacts was being shown to the employees of

Reva St. James's apartment building. They all agreed she was the gigglepuss who had come in with the Japanese restaurateur. Meanwhile, the highway patrol had recovered the other items of Athena's wardrobe—the wig, the cape, the boots—from the house. That was enough to get Lieutenant John Duffy on a plane to California. His was the first face I saw when I regained consciousness, which might explain why I immediately went into a relapse.

I gave Duffy a three-hour version of my adventures with Athena and the Glitterburners. In the next two hours, I told the same story to the LAPD, FBI, CIA, NSC, DIA and probably the ILGWU guy who was visiting his sick mother next door. It got so bad I would go into a recitation of my ordeal at the sight of a monogrammed handkerchief. Interpol; the Sureté National; M15; a group of bowing, smiling Orientals, each with his own tape recorder; a polite German who stared out of the window during my story; the intelligence services of every country in the free world beat a path to my door.

That night Grissom showed up for a page-one photo at my bedside. He had a tear sheet from the *Event* edition of the next day, showing how thoroughly I had been exonerated. He had even gone so far as to create an image for me. "I Work Alone. . . ." an overline over my photo proclaimed, and there was a long, totally fabricated piece about how I had kept my superiors in the dark about this story even after I had been disgraced because I was afraid that any leak would compromise my sources.

The same editorialists who had pilloried me now rang in with encomiums to my courage and integrity. "The very embodiment of the First Amendment," one of them called me. "When you have a free press in a free society, you get men like Josh Krales," another said. "To risk life and reputation in pursuit of a story, that's what American journalism is all about. And that kind of devotion to truth has found its incarnation in Josh Krales of the New York *Event*," declared a page-one editorial in, of all places, the New York *Event*.

"You're a hero," the night nurse told me. But not heroic enough to get her to climb into my electrically controlled bed with me.

"You're a hero," my ex-wife said when she called collect. But my heroism didn't merit even a temporary decrease in alimony.

"You're a hero," Grissom assured me, but his secret smile showed how much my heroism would be worth in the week it would take for this thing to blow over. It would be Brooklyn Police Headquarters for me. Nothing like rice and beans and purse snatchings to take the hubris out of a man.

But for the moment I was the undisputed star of the staff. They were saving a square-off at the bottom of page one for the Saturday edition, and for the next five days to come. I was to write my story just as it had happened, in whatever style I chose. They already had it syndicated throughout the world. Everyone was waiting with their tongues hanging out. "Go to town," Grissom told me. "We've got a big paper for the weekend, and we can always jump to the back pages. Write as much as you want."

"Write as much as you want": words calculated to turn any newspaperman into a yammering aphasic. Long had I craved a chance to break the bonds of daily journalism; to expatiate and define, even meander a bit; to get to the philosophical core of an issue, instead of just giving names, ages and counting stab wounds. Well, now I had it; *carte blanche,* poetic license. Plus an important subject that did no less than address itself to the very future of Western democracy. They wheeled a typewriter into my hospital room. Grissom arranged for a secretary in case I needed one. It seemed that the whole world was hovering at my bedside, waiting to catch the pearls.

About 1 A.M. the Demerol wore off, and I began to work. An hour later there was a mound of crumpled paper on the floor. I had managed one paragraph, which was about to take its place among the discards. It wasn't profound enough; it didn't encompass all. I kept thinking about all the people who had died because of the lunatic whims of a few unbalanced celebrities. How could such drugged, feeble incompetents accomplish this? What did this all say about our society? There was something big here, all right. I had a chance to make a statement, to influence, to change. This was the most significant story of my career.

"All you have to do is put one little word after another."

I looked up and almost dropped my bedpan. Potosky was in the doorway, her arm in a sling, a bandage wrapped turban-style around her head, wearing a hospital robe with a plunging neckline. Always the stylish one; her burial shroud would probably have a slit up the middle.

"This isn't one of those stories," I said, trying to kick my outtakes under the bed. "What happened to you anyway?"

"The most bizarre thing. I went to cover a press conference, and the building exploded. Know anything about that?"

I sat back and folded my arms smugly. "Everything."

She scuffed over to the typewriter and peered down at my lead. "Society's spoiled children gathered this weekend at a house on Malibu Beach, the symbol of Hollywood luxury and corruption, to plan the destruction of the world as we know it."

I suddenly needed more Demerol. "It wasn't meant to be read aloud."

"Don't be silly," Potosky said. "Add a few more stanzas, and we can make it an oratorio."

"Listen, this isn't just another crackpot murder story. . . ."

She agreed. "That's right. It's the biggest crackpot murder story of the year, possibly of the decade. . . ."

"There are a lot of important questions to be asked here," I said. "What are the cultural implications? What motivated these people? What does this say about the future of the American system?"

She agreed again. "Oh, you're absolutely right. So why don't you ask all those questions in *your* piece. I just want to know all the gory details. You know, like who was there, what kind of dope they were taking, who was screwing whom, how did they actually do all those murders. You know, all that trivial stuff." She shrugged modestly. "I mean, I haven't got the mental equipment to deal with these momentous issues. So if you just give me all that cheap, sensational stuff . . ."

"This is an exclusive, Potosky. My exclusive. And there's no way you can steal it or beat me because it's all inside my head."

She sat on the bed. "Then I'll just have to pick your brains, won't I?" she said, laying her cool hands on my fevered brow.

I looked straight into her eyes, a bad habit Athena had gotten me into. There was no gray, primeval murk there, just sardonic, challenging laughter—and the unmistakable glint of larceny. I lunged for her, but she fended me off with her sling. "For a philosopher, you're not very platonic."

"Oh, yeah, did you ever hear of Plato's Retreat?"

She slapped me playfully. "Down, boy. First we negotiate. I want an exclusive interview with you."

"Uh huh, you want me to compromise my own story. The nightmare I lived through. My chance for journalistic stardom."

"That's right."

"Well, what do I get out of it?"

Potosky lay back on the bed with a dreamy smile. "It'll be great. They'll ask me how I got the story, and I'll say, 'It was Hollywood. I got it on my back.'"

I looked around. Visiting hours were over. The halls were empty. I could close the door, keep her here all night. I was a little run-down, but I might even be able to get a couple of exclusives out of her.

"I'm on deadline," I said.

Potosky pouted. "Oh, great, the masterpiece . . ."

"Don't worry, it'll only take a second."

I shoved a fresh piece of copy paper in the typewriter and put myself on automatic pilot.

"A den of sex, drugs, rock and roll and murder came to an explosive end yesterday in exclusive Beverly Hills," I wrote.

Potosky sat up and looked over my shoulder. "That's a good boy. Just let your fingers do the writing."

I was typing like a fiend. "It's amazing what a little incentive can do.

"I can't believe it," Bessie Schildkraut, 57, a longtime Los Angeles resident said. "All those beautiful people . . ."